ACKNOWLEDGMENTS

There are far too many friends who encouraged and supported me to list.

There are a few who deserve recognition.

Donna Backes has been a true friend in proofreading my work brutally. I do appreciate her efforts and encouragement.

Dede Hammond organized our writing group and has been a faithful encourager. I appreciate her more than I can express and apologize to her for playing such lousy golf with her.

My sisters, Ellen Cooley and Bonnie Rutherford have always been true friends as well as sisters. They have cared for me and encouraged me all my life.

My daughter, Verta Lynn, is the best daughter in the world. She thinks whatever I do is great and loves me unconditionally.

I love all the people who have worked with me in the school teaching and my horse work. I have some great memories of the heart of the horses and other animals with which I've worked. My Cherokee Challenge (on the cover) is the great grandson of Man O' War and was as near human as a horse can get. He proved his love for me in many ways and many times.

Last, but far from least, all the people in my church who cared and laughed with me. Peggy and Dennis Kissinger were two who sincerely took an interest and encouraged me.

Thank all of you from the bottom of my heart. I am so blessed.

PROLOGUE

Squirming to relieve her aching back, Sharon continued her drive from San Antonio, Texas to Zephyrhills, Florida. What a way to spend her twenty-first birthday. A new widow, hurt, confused and a tiny bit afraid of her life ahead, she drove bravely on.

I can remember Grandmother McGregor saying, 'When you find yourself knocked to your knees, you're in a good position to pray.' She smiled to herself as she remembered her lovable, feisty Scots Grandmother. Her beloved maternal grandmother had died four years before and was still missed. *I've sure been knocked to my knees a lot the past few months, and I've prayed a lot, but I still am not sure that I'm making the right decision. Guess I'll just have to keep on keeping on and have a lot of faith and trust. I do trust you, Lord.*

Pewter-bottomed clouds didn't allow much of the blazing sun through while heat covered everything as if it were a thick comforter on a feather bed. *Aw gee! More road construction. Someone must have told them I'd be coming through. Trials and tribulations seem to follow me. Stop it, Sharon! You're getting paranoid.*

Sharon breathed a deep sigh and dropped her head against the backrest of the seat. Her aching heart, matching her aching back, brought the past two years to her mind.

She whispered, "Heavenly Father, help me to put the past behind me and make the future strong for me. I still don't understand how so much evil happened as it did, but I'm so thankful you were there to cushion me. I know that you will take charge and lead me from now on." She closed her eyes thinking of the past two years.

CHAPTER ONE

"Hey! Hey! Ole!" Sharon Donnelly sang as she snapped her fingers and moved her feet in rhythm with the Latin beat that the band played. Waist-length strawberry-blond hair swirled out in waves and curls as bright, jade eyes sparkled with excitement and happiness.

Her parents, Sean and Megan Donnelly, had arranged to give her this surprise nineteenth birthday party. Vivid blue and gold streamers and multi-colored balloons decorated the Silver Pines Country Club in Fort Lauderdale, Florida. College friends and neighbors were celebrating with her. Lightning bursts of happiness raced through her heart as she walked smiling through the crowd and feeling blessed.

"Wow! What a grrreat party!" Lynn Yates burbled as she gyrated by Sharon in rhythm to the beat of the rollicking music.

Lynn's mother was Sean Donnelly's sister. When Lynn was five years old, her parents died in an automobile accident, and the Donnellys had taken Lynn to raise as another daughter. Three year old Sharon had idolized Lynn and they were much closer than most biological sisters.

Although Sharon smiled at guests, and sometimes made a comment, her thoughts took her away. She smiled lovingly after Lynn. *Oh, Lynn and I were such brats. We were, and still are, horse crazy and practically lived in the stable. Poor mom. She's such a lady, and she despaired of us ever growing to be more than tomboys. Now look at us. I've finished my second year of college to become a teacher and*

1

Lynn's finished veterinarian school and Master Instructor so she can open a riding school for the handicapped. We'll both be teaching and we both adore children.

"Sharon, darling, are you with us?" Megan Donnelly giggled. "You're in another world and haven't answered me."

"Earth to Sharon." Sean Donnelly laughed as he put his arms around her waist and lifted her to twirl around.

"Daddy! Put me down this instant." Sharon didn't succeed in sounding firm or angry. "Thank you, Mom and Dad," she exclaimed as she hugged each one. "I don't know when I've had more fun. This truly is a wonderful party."

She smiled at her parents thinking, *daddy's only forty-two and mom's forty. They* both *look marvelous and they've been the world's best parents for Lynn and me.*

"We're happy if you are," Megan said. "Why don't we get to that delicious looking buffet while we have a few minutes to ourselves."

"Lead me to food anytime," Sean chuckled. "Mom's right. Better grab a bite while we can."

"Oh, no," Sharon groaned. "I'd better not eat. If I put anything inside, it'll be outside real quick. The grasshoppers and butterflies in my stomach aren't mixing too well."

"Too late," Sean whispered. He reluctantly turned, with a smile, to shake hands with the two men who stood by him. Megan talked politely to the men's wives while slowly moving toward the buffet table.

"Thank you for coming to my party," Sharon told the two couples. "Please excuse me. My roommate and other college friends are wondering why I don't spend some time with them." She walked over to a group of young people that included Amanda Rawlings, her college roommate.

"Yoweee! I'm having a hard time closing my mouth. This is so amazing. See my big eyes," Amanda laughed. "My family is socially active in Virginia, but we never belonged to a club like this. It feels as if I'm in the middle of 'Gone With the Wind' in this plantation setting. Your folks sure went all out for you."

Sharon put her arm through Amanda's arm. "Remember, I grew up with this. It ain't all that hot to me. Besides, you know how I feel. It's what a person is inside that's important, and not what they belong to or how much they have."

"Oh, I know how you feel, and I'm not envious," Amanda continued. "You're one of the most down to earth people I know. They would soon throw me out of here with my cut-off jeans and ratty sneakers."

"You think you have ratty clothing? You should have seen Lynn and me when we were little. My dad almost got kicked out of the country club because we would ride our horses, bareback, straight across the golf course while looking worse than street urchins. We were barefoot, wearing dirty shorts and torn T-shirts. There's a lake by the golf course for boating and an area for swimming. Can you imagine how those proper ladies felt as they leisurely drifted around in a canoe and here came Lynn and I swimming our horses toward them and yelling like savages." The group of young people was laughing hysterically. "But at church we were angels. Mom dressed us at least to look like ladies and we were afraid to behave differently. Lynn was always better behaved than I.

"Did I hear my name taken in vain?" Lynn walked to stand beside Amanda. "Are we telling stories? Boy, could I tell you folks stories about this one," she laughed gesturing toward Sharon.

"Okay, old lady. That's enough out of you," Sharon chuckled.

"Who'er you calling an old lady?" Lynn teased trying to look angry and failing. The group laughed and asked to be let in on the joke.

"There's no joke," Sharon answered. "Lynn's two years older, and I like to tease her about being the oldest." She turned to a neighbor girl. "Remember the party mom and dad gave Lynn for her twenty-first birthday here at the club a couple of months ago?" She explained to Amanda and the group. "This place was decorated horsey. Some of our hunt club friends and riding buddies even rode their horses right up the driveway to the club house. One boy tried to ride into the social room, but the club officers were present and threatened to have him arrested if he didn't leave. Mom and dad were mortified Lynn spoke through the laughter, "Well, as long as we're telling stories ---"

"Never you mind," Sharon shook her head. "Why don't we get this crowd into a line dance. The romantic couples have been swinging and swaying long enough." She went to the band and talked to the leader. In a minute the music changed from pop to western.

Sharon was in a line dance doing the 'Boot Scooting Boogie' when Amanda twisted and scooted near her. "Fan me quick, mamma. I've died and gone where good little girls go to meet sexy, handsome men," she gushed.

Sharon glanced up to see the Taylors entering the room. Her dad's law partner, Malcolm Taylor, and his wife, Agnes Taylor, and their son, Jeremy, were at the door. She knew Jeremy was home on leave from the air force. He was a pilot, a lieutenant, and looked great in his uniform. She started walking toward them, happy to welcome them.

I'm sure Jeremy won't remember me, Sharon thought. *He was four years ahead of me; a football hero and in the ROTC. There were scads of beautiful girls hanging around him, and he had a wild reputation. Why would he remember me, a plain girl who was too shy to try to be part of his group.*

Lynn caught up with Sharon just as she reached the Taylors. Malcolm Taylor hugged both girls. Agnes Taylor floated in, her head high, expecting adoration from everyone. She ignored Sharon and Lynn. Agnes loved to have people think she was Jeremy's older sister, therefore, pretty girls were discouraged. They might take attention from her.

"Jeremy," Malcolm's deep voice boomed. "This gorgeous young lady is the birthday girl. Do you remember Sharon?"

"How could I forget?" Jeremy's deep, sensuous voice made Sharon's knees weak. Black, curly hair; midnight blue eyes and olive skin made a heart-fluttering impression on Sharon. Jeremy took Sharon's hand and tucked it into the bend of his arm with a slow, seductive smile. Her five feet six looked tiny beside his six feet two muscular build.

"I'm glad you could come," she stammered. "Oh, you remember Lynn."

"I sure do.," He turned a smile on Lynn as he took her hand and drew it slowly to his lips.

Lynn firmly pulled her hand back before he could kiss it. "I know your parents are happy to have you home," she said politely with no expression.

Jeremy's eyes narrowed. He gave a small nod to Lynn before turning to smile at Sharon. He kept looking quizzically and slightly angry at Lynn.

Malcolm took his son's arm. "Sorry, girls. I know you'd love to get reacquainted and play catch-up, but I'd like to introduce Jeremy to some business friends." Jeremy looked back at Sharon with a practiced, pained look as his father took him off, his mother still floating after them with her head high. "Jeremy will catch you again later."

Lynn snapped her fingers in front of Sharon's eyes. "Wake up and dust the cobwebs off your brain. Use the common sense God gave you, and don't let that loser reel you in. Never forget that he's momma's little darling and she's spoiled him rotten. Surely you remember all the foolish girls who did his assignments so that he could be a football hero and stay in the ROTC." Lynn viewed Sharon with a worried, but loving, expression.

"Oh, for heaven's sake," Sharon snapped. "Of course I remember. I was one of those foolish girls for a short time. I helped him with literature classes. But -- I'm sure the military has helped him to mature."

"Don't count on it. You know what they say about leopards," Lynn winked.

6

Leopards? Sharon looked puzzled at Lynn as they walked over to join some of their friends. One of her dad's friends asked her to dance. Sharon looked over the man's shoulder to see Jeremy staring at her. He grinned and winked. Nervously she looked away pretending not to see him.

Jeremy's mother had taught him to cultivate rich girls in high social positions, and Sharon qualified. As weeks flew by, Sharon fell under Jeremy's charm. They kept in touch through phone calls and letters. In one of Jeremy's letters, he had invited Sharon and her parents to be his guest at dinner in a famous French restaurant in Fort Lauderdale the following Friday.

"Mrs. Donnelly, how beautiful you look tonight. Everyone will think you're Sharon's sister. Let me help you." Jeremy rushed to hold her chair and then hurried to hold Sharon's, but Sean had already seated his daughter.

"Mr. Donnelly, my dad is so fortunate to have you for a partner."

"Jeremy, I'm the fortunate one. Let's hope you make half the man your dad is. I'm sure it's hard to follow his example. You should count your blessings that you have such an excellent role model in your father. I'm sure you're thankful you have the advantage of such an outstanding parent."

Jeremy was thankful that the waiter came to take their order. He wasn't sure what his reply should be. He had known the Donnellys all of his life and knew how close his father and Sean Donnelly were, but he really had no feelings for his father.

Malcolm Taylor and Sean Donnelly had been friends during college and through law school and had been partners for many years. They were as close as most brothers were. However, Agnes Taylor and Megan Donnelly were only polite to each other. Agnes did no work of any kind, leaving her house to servants, and attended all social functions possible. Megan volunteered for several charity groups and loved to take care of her own house and family. She only had help with window washing and heavy cleaning.

Ignoring Lynn's, and other friends' warnings, Sharon dated Jeremy and kept in touch.

Seven months after her party, she fell completely under Jeremy's spell, and one of the most publicized weddings of Fort Lauderdale took place in the Baptist Church. It was an event fit for royalty.

Following their wedding, three hundred guests were served at a sit-down dinner and a well-known group of musicians entertained at a reception held at the Silver Pines Country Club. Jeremy and Sharon, on the floor for the first dance, glided through the bubbles floating through the air from a machine. Her head just reached his shoulder. An arch of white roses on a long veil was placed across her head. The white lace and satin gown made her look as if she had stepped out of a picture of the middle 1800s.

"This must be costing Sean a fortune," a golfing buddy remarked to Agnes Taylor, sitting beside her at the dinner.

"Don't worry about the cost," Agnes Taylor replied, happy to supply gossip. "Sean's family owned a successful shipping business and importing and exporting for several generations. When Sean's father died, the entire fortune went to Sean and his sister. He has invested wisely. He and Malcolm, my husband, have a lucrative law practice. I think Sean must have descended from King Midas," she laughed strangely. "Sean Donnelly makes no financial mistakes. Of course his sister's share of the inheritance went to Lynn under Sean's guardianship. He comes out on top regardless of what he does."

The man quickly excused himself and left as if he were uneasy in Agnes' presence.

"Look at the newly weds," Ellen Turner sitting across the table sighed. "Aren't they a beautiful couple."

"Oh, to be young and foolish again," her husband quipped.

"They are sweet," Bonnie Stallard spoke. "I bet they will have a long, happy marriage and beautiful children. They are so right together."

Two days later the wedding seemed like a beautiful dream as Sharon gazed out of the hotel window enjoying the view of the ocean and the beach.

"Darling, I'm sorry we'll only have a week here in Bermuda. I want to share so much with you." Jeremy slouched in a big chair and watched Sharon.

"Oh, Jeremy." Sharon twirled around as if she were dancing and sat on his lap. "That's not important. Just being with you is wonderful and our honeymoon will last a lifetime, wherever we are."

A knock sounded on the door as a maid opened it and walked in. Smiling she asked, "Do you need anything; towels, soap, shampoo, anything?"

"Hey!" Jeremy roared jumping up and dumping Sharon on the floor. He stormed at the maid. "Did we ring for you? Did I invite you into this room?"

Frightened, the woman shook her head and shuffled backwards.

"Then get out of here and don't come in this room unless you're invited." The maid ran out leaving the door open.

Walking to close the door, Sharon said, "That wasn't nice. She's just doing her job."

"Shut up!" Jeremy shouted pointing his finger in her face. "You let me handle the hired help. Do you understand?"

Although Sharon was shocked at his behavior, she choked back a response. It hurt her for him to speak in that tone of voice, but she was too much in love to allow it to become an argument. She was so naïve that she didn't recognize Jeremy was doing as his mother had taught him. She had yet to learn he had no respect or compassion for others.

After their week in Bermuda, they reported to the Air Force Base in San Antonio, Texas. This would be a complete change in life style for Sharon because, instead of a single family residence, they were assigned one side of a lovely brick duplex. There were a few apartments and single dwellings for higher officers, but all of the housing was much closer together than she was accustomed to living.

Their furniture would be issued from a billeting and they would be responsible for even a scratch on a piece. They would pay their own phone and cable TV bills, but all other utilities were provided.

"Can I work in that miniscule yard and plant my own flowers?" Sharon inquired eagerly. "I want to make this look truly like our home."

"No," Jeremy answered irritably. "The post engineers do all the lawn work and planting. You would have to ask permission and fill out papers in triplicate. You know how the government is."

"Can I at least choose curtains and items to make this seem more like a home?"

"Yeah. Yeah. If it means that much to you, do what you please. I'll be in later. I have people to see." Jeremy snapped and strode out without any explanation.

Heavenly Father, I love my husband and am trying to be a good wife. I'll need your help a lot because all of this is new to me. I wish Jeremy would confide in me and tell me what's worrying him. He hasn't been the same since we married. I'm sure going to need my guardian angels. Guide me, please.

Sharon was grateful to those who came to welcome her to the base and offer help if needed. Some even brought prepared food so that she wouldn't have to cook much until she was settled in.

Linda Pallister introduced herself as a neighbor across the section facing Sharon, and two houses down. "My husband is a military attorney, Captain Philip Pallister," she said more proudly than she intended to. "And you might as well know, I am silly in love with him, possibly even more than I was when we married eight years ago."

Laughing at the woman's confession, Sharon felt herself drawn to Linda. *I like all of the wives who came today to welcome me, but, for some reason, I feel that Linda and I are going to be great friends.*

Jets taking off and landing actually caused a vibration in the house. "I'm not sure I can ever learn to sleep through the unfamiliar noises. I may even have to buy ear plugs," she told Jeremy one morning and that day she did buy them.

One morning at breakfast she asked a silent grace as usual. It disturbed her that Jeremy objected to praying before meals. She quietly studied the stern face of her husband. "Darling, why haven't you told me exactly what you do."

"Why? I thought you knew. Lady, you have an important husband," he leaned back in his chair. "I'm a flight instructor for the new soldiers. Their first few days are spent in the classroom and then I take them out to teach them to fly our planes."

"How exciting. Are you the only instructor?"

"Of course not. There's too many new recruits coming in for one instructor to handle. I'm the best though."

"You don't have to tell me something I already know. What else do you do?"

"I fly the big brass wherever I'm told to take them."

"My goodness. That's a big responsibility. Does it mean you'll be gone overnight sometimes?"

"Sure. For instance, if I fly to Washington, D.C., it could mean two or three days."

"I am in awe of you, my darling. Your job is much more important than I realized.

Could you teach me to fly?"

"No! I can't use military equipment for personal reasons and besides, you don't need to know how to fly." His unreasonable temper was confusing.

Disturbed at his anger, she changed the subject. "Oh, look at the time. We have to hurry and get ready for the orientation meeting."

"You don't mind going alone, do you? I have some things I must take care of."

"Jeremy, please come with me. I'll fell awkward going by myself."

"There'll be plenty of wives there alone. Not all husbands can have free time whenever they wish. Gotta go. Enjoy." He was gone in a rush without a hug or a kiss.

"Linda, I can't tell you how grateful I am that you volunteered to go to this meeting with me. " Sharon was grateful for Linda, but embarrassed that Jeremy was not there.

"Think nothing of it. There'll be many new wives, or rather new to the base, but I'm already acquainted with the base and people and thought I might be a help to you."

"You've helped me just by accompanying me. Thank you."

The Commanding Officer, General James Huff, made all of them feel welcome and at ease. *He reminds me of a sweet, old grandfather*, Sharon thought and smiled to herself.

After the orientation meeting and refreshments, Linda took Sharon and two other new wives for a drive around town to sightsee.

The sun had just gone down over San Antonio as a tall, thin man, in a rumpled suit, hurried along Nogalitos Street.

He looked furtively around and then stepped quickly into a phone booth. He asked for reverse charges on a number he wanted in northern Florida.

"Hey, Hank, it's me, Duke. You won't believe it. The Fool has went and got hisself married and he never said nothing to me about it."

Strong profanity came over the phone before the person said, "Well --keep an eye on him."

"Sure thing. Do you want me to tell him to talk to you?"

"No. Don't say anything. Report to me as soon as you find out anything more. I want to know all about the woman he married and what they're doing. Be sure he understands you're still his contact."

"Gotcha. Ring you later."

Sharon happily made a home for Jeremy while learning how to cook and sew. She hoped that Jeremy would change his mind about having children. *I would love to start a family, and I bet Jeremy would love a child of his own.*

Gradually Sharon began to notice abrupt mood changes in Jeremy; his sulking and his hurtful words to her. Although her heart was heavy, pride, self-respect and loyalty to her husband, helped her to hide her feeling from others behind a brave smile.

On Sharon's twentieth birthday, some of the women took her out to dinner and gave her gifts. Linda Pallister had planned the evening. Although she was nine years older than Sharon, they had become close friends. Linda and Philip often took short trips with Jeremy and Sharon and ate out together as often as possible.

Jeremy was disturbed that Sharon was out with the women and he could not hear their conversations. When Sharon came home, she was shocked to find him drunk and passed out on the couch. *If I wake him, he might be too angry for me to handle. I'll just leave him alone and let him sleep it off. I don't know when he started drinking. He wasn't raised to indulge. Why is he unhappy? Am I doing something wrong?*

CHAPTER TWO

Their first wedding anniversary soon followed, which Jeremy ignored. Sharon's parents and Malcolm Taylor sent gifts and best wishes. The days came and went, but Jeremy wasn't seen or heard from for two days. It was late when he staggered in disheveled, smelling of alcohol and cheap perfume. She was hurt and confused when she got the brunt of his unreasonable anger. She had never experienced a male, in her life, being so cruel and unreasonable.

As time passed, Jeremy was seen in town with a variety of questionable women. The military men, who saw him, told their wives, but Sharon didn't hear of it.

Sharon wrote to both of their parents regularly. Agnes wrote letters only to Jeremy and never acknowledged Sharon. Agnes was angry because Sharon had a more enviable social position. Even though Sharon didn't seek the spotlight, Agnes was jealous because Sharon was younger and prettier. Too, Sharon was with Agnes' son, and she wanted him all to herself.

Sharon was careful never to hint at her troubles with Jeremy. Her parents were not suspicious because she always kept her letters and phone calls light and cheerful.

Malcolm Taylor, however, knew his son. He called Sharon every week and asked her questions, as a good attorney would, that made her scramble for answers. He realized that she was being evasive, and it worried him.

After talking to Sharon one day and not getting satisfactory answers, Malcolm leaned back in his chair and placed his feet on his desk. *I have a feeling that everything is not roses and light, but I can't help Sharon if she won't confide in me. Lord, be with them.*

As time passed, Sharon became more tempted to discuss Jeremy's disturbing behavior with his dad. Her loyalty to her husband kept her quiet as well as her hope and prayers that he would change and be as he was when she first married him.

Gradually, as weeks passed, Sharon became aware that she was actually afraid of Jeremy. One day he would be outgoing and cheerful then, without warning, he became quick tempered and moody. One night he came home sullen and brooding. Sharon, trying to lighten the atmosphere, was caring and loving. She hurried to the door to meet him. "Hello, darling. Did you have a good day?" She smiled reaching to hug him, and realized he smelled of alcohol.

"Why? What d'ya want to know for?" Jeremy yelled, pushing her away. "Are you spying on me?"

"Jeremy! No!" Sharon protested. "I am truly interested in your work. You're my husband. I love you and am proud of you."

"You're meddling in my business. Shut up before your nose gets you into trouble."

It was out of character for Sharon, but she became impatient with his currish, childish behavior. "At least I stay out of trouble. No one will ever be able to accuse me of not honoring our marriage vows."

"Are you accusing me?" Jeremy screamed, jumping right in her face.

"I'm not accusing you of anything. Something is very wrong. Won't you talk to a doctor or go with me to talk to the chaplain?"

"So. You think I'm unfaithful and that everything is my fault. Come here. I'll give you what you really want."

Sharon was too stunned to protect herself. Never in her life had she been around a man or woman who acted as Jeremy had been. He slapped her so hard that she fell.

Grabbing her by the hair with one hand, he dug the fingers of the other hand painfully in her upper arm and dragged her into the bedroom.

"Jeremy! You're hurting me! Please! Stop!" Sharon's efforts were in vain as she struggled to gain a release from him.

Laughing maniacally Jeremy threw her on the bed and literally tore her clothes off her.

"Please don't do this, Jeremy," she sobbed. Pain, both physical and emotional swept over her as he raped her without mercy. He carelessly climbed off her tormented body where she lay in twisted sheets. She didn't move as he showered and dressed.

"That's the way women like you want it," he sneered as he swaggered out of the bedroom and left the house.

As soon as she heard the outer door slam, she gulped for air like a drowning person, realizing that she had been holding her breath against the shock and pain. She then drifted into the blackness that would take her away from the horror of Jeremy's cruelty.

Waking later she found herself in the dark room and, thankfully, alone. Groggily she stumbled to the bathroom and washed her mouth out with water. Weakly she staggered back to bed and fell into a fitful sleep.

During the early morning hours, Sharon awoke and went into the living room to sit in the dark and think. Miserable and confused, her thoughts flew wildly. *Is it possible Jeremy has a serious illness he isn't facing or telling me? Maybe, in the past, he had a head injury or a trauma that's causing his erratic behavior.* She could not, and would not, accept that Jeremy was just mean natured and was violent. She didn't realize Jeremy's true nature was showing -- one that he had kept hidden from Sharon while they were planning their marriage. Her heart ached thinking of how helpless she felt. Putting her head back against the chair, she drifted into an uneasy sleep.

Sharon woke the next morning feeling sore and lonely. Sad and bewildered, she took a shower and prepared to brush her teeth. Her reflection in the mirror filled her with horror. Both eyes black, cheeks red and swollen, bruises all over her body. Even her heart felt bruised. Jeremy had not come home.

Going into the kitchen, she hoped she would be outside, and with sunglasses on, before the women saw her. Linda and two other wives were going shopping and Sharon had offered to drive this time. *How I wish I were not obligated to go, but I can't hide forever. Dear God, what can I do?*

Listening to the radio usually made washing dishes and cleaning house more pleasurable, except this morning. As she worked, she agonized over the previous evening, grateful that Jeremy was not at home.

She whispered, "Heavenly Father, is it something I'm doing wrong, or neglecting to do? What can I do to help my marriage? How can I persuade Jeremy to get help for his behavior? He won't admit that he needs help. Please show me the way."

Deep in her sorrow, Sharon didn't hear Linda knock lightly, open the door and walk in. "Good morning, merry sunshine," chimed the lovely, lilting voice of her friend. Surprised, Sharon whirled with a gasp and grabbed for the sunglasses on the table.

"Sharon!" Linda shrieked. "What happened? Did Jeremy do that to you?" she asked through tight lips and a clenched jaw. Linda knew the gossip about Jeremy.

"What? Oh, you mean this?" Sharon answered with a small, nervous laugh. "Heavens no, just clumsy me. I --uh -- tripped in the dark and fell against the uh -- coffee table. Unfamiliar house, you know. I've done that a lot lately."

"Honey, you'd be surprised at the number of women who claim to have tripped or run into something. It is common knowledge that darling Jeremy is not such a darling. It's also common knowledge that he's drinking heavily and is constantly in hot water with Gen. Huff. Girl friend, you know I'm not fooled. Now give."

A couple of tears escaped and rolled down Sharon's cheek as she ducked her head and turned to walk out of the kitchen. "I'll get my purse. Linda, you're a dear to worry about me, but really, I'm fine. Give me a couple of minutes and I'll be ready."

"Sharon, you need help, but I can't help you unless you're willing to admit it and cooperate." Sharon waved a hand over her shoulder and went into her bedroom.

When Sharon and Linda met the other two wives, Sharon told them the same story she had told Linda. The women looked at Linda with raised eyebrows and frowns, but she shook her head in warning and started an upbeat conversation. There was some good-natured arguing about what they would do first before they got to the serious business of shopping.

Feeling very protective toward Sharon, Linda declared to herself that she would discuss the situation with Philip that night. *He'll know how to deal with it,* she thought.

That evening Linda waited impatiently for Philip to come home. She ran and jumped into his arms talking excitedly and trying not to cry, but babbling in her distress.

"Shh. Calm down, sweetheart. I can't understand what you're saying," He cuddled her closer. It was several minutes before she was able to tell him about the sweet young girl they had learned to love like a little sister.

"Sweetheart," Philip comforted her. "I know how upset you are. I'm furious. Sharon is a sweet, decent young lady. Several of us have been discussing Jeremy's drinking, womanizing and irresponsible behavior. He has enough warnings to take him out of the flying program entirely. A man with his behavior is too dangerous to himself, and others, to be allowed to fly. Gen. Huff needs to know of this latest episode."

Jeremy didn't come home until late the following afternoon and found orders to report to Gen. Huff. Capt. Pallister had asked permission to be included in the meeting.

"Lt. Taylor, looking at your record I can see you're not a stranger to breaking rules and getting into trouble. You've been given many advantages and you still don't use common sense. Can you explain to me what is wrong with you?" General Huff asked angrily.

"There's nothing wrong with me, Sir. People are jealous of me," he glared at Philip. "My wife is not a good military wife and I'm having problems with her. I'll take care of it and you'll not have to see me in here again."

"I've heard that story before. Due to the fact that you're in a security position, I had your wife investigated as soon as you married. I'm impressed with the excellent report on her. It so happens I know her parents, and yours. Both families are above reproach. You, on the other hand, are a black eye to the service and an embarrassment to this base. The next time you're brought before me, you WILL receive maximum punishment which will be a demotion in all possible forms. Do I make myself clear?"

"Yes, Sir," Jeremy snapped angrily and jerked a salute. He backed up to turn and leave.

"Hold it, soldier," the General went on. "Capt. Pallister, did you have something to add?"

"Yes, thank you, Sir. Knowing the serious trouble Lt. Taylor has been in, and knowing the ungentlemanly manner with which he has treated his wife, my staff and I have arrived at a decision. Our recommendation is that Lt. Taylor be required to see Dr. Harrison, who is an excellent psychiatrist."

"I concur," Gen. Huff looked at Jeremy. "This will go into your records. Make sure you make the appointment with Dr. Harrison and --"

"That's not fair," Jeremy interrupted heatedly.

Gen. Huff continued firmly. "Lt. Taylor, you'd better count your blessings, keep quiet and cooperate. You're in enough trouble. If your present behavior continues, your rank will be reduced and you could face a dishonorable discharge. You WILL see the psychiatrist. You WILL abide by rules and regulations. You WILL get help for your drinking. You WILL treat your wife with the respect she deserves. You WILL cooperate or what happens to you won't be anyone's fault but your own. DO YOU UNDERSTAND?" His blue eyes were snapping.

"Yes, Sir!" Jeremy said with a brazen expression. He again saluted, turned smartly and marched out with stiff, angry strides.

"I'm surprised he got this far in the Air Force. There's a young man with a lot of emotional problems. He's had the world at his feet and doesn't have the maturity to deal with it," Gen Huff observed. He sighed and ran his fingers through thick, wavy, gray hair. At five-eleven he was in excellent physical condition.

Jeremy was in a murderous mood. He accepted the fact that not everyone agreed with him, but chalked it up to their ignorance. He could not accept the fact that he had been disciplined and not allowed to do as he pleased. Too, he was irate that Philip had witnessed his correction and had given his suggestions. Most of all, he was angry at Sharon and blamed her for all that had occurred. Philip outranked him and he could not rave at a superior officer, even one considered a friend. He grinned evilly as he thought of Sharon.

When Jeremy staggered in the door late that evening, Sharon was hoping for peace. She wanted to know what happened at the hearing, but knew better than to ask. Before she could speak he was screaming at her.

"Little Miss Puritan," he raved drunkenly. "You may have other people fooled, but I know you for what you are, and so does my mother. Your friend, old pretty boy Philip, recommended a psychiatrist for me. He must have gotten the idea from you."

"Jeremy, what idea do you think Philip got from me? I've always been proud of you and supported you."

"Not like mom does."

Much to Sharon's relief, Jeremy staggered over to the couch and passed out. She tried to think through what was happening. *Obviously Jeremy has told his mother lies and she has encouraged him in his irresponsible behavior. Dear Lord, what shall I do? Maybe it's time to confide in Dad Taylor, and maybe my dad. I can't shoulder this alone. Father, where are you? Why have you forsaken me? Oh, forgive me. I know you never leave us. It's we that leave you. I've tried too long on my own. I'm now leaving it in your hands.*

Jeremy roused to see Sharon walking the floor and crying. With a roar he leaped up and jumped at Sharon, landing several blows and kicks as she fell. She rolled screaming across the floor. Jeremy fell over an ottoman as she drug herself up and wobbled out of the house, unaware of where she was going--just trying to get away.

Jeremy ran out of the house as Sharon fell down the front steps and onto the lawn. He was shocked to see Linda and Philip running toward them as well as other neighbors gathering around.

He knelt quickly beside Sharon. "Sharon, oh baby, forgive me," he whispered. "I don't want to hurt you, but you make me so mad sometimes. It's your fault. I know I've drunk more than I should, but everybody has picked on me today. You should have more faith in me. It won't happen again, I swear. Please don't tell anyone or I'll be in serious trouble. Gen. Huff said --"

"Sharon! What has happened?" Linda broke in as she fell on her knees beside Sharon. "We heard you screaming." Tears streamed down her cheeks.

"What's going on here?" Philip demanded through gritted teeth.

"Oh, dear God," Jeremy groaned. "Sharon, sweetheart, what did happen to you?"

Sharon could hardly believe that Jeremy was denying what he had done. *It's almost as if he doesn't know. This is a chance for me to prove to him that I do love him and support him.*

"I--um-- started down the steps and some animal ran in front of me. It startled me and I fell," she said haltingly trying to breathe through the pain.

Someone had called for help. Military police and paramedics arrived. Philip's lips were a tight slash as he pulled Linda to her feet so that medical assistance could be given to Sharon.

"Capt. Pallister," Philip turned to acknowledge the lieutenant who lived on the other side of the duplex with Jeremy and Sharon. "My wife and I heard Mrs. Taylor screaming and Lt. Taylor yelling inside the house several minutes before she came out. She was begging him to stop and then we saw her run out and fall off the steps."

"Thank you for the information. Will you please tell this to the M. P.? If you know, for a fact, about any other unpleasant incidences in the past, please give that information, also." Philip was sure this was not the first incident.

"Yes, Sir. We'll be happy to help. We've heard her begging for mercy before this."

Linda and Philip followed Sharon to the hospital. The doctor could not give them much information because the injuries were too fresh and the flesh swollen. Philip explained to the medical staff why Jeremy should not be allowed to see Sharon. He and Linda stayed until midnight and then reluctantly went home.

Sharon woke the next morning feeling sore and stiff. Her aching heart felt worse than her physical injuries. She hazily became aware of a nurse standing by her bed.

"Good morning, Mrs. Taylor," the nurse spoke kindly. "I need to bother you a little to take stats. Your breakfast is on the way."

"Thank you, but I don't think I can eat anything."

"You need to build your strength. Besides, putting it in your mouth is a lot more pleasant than putting it through needles and tubes," the nurse chuckled.

"I suppose you're right. What's wrong with me?"

"The doctor will be here in a few minutes and he can answer your questions a lot better than I can." The nurse patted Sharon's foot and quietly left. Sharon slept.

"Good morning, Sharon." She slowly opened her eyes. "How do you feel?" Squinting, she recognized Col Ben Davis, her doctor. "How do you feel," he repeated.

"Like I've been hit by a speeding train."

"That good, huh?" He smiled at her as he sat in a chair by her bed. "Honey, I wish I could say you just need a rest, but it's obvious you've suffered a beating. According to your neighbors, this isn't the first time. I can't for the life of me understand why you've put up with such cruel, inhuman treatment. Why didn't you leave him or confide in someone who could help?"

"You've heard it all before," she sighed. "I truly love my husband and keep hoping he'll be like he was when we were newly married. Too, I'm not sure how much of the guilt is mine. I knew he had emotional problems while growing up, but I assumed his military training had helped him to mature. Please don't tell anyone what I've said. I must try to help him. Now, what is wrong with me?"

"First, you can't help your husband do anything. He's an adult and responsible for his own actions. He has to recognize that he needs help and ask for it. As for you, you have three broken ribs, a broken finger and numerous cuts and bruises. I'm keeping you on painkillers for a couple of days until you can breathe easier and feel like sitting up for a short period of time. I have to go on rounds, but I'll be back. We need to have a long talk. Good. Here's your breakfast, and I want you to eat every bite."

Sharon dutifully tried to eat the oatmeal, milk and bowl of applesauce, but she choked when she tried to swallow around the catch in her throat.

Although Sharon slept through Linda and Philip's brief visit, she was wakening when Jeremy came just before lunch. He placed a vase of her favorite peach-colored roses on the stand by her bed. "Hi beautiful. Wanta' see these blush with shame? They know they'd never match your beauty." He continued to babble, but Sharon was too groggy to respond. Too, she wasn't sure what she wanted to say to him.

"I'll come back another time when you're more alert," Jeremy said as he leaned to kiss her cheek. He left, and Sharon relaxed into the cottony feeling of the painkillers.

A soft voice repeatedly speaking her name roused her from troubled dreams. She slowly opened her eyes to see a chaplain, Col. Mark Kirkpatrick.

"Hello, there," he said softly. "We've all been so worried about you. How are you feeling, or is it too soon for you to know how you feel?" he smiled.

She tried to smile but a groan escaped.

"Be still, please. I'll do the talking. I don't want to add to your hurts and heartaches, but I know what happened regardless of what you've said, or haven't said. People heard the ruckus from inside your house, and the M.P. s saw Lt. Taylor's bruised hands the night you were injured. You may not realize how loudly you were screaming and begging him to stop, but several people came out in time to see you running out of the front door and fall down the steps."

Sharon began to sob and shake, cringing against the pain.

"Please try not to cry. I know it upsets you, but for your sake, and your husband's, you must tell the truth. We all know he desperately needs professional help, and the only way he's going to face facts is for you to be strong enough to tell the truth."

Sharon shook her head and turned her face away from him. She was sobbing aloud as a nurse hurried in.

"Colonel, you'll have to leave. This is a very sick woman. She must have rest and remain free from stress as much as possible." He patted Sharon's shoulder, said a quick prayer and left.

That evening, gritting her teeth against the pain, Sharon made a person-to-person call to Malcolm Taylor. It wasn't something she wanted to do, but common sense told her he needed to know what had been happening.

"Dad Taylor, you don't know how sweet your voice is. First I want you to promise you'll not tell my parents what I'm going to say. I don't want them to worry. I can't ask you not to tell your wife, but I hope you won't. Just listen, please." Haltingly she told him all that had occurred even to the men talking downtown and Jeremy's anger as he shook her.

Malcolm made a strangled sound, and his mounting anger was palpable over the phone when she told him why she was in the hospital. Telling him the entire truth, she sensed it was taking all his strength to try to remain calm.

Sharon

"Honey, I've suspected that all was not well, but I had no idea it was this serious. I'm heart-broken. I've known and loved you all of your life and was ecstatic to welcome you into the family as my daughter. I can't answer for my wife. She's been wrong in spoiling Jeremy. Honey, your parents need to know. They love you with all their heart, and regardless of how old you are or how far away you live, you're still their little girl. Your dad is not only my partner, but he's like a brother to me. They'll be deeply hurt to learn you told me and kept it from them. However, Jeremy is my son, and I'm partly responsible for his actions. That's why you called me first. Honey, you need all of us loving you and supporting you as you deserve." Malcolm could hardly stop talking for his anger. He wanted to be there to hug Sharon and comfort her.

Sharon couldn't control her tears with Dad Taylor being so sweet and understanding. Through her wrenching sobs, she reluctantly agreed that he could tell her parents.

The next day when Jeremy came in, Sharon was prepared to discuss their future, hopefully without breaking down.

"Darling, something is seriously wrong. Regardless of what you think, I'm on your side. I've not told anyone here what happened, but they're not fools. They guessed, and heard for themselves."

"Yeah," he sneered. "Everyone's guessed. They guessed after you told them what a monster you married."

"No, Jeremy. I've never said anything negative about you. Why have you turned against me? No one here knows for sure how badly you've treated me."

30

"I've treated you!" He jumped up raising his voice. "What about the way you've treated me; your neglect of me."

"How have I mistreated you, Jeremy?" she asked in surprise.

"You expect too much from me. I should never have married you, and mom thinks so, too."

Sharon looked him straight in the eyes. "You can go on pretending, but you're not fooling anyone. You're only fooling yourself. I've been willing to lie and cover up for you. I married you because I believed in you and I loved you. Why did you marry me?"

"Because Miss Pure and Proper would not go to bed with me without being married," he answered insolently. "And mom thought you'd make good connections."

"Is that the only reason?" she gasped.

He laughed and then like a bolt of electricity it dawned on Jeremy. "No one here knows. What do you mean, no one *here* knows. Who does know?" he snarled.

"Your dad knows and by now my parents and Lynn."

"How does dad know? Who told him?" he shouted.

Two nurses, working on records at their station, had looked up when Jeremy raised his voice. One ran into Sharon's room while the other one called security. They struggled with Jeremy to keep him off Sharon's bed until security came. He had just slung one nurse to the floor when the M.P.s rushed in. Jeremy fought the two guards while yelling incoherent phrases and profanity as they wrestled him out of the room. They fell to the floor in the hall while they placed handcuffs on Jeremy.

"Please don't hurt him," Sharon sobbed. She was so upset that a nurse called the doctor who immediately ordered a sedative.

Sharon was awakened in the late afternoon by the sound of the nurses' starched uniforms moving around. She slowly opened her eyes and then shrieked.

CHAPTER THREE

"Glory be! It's an angel!" Tears of joy streamed from Sharon's eyes.

Lynn was standing by Sharon's bed with misty green eyes. Lynn's long, dark eyelashes grazed a smooth complexion tanned lightly by her outdoor activities. Shoulder-length honey-colored hair fell in soft curls with a wavy bang over her right eyebrow.

"That's enough," Lynn broke in after several minutes. "We've shed enough tears, and they'll stop right now. Sharon, you're a beautiful person, inside and out, who has done no wrong. You're an intelligent person with a tremendous amount of common sense even if you did lose your mind temporarily," she smiled. "By the way, I want to meet your friend, Linda, and thank her for calling me. She sure is concerned about you."

"I know. She and Philip have been great friends. They're worth a million. You'll meet them soon."

The next day Sharon felt a little better. The two vivacious girls put a sparkle on the whole floor much to the delight of patients and medical staff as Lynn wheeled Sharon through the halls greeting everyone. Sharon rested peacefully that night.

The next morning, after a bath and breakfast, Sharon was just settled in bed when she heard Jeremy's voice at the nurses' station.

Col. Kirkpatrick and an M.P. were with him as they entered her room. Jeremy sat subdued in a chair by her bed.

"I guess you know I'm under arrest. I've also lost my officer's rank and--. Well, never mind. Tell me, how does dad know?"

Sharon told him of the phone call. Sitting with bowed head in his hands, he said, "I truly am sorry that I hurt you. I hope you heal quickly." He stood up.

"Jeremy, I meant it when I said I wanted to save our marriage. Will you go with me to a marriage counselor?'

He stared down at her, shook his head, then left without looking back.

Megan and Sean came in the afternoon while Lynn was there. "How lovely to see both my girls," Megan tried to smile. There were hugs all around, but Sharon noticed how her dad was shaking while trying to control his anger.

Gritting his teeth and clearing his throat, Sean finally spoke. "We talked to Dr. Davis and a Capt. Pallister before we came to the hospital. I hope I don't see Jeremy or I'm afraid I'd be arrested for what I feel like doing."

Dr. Davis walked in. "Good news. If our girl has a good night's rest and a good check-up tomorrow, it might be possible for her to leave the hospital. I didn't want to send her back to the base alone, so we've kept her here to make sure she started healing well. Too, I was hoping someone would be with her that would love her and care for her."

"Dr. Davis, you've earned my undying gratitude." Sean shook hands with him.

Everything did go well and the next day Sean and Megan took Sharon and Lynn to a hotel where they had rented a suite. Lynn brought them up-to-date on her horse program with the handicapped.

Later the two girls were alone in their bedroom. "Sharon, are you returning to Ft. Lauderdale or would you be willing to give Zephyrhills a chance and stay with me?"

"I know I don't have a future with Jeremy. As much as I hate to, I'm going to file for divorce as soon as possible. Philip has offered to represent me. The University in Tampa sounds good so that I can finish my education and get my degree to teach. If you're willing to put up with me, why don't you find a house for me in Zephyrhills and take care of opening it for me. I'll come as soon as I can."

"Save your money and stay with me. You can help with the horses until you're ready to make permanent plans for your future. The children will love you and you'll love them."

"Thanks a million, Lynn, but I need to be on my own." Lynn reluctantly accepted Sharon's decision making it clear that she was always available, if needed.

"Now that mom and dad are here, I'll go back home in the morning and get started looking for your house. I'm thrilled that you'll come to Zephyrhills, but I'm very anxious for you to be safely with me." Lynn spoke softly and kissed Sharon's cheek.

The next afternoon Sharon was resting while her parents cleaned up after their lunch. A knock sounded at the door. Sean opened the door to see Malcolm and Agnes. They were warmly welcomed and taken into Sharon's bedroom. Agnes, as usual, was stern and holding her head high, acknowledging no one. She sniffed as if at a bad odor.

Malcolm could hardly speak around the lump in his throat as he hugged Sharon and kissed her cheek. "Sharon, darling, I hope you know you can depend upon my complete support."

"Well, Malcolm," Agnes sneered. "The little tramp has fooled you, too. It looks as if she has you wrapped around her finger. Why is it that only men are taken in by her?"

"You vile woman," Megan gasped walking toward Agnes with clinched fists.

"Agnes!" Malcolm choked astonished. "For once in your miserable life get your mind off your selfish existence and our son that *you* sinfully spoiled." He looked angry but more embarrassed.

"Please don't quarrel over me," Sharon's voice trembled. "I know it's difficult for you to accept," she continued, trying to calm Agnes. "Jeremy does need professional help and your denying it won't change him."

"Sharon, you were too young to get married," Agnes snapped. "You're too spoiled, sheltered, immature, and selfish, and the only problem Jeremy has is **you**." Spittle was flying from Agnes' mouth and she was shaking visibly as she spat out the words.

Sean was livid. "Agnes, these may be rented rooms, but for the time being it is our home. Either conduct yourself as a lady, face the truth about your son, and leave my daughter alone, or get out. Sharon has suffered enough."

"Jeremy has suffered the most, and it's all her fault." Agnes shot back.

"Malcolm I'm truly sorry, but of course you'll have to leave with her. You and I are partners and friends, but Agnes is not welcome." Sean spoke firmly.

"Just wait until I get back home and tell everyone about Miss Squeaky Clean. She'll be the laughing stock of the whole city, especially the country club," Agnes laughed as if she were demented. Her bleached-blonde hair was shaking loose from a twist.

"Agnes, it's times like this that makes me wonder what I ever saw in you. Megan, Sean, Sharon, I'm so sorry. Come on Agnes. We need to have a serious talk and then have one with our son. It's long overdue."

Two days later Jeremy agreed to give Sharon an uncontested divorce. He was facing a dishonorable discharge and was angry with everyone. By unspoken agreement everyone was careful to keep Jeremy's activities from Sharon. Everyone felt she had suffered enough without learning of his continued self-destruction.

Gen. Huff issued orders that Jeremy was not to pilot any planes or drive any military vehicle. He was relieved from all duties. He was fortunate that it was peacetime, otherwise, he might face a court martial.

The next day Colonel Kirkpatrick came with Linda and Philip. "Sharon, I hardly know how to tell you," the Colonel began.

Linda broke in. "Please. Let me, Sir. You and Philip can leave or stay, but I think I should tell her."

"Well, someone tell me. You're scaring me."

Linda reached and took Sharon's hand. "Honey, I guess the good news is that your immediate problems have been solved. The bad news is the way it happened. Jeremy, during one of his drunken flings, stole a plane, but he didn't get off the ground. At the end of the runway, the plane flipped over bursting into flames. Jeremy didn't make it."

Sharon sat stunned and then dissolved in wrenching sobs. Philip motioned for Col. Kirkpatrick and they quietly left. Linda gathered Sharon in her arms. "Where are your parents?"

"With Dad Taylor," Sharon was finally able to say.

Duke hurried into a phone booth in a shabby section of town. He made a call to northern Florida, again reversing charges.

"Gee, Hank, our problem was taken care of and my hands are clean. The Fool crashed a plane and killed hisself."

"Yea! Score one for us."

"We still don't know if his wife knows about us."

"Keep an eye on her, but don't do anything until you check with me. I have to talk to the Boss. I'll get back to you."

Hank chuckled to himself and then picked up the phone. He was the only one who knew this number even if he'd never met the man on the other end.

"Good news, Boss. Great news. Duke called and said Jeremy crashed a plane and killed himself. I don't know all the particulars, but it's a break for us."

"I'll say. What are you doing about the wife?"

"I told Duke to follow her but not to do anything until he checked with me."

"Good enough. I'll get in touch soon about our next development."

"Okay. You know where to find me."

Sharon and her parents met with Philip in his office on the base. "Sharon, Jeremy had not signed the final divorce papers, so, legally you're his widow. You need to make arrangements for a funeral"

"Agnes wants to take the body to Fort Lauderdale where she can grieve publicly," Megan spoke quickly.

"Too bad. It's Sharon's decision," Philip smiled.

"If I may, I'll have the funeral in the chapel on the base so our military friends can attend. Will you see to that for me, please?" Sharon spoke softly.

"You don't need to ask, Sharon. I'll do whatever is necessary to help you."

Sharon and Linda were standing by the coffin when Agnes entered and approached, facing them across the coffin. There were several people already in the chapel.

"Get her away from here," Agnes demanded loudly, throwing her arm out and pointing at Sharon. "You don't belong here. Murderer! Murderer!"

Agnes became angrier when Sharon remained calm. She continued shouting as Malcolm practically carried her out. He looked back sadly at Sharon. She felt sorry for him and knew it was difficult for him to deal with his grief because of Agnes.

Two days after the funeral Philip had Sharon come to his office. Both sets of parents were present. Agnes again staged an unpleasant scene.

"What do you mean she gets his money and his insurance? She didn't love him, never did, and she was trying to divorce him. She's glad he's dead." She stormed out.

Malcolm hung his head. "I'm so sorry. For years I've been thinking my son was spoiled and thoughtless. I'm ashamed of myself for allowing his mother to influence him. I haven't wanted to face the fact that Jeremy was plain mean, or might have a mental problem. Agnes' actions make me wonder about her, too. Sharon, you will always have my complete support." His shoulders shook with silent sobs.

"It's over for Jeremy," Sean spoke soothingly to his friend. "Maybe Agnes will settle down now. It's a shame that she had to be tranquilized for the funeral. I hope she'll forgive all of us for not allowing her to take charge."

"Thank you for being my other dad," Sharon hugged Malcolm. He left, shuffling along like an old man. His six feet two frame bent and sad.

The next morning the Taylors went back to Fort Lauderdale. The Donnellys left also after Sean had Sharon's car checked and filled with gas before he left.

"Darling," Sean said, "your mom and I don't want to leave you, but it's your decision. Keep your cell phone handy and call me if there's any problems. It won't take me long to get to you." She hugged both of her parents and they reluctantly left.

Sharon loaded her car and looked around the neighborhood as she prepared to leave. *Will I ever return to Texas? I've made the most wonderful friends and hate to*

leave them, but with God's help my future will be brighter.
She went in to make a last phone call.

"Hi, Lynn. It's just me. Are you sure you're ready for me?"

"Silly, you're wasting time talking. Boogie on over, but get here safely. Are you sure you don't mind traveling alone? I can always come to meet you."

"No. I'll be fine. Thanks for offering though."

"Did you get the package I sent?"

"Sure did. Just saying thanks isn't enough. See you in a couple of days."

Sharon went out to find Linda, Philip and numerous friends and neighbors waiting. Linda smiled through her tears. "You're like a little sister to us. We both love you and want the best for you."

"Call us as soon as you get home. We'll be anxious about you. We may even hop over and visit," Philip hugged her.

"I love you both and have been so blessed to add you to my extended family. Do visit, and soon."

"If you need me, I'll catch up with you wherever you are," Philip hugged her again.

The Pallisters moved aside so others could speak to Sharon and hug her. Several had goodies for her to snack on and gifts to remember them. Everyone loved Sharon's gentle nature and her obvious caring about others. Some of the men had privately discussed how they should have taken care of Jeremy before he had hurt Sharon so badly.

With a lump in her throat, Sharon drove off the base waving to everyone and feeling a little like she did the first time she left home.

Sharon

Will I see these wonderful people again? Will I ever return to Texas?

CHAPTER FOUR

Blasts of angry horns brought Sharon back to reality. She was embarrassed to see the cars ahead of her had moved on and she was holding up traffic while daydreaming. In her little green Corsica she had driven over five hundred miles and now the dusk was covering the earth like a soft blanket over a sleeping baby.

Sharon hadn't noticed that the pewter clouds had become black. Suddenly they erupted in a downpour accompanied by crashing thunder and blinding lightning. Heavy rain, coupled with forceful wind made it impossible to drive at the allowed speed. The wind increased causing the rain to hit the windshield like pebbles. She drove slowly and carefully, leaning forward to gain better vision.

She was concerned because other cars were driving by her too fast on the slick road.

She felt her scalp prickling and cold fingers crawled across the back of her neck. This feeling had come over her previously, and although she wasn't psychic, she seemed to sense danger.

Telling herself it was just the weather and tension, she was unprepared when she was struck from the rear. Her car fishtailed, then swerved and headed for the steep bank beside the expressway where a deep river leaped and roared below.

Working automatically she quickly took her foot off the accelerator and turned the car in the direction of the skid. Finally able to straighten the car, she drove on the shoulder until she could get back on the highway. *Thank God dad taught me to drive under these conditions and not lose my head in an emergency.*

"Some idiot driving too fast rear-ended me," she fumed aloud. "Why didn't the driver stop to see if there was any damage or injury?" Scrutinizing the side mirrors and rear-view mirror, she was not able to see the car that might have hit her. All other traffic was moving on and none looked suspicious.

"Okay, Steamboat," she patted the steering wheel, "it's time to find a motel. I wish I could drive all the way through, but it's safer to stop during this storm. After all, there's lots of miles to cover yet. Boy! If Agnes could hear me talking to you, she'd really doubt my sanity and be happy to shout it to the world." She chuckled. Talking her thoughts aloud had always helped her to think more clearly.

After about half an hour, several neon signs flickered 'no vacancy' before she saw one in the distance that looked promising. Leaving I-10 she exited into Midway, Florida.

Ahead, and to the right, was a Rest Best Motel and Restaurant. Sharon pulled under the canopy in front of the motel office.

She eased out of the car still too stiff to move quickly. Her ribs were still tender and she felt the strain of the drive. *At least the rain has let up*, she thought thankfully.

Sharon heard the blaring television before she opened the motel office door. Inside, the noise was almost unbearable. Clearing her throat didn't get the man's attention that she could see in the open room next to the office. He was sitting forward, on the edge of his chair, intently watching "True Stories Of The Highway Patrol."

"Excuse me," she spoke loudly. No response. "Sir, I need a room," she stated a little louder, tempted to pound on the desk. She was exhausted.

A short, obese woman came shuffling out of a back room chewing on a thick ham sandwich. Her backless house slippers slapped the floor as she moved.

"That ole fool can't hear you. He has hearing aids and won't wear them. He just drives the rest of us crazy. Herman," she screamed. "Consarn it. Turn that fool thing down."

The man waved his hand over his head without turning around and leaned forward. Sharon was astonished to hear him cheering for the criminals.

"Whatcha want, honey? A room for the night?" The woman grinned at Sharon.

"Yes, please."

"Wherjha come from?" The woman handed a registration card across the desk to Sharon.

"I --I've been in Texas." Sharon felt uncomfortable giving information about herself to strangers, especially when traveling alone.

"Oh, you're from Zephyrhills. 1818 North 18th St.," she read Sharon's new address on the card. Sharon just smiled and reached for the key. "I'll pay you now because I don't know how early I'll leave."

Stupid, Sharon, you're stupid. Why didn't I give my parents' address in Fort Lauderdale? Oh, well. It's too late now. At least I took my maiden name back. She reached for the door to go out.

"It's room five and you can git ice from the machine there in the hall outside this office," the woman called belatedly.

Sharon smiled and thanked her as she went out the door. She got in her car and drove about sixty feet to the left, then turned to back against the curb. Getting out of the car she was thinking how tired she felt and how thankful she would be to get to Zephyrhills the next day. She walked to the back intending to get an overnight bag out of the trunk. One foot raised to step on the curb, she grunted in pain as she felt the sidewalk slam against the right side of her head and her right knee plowed into the side of the curb.

"Oh, great! Are you hurt? I crashed into you. Can you move? I'm sure sorry." A deep, contrite voice spoke somewhere above her head.

"Ooo. I'm going to have a doozy of a headache. Ouch! My knee. What happened? I was minding my own business and innocently going to my room, then this --. What else is going to happen to me?"

"Come on, idiot!"

Sharon was startled when another man's voice barked angrily nearby. Through blurred vision she could only see dark shapes. The light from the open door behind the man kept her from seeing clearly.

"Let me help you up." A hand reached down to her. *What an odd ring. A coiled snake with ruby eyes and it looks to be solid gold.*

"Thank you." She put her hand in his and struggled to her feet. Hearing the second man cursing loudly, the man, who had helped her to her feet, dropped her hand and ran across the parking area. She saw him open the door of the car and jump in as it took off.

Turning north, the car sped into the darkness.

Sharon limped gingerly to the trunk and got an overnight bag, then hobbled to the door of room five. Unlocking the door, and stepping inside, she drew a relieved breath and turned on the lights.

What else is going to happen? All I need now is for a building to fall on me. Shut your mouth, Sharon. With your luck that's the next thing that will occur. What's that old saying? Oh, yes, 'if I didn't have bad luck I wouldn't have any luck at all'. No. I won't allow myself to sink into despair. I did ask God to help me and I believe that He'll help me every way that I need. She took a deep, shuddering breath and gave herself a mental shake.

Limping and feeling slightly nauseated, Sharon went to get a bucket of ice and two Diet Cokes then hobbled painfully back to the room. She put ice in a glass and poured one can of coke over the ice, drinking it with two aspirin.

After a warm, relaxing shower, she dressed in lime green silk pajamas. She brushed her teeth and slipped into bed. The remote control was handy for her to turn on the television, select a movie, set the sleep timer and settle down. She ate some of the snacks her friends had given her and slowly began to feel more comfortable.

Sharon appreciated the soft bed that helped her to relax. Before slipping down against the pillows, she glanced in the horizontal mirror over the long dresser. Seeing her red, swollen cheek, she chuckled aloud. "Beautiful. No wonder the man ran from you, Sharon ole gal."

Giggling to herself, in spite of her aches and pains, she snuggled down to enjoy the movie. In a short time she drifted into a deep, peaceful sleep letting the sleep timer turn the television off.

Sharon groaned and slowly opened her eyes to an irritating noise. Her head hurt and she ached all over. There was that noise again. *Wha -- is someone knocking at my door?*

"What is it?" she snapped.

"Police. Open up. We need to talk to you."

She groaned again and dragged her aching body out of bed. Slipping on a peignoir matching her pajamas, and fighting to wake up, she hobbled to the door. Jerking the door open only as far as the chain would allow, she asked irritably, "What do you want? I was sound asleep."

"Good morning." A man smiled and touched two fingers to the brim of a western hat. "I'm sorry to disturb you, but I need some information. It's vitally important that we talk." He showed a badge and a card identifying him as Lt. Larry Dauber, Police Detective as he introduced himself. "May I come in or would you rather come out here?"

Sharon hesitated. "I'll dress as quickly as I can and I'll be out." Shutting the door firmly, she turned and limped to the luggage to get clean clothing. After a quick shower, she dressed in a peach-colored shorts and shirt set, then slipped her feet into cream-colored leather moccasins.

The bright sun made her squint as she stepped on the hot sidewalk. "Excuse me a moment. I'm going back for my sunglasses." She went back into the room for her glasses and came out to stand quietly in front of Lieutenant Dauber. Uniformed police stood around with a short, thin man whom she recognized as the man in the office. His wife was beside him with a few curious bystanders.

I don't know what I really expected, but not this. She looked up with surprise when Lt. Dauber took a step closer. He stood at least six three. His dark brown hair came to the top of his collar and gray eyes seemed to look right through her. She had to bite her lip to keep from laughing aloud when she looked at his neatly trimmed mustache and thought of Zorro.

"Miss Donnelly, I'm sorry to awaken you in this manner, but we do have a major concern." She crossed her arms over her chest and just looked straight at him. She could not think of any way she would be involved in a major concern of his. "Do you know, or have you heard of, a man by the name of Arnold Millhouse?"

"No. The name is not familiar. If I ever met him, I don't remember him, but I don't think I've ever met him."

"Did you see anyone around room four, the room to the left of your room, when you came in last night?"

She frowned. "I didn't exactly see anyone, but I know someone was near there."

"Who was it?" snapped the man from the office aggressively.

"Mr. Morrison. Please allow me to ask the questions." Lt. Dauber glared at him and spoke firmly.

"Can you describe who you saw?"

"Not really." she answered truthfully.

"Maybe she's in on it," snarled Morrison.

"Mr. Morrison," Lt. Dauber spoke with disgust in his voice, "remain silent or go back to the office with a policeman and wait for me there."

"Herman," his wife said softly and reached for his arm. He mumbled and jerked away from her but did stay quiet. His beady, black eyes stayed on Sharon.

"Can you tell me what, or whom, you did see?" Lt. Dauber questioned Sharon.

Sharon explained what happened when the man bumped into her and how he left. "I can't prove the men had been in room four, only that the door was open and the light was on. Oh, now I remember. Several minutes later when I went for ice, the door was shut and it was dark, but I thought nothing about it."

"I'm sorry you've been hurt, Miss Donnelly. To tell the truth, I was a little suspicious when I saw the bruises on your face and that you are limping."

"Why in the world would my injuries make you suspicious of me?" Sharon asked disturbed. "It is only common courtesy that you tell me what these questions are about."

"You're right, of course. I needed to determine if you were involved or knew something about the murder."

"Involved in what?! And why would I know anything about a local murder when I'm just passing through?"

"The man in room four, Arnold Millhouse, was found dead this morning when the maid went in to clean. It is unfortunate, but it looks as if you checked in about the time it happened. It's just standard procedure to ask anyone around for information."

"So you think the men that I saw could be involved?"

"I have no way of knowing. I need to talk to anyone who might give us even a tiny scrap of information. I can't be sure those men knew anything until I can question them. Can you identify the car they were in?"

"I didn't see the car enough to identify it. It was just a dark shade parked over there in the shadows. The light from here doesn't reach over there."

"Did you observe anything about either man? Did either one have a noticeable accent or speech pattern? Was there an odor of any kind such as shaving lotion or something they wore? Can you think of anything more to tell me?"

"Nothing. I'm sorry. The man that ran into me was polite, had a deep voice and was very tall. The other man was angry at him for stopping to help me."

"Thank you, Miss Donnelly. Please give this officer your name, address and phone number where we can contact you. Here's my card. Remember, no matter how insignificant something might appear to you, it may be just the break we need. Feel free to contact me at any time."

Feeling prickles at the back of her neck, Sharon turned around to see Herman Morrison glaring at her, but his wife was smiling.

Sharon went back into the room and prepared to leave. She puzzled over Herman Morrison and his obvious dislike of her. *Why? He doesn't even know me. Why do I feel so uncomfortable to be around these people?* So many troubling thoughts raced through Sharon's mind.

She put her bag in the trunk of her car and then walked over to the restaurant. After breakfast she got into her car, clicked the seat belt in place, and pulled out to get back up on I-10. She turned toward the southeast thinking she would more than likely reach I-75 in a little less than an hour.

A little more than half an hour later the heavy rain started. *First beatings from Jeremy, then the stupid fall, knock-down, whatever, last night. I sure don't need an auto accident to finish me off.* She drove carefully on her way, her heart becoming lighter as she came closer to her new home.

Sharon turned the radio on hoping to get a weather report, but static forced her to turn it off. About an hour and a half after she had left the motel, Sharon turned south on I-75. The miles had taken longer than she expected because the pounding rain had forced her to drive slowly, and even stop once until she could see more clearly.

She pulled into a service station for gas and a rest stop. The Snack Mart had cold soft drinks and snacks. She thought a sweet cake and the caffeine in the coke would give her some much needed quick energy. *At this rate I'll probably reach my new home by about ten tonight. It's too bad I was held up until eleven before I could leave the motel this morning. I sure thought I'd make better time than this. It's okay though just as long as I arrive safely.*

I sure am glad Lynn sent me directions along with a house key and garage door opener. I can hardly wait to get there. How wonderful it will be to live near Lynn and be stress free.

The rain became a light mist and then stopped, but the sky still looked threatening As Sharon drove through the Ocala area, she decided to stop and rest. Pulling in front of a restaurant she sat quietly with closed eyes and rolled her head gently on her shoulders. Getting out of the car the muggy heat seemed to hit her like a slap in the face. Walking slowly to keep from limping, she went into the restaurant.

The air conditioning was welcome after the slow walk across the hot pavement. She found a table near a window. A middle-aged woman came to take Sharon's order.

"Your dinners look delicious, but I can't decide whether I want a full meal or just a sandwich. Can you give me a minute?"

"Sure, love," the waitress answered with a British accent. "Take all the time you need. Would you like something to drink while you're deciding?"

"Yes, please. A big, tall, cold glass of ice tea with lemon would be heavenly."

The waitress brought the tea with two big chucks of lemon hanging on the side of the glass. Taking her pad and pencil from her pocket, she asked, "Have you decided what you want?"

"Yes. I would like the chicken salad platter and blueberry pie. Could you please heat the pie when I'm ready for it?"

"Absolutely. We're here to please." She smiled and walked away.

The food was delicious. Leaving a generous tip, and then paying the bill, Sharon walked toward the ladies' room. As she passed a booth, she deftly stepped aside to avoid a man who stood quickly. He reached out to steady her as she staggered.

"Gee, I'm sorry. That was careless of me to get up without looking. Are you okay?"

Sharon broke into nervous giggles. "That's the second time in as many days that a man has asked me that?"

He looked strangely at her and dropped her arm as if she were a threat to his life. She quickly excused herself and, blushing with embarrassment, hurried to the ladies' room.

Back in the car, Sharon cheered. "Hurrah, Steamboat! You sure are a good little buddy." She grinned as she patted the dashboard. "We're almost home and you can have the rest you deserve. Me ,too. Wonder why I'm accident prone lately? Must be getting old," she chuckled.

The trip continued uneventfully. Sharon exited off I-75 on to S.R. 54 for the last twelve miles into Zephyrhills. A few minutes before ten pm, she drove by the city limit sign. West 54 became Fifth Avenue as she drove across the little bridge over Zephyr Lake. Driving across Gall Blvd., known as Highway 301, she soon reached Eighteenth Street. Turning left she quickly covered the few blocks to her new home.

What a relief and how exciting to push the remote control for her very own garage door to slide smoothly open.

"Hallelujah! My compliments to you Steamboat. We did it."

Remembering the floor plan that Lynn sent, Sharon stepped from the garage into the house. Turning left she walked down a short hallway to the master bedroom. With a sigh of contentment she slipped out of her shoes and then toured her new house.

Lynn had left a beautiful vase of sweet-smelling roses on a credenza. As Sharon bent to smell the flowers, her eyes were drawn to the blinking light on the telephone answering machine. She turned it on for her message.

"Hey, Sharon. It's about time you got here. Call me as soon as you get in. I've been worried about you. I'm expecting you to spend the day with me tomorrow. You'll love the two new young horses I bought. Are you going to ride with my hunt club? Oh, there's so much to talk about. Call me before I zonk out. I'm exhausted, but I'm so anxious to hear from you."

Sharon smiled at Lynn's message but phoned her parents first.

"Darling, I'm so relieved to know you're in Florida safely. How are you? How was your trip?"

"I'm fine, Mom. It's so good to hear your voice. The trip was tiring and I'm thankful it's over."

"Hi, beautiful!" Sean Donnelly's voice boomed out on the extension. "How soon am I going to get to hug my daughter? Honey, we're thrilled that you're living closer to us. Grab Lynn and both of you come home here for awhile."

"I love you guys. I'm the luckiest person in the world to have you two for parents. I know Lynn would love to come, but she has to work. After all, when you're the owner it isn't as easy to take time off. You know that, Dad. Lynn is responsible for people as well as animals. I can't answer for Lynn, but I'll try to come at the end of this week."

"Sharon," her mother interrupted. "Don't you think it would be wise if you came here to stay for a few weeks. Better still, just come here to live."

"No, Mom. I need to keep busy and take charge of my own life. I'll be taking college courses in Tampa at the University of South Florida and helping Lynn as much as I can. Besides, I don't want to be in the same town with Agnes Taylor until I do some healing. It's bad enough that I'm in the same state."

"Baby, I applaud your common sense and wish the best for you. Agnes did as she threatened. She's told everyone that will listen how you let Jeremy down and that you're responsible for his death. Of course none of the people who are worth anything pay any attention to her," Sean laughed. "She even tried to get the newspapers to carry a story on Jeremy's life and death and how you were the worst excuse for a wife. One editor called me and was furious with her. He assured me that no reputable paper would print any such thing. Since none of the others did either, I can only assume that they chalked her up as demented and refused to play along with her. You can count on Malcolm, but you're right, honey. You're an adult and need to make your own decisions. Just don't let pride lead you into deciding something you're not sure of when we're here for you," her dad finished.

"Thanks, Dad. I know I can count on you and Malcolm. I hope I never have to ask him to choose between Agnes and me."

Sharon hung up and immediately called Lynn. Happy sounds came from both young women. "Yes, I plan to come see you tomorrow, but I can't take time to ride. I'm sure my aching bones wouldn't allow me to ride, but thanks anyway. I have lots to do. I love the house and furniture you've chosen for me. Thanks again until you're better paid."

Her last call was to Linda and Philip Pallister. "Sharon, what a relief to hear from you. Honey, it's dead here without you. Oops. Forgive me. I meant it isn't the same without you. In fact, it's downright dull," Linda choked.

"How's my other best girl?" Philip broke in. "It's true. We all miss you and it isn't the same. People on the base grew fond of your sweet smile and sunny personality. We want you to be happy -- and safe."

"I know. How blessed I am to have friends like you. Know something? I missed you folks as soon as I drove away. Let's keep in touch. I hope we'll still be prayer partners. Remember, I expect a visit from you as soon as you can get here."

Goodbyes were said and Sharon recognized that she was too tired to do more. She found fruit, milk, soft drinks, sandwich materials, frozen dinners and goodies of all kinds as well as dry cereal and microwave popcorn. *Bless you, Lynn.*

An apple cut into thin slices, some cheese and vegetable crackers were placed on a saucer. Picking up the plate and a cold glass of milk, she went into the bedroom. She placed the food on a night stand and propped up against king-sized pillows on the bed.

After watching a late news program and checking on the weather for tomorrow, she took a quick shower, brushed her teeth and dressed for bed. Her prayer was one of thankfulness. Exhausted, she turned off the light and snuggled down to sleep.

Bright lights stung Sharon's eyes. Dark forms of people moved around her in slow motion. Distorted voices came floating at her as if they were sounds on a very slow tape.

A short, thin man stalked her snarling and threatening. She tried to run and found Jeremy facing her with his twisted mouth grin and his fist raised to strike her. She screamed so loudly that she woke up.

Still panting for breath, she drug out of bed and went into the adjoining bathroom to wash her face in cold water.

Will I ever get over this feeling of fright and sadness? Oh, grow up. You're silly Sharon. I have so many blessings and too much to be thankful for. Oh, I know I'm going to love Zephyrhills and working with Lynn.

CHAPTER FIVE

Sharon's eyes felt gritty as she laboriously crawled out of bed. After a leisure breakfast, she unpacked and hung clothes in a large walk-in closet in the master bedroom. While dusting and doing small chores, she called Lynn and made plans for a visit, then went outside to walk around the house and see what flowers could be planted.

Following Lynn's directions, Sharon drove down Eighteenth St. south to Fifth Ave. and turned west. She enjoyed driving through the peaceful city of Zephyrhills. Cruising slowly so she could enjoy the almost old-fashioned city, she observed that the main street had two wide traffic lanes on either side of a wide, grassy medium. On the medium were holly trees, loaded with red berries, planted every few feet and covering about two miles. Baskets of colorful flowers hung on the arms of each light post. Old-fashioned bricks were laid in an attractive pattern at a wide intersection.

What a lovely, restful city. I can almost see the Calusa Indians proudly living and walking around here as they did in the 1500s.

Leaving the business district, Sharon drove through miles of citrus groves. *I remember reading that Zephyrhills once depended on tobacco and peanuts for money crops, but blights and bad weather destroyed them. Now the orange groves and other citrus fruits have made Florida famous. Good, here's Morris Bridge Road. I'm supposed to turn left on to it.* About half a mile on the right she   saw a large vertical sign reading SOARING EAGLE THERAPEUTIC EQUESTRIAN CENTER.

As she pulled into the visitors parking area, a man came out of the stables pushing a wheelbarrow filled with dirty straw and stable droppings.

"Morning, miss," he greeted her politely. "What can I do for you?"

"I'm Lynn Yates' sister. Do you know where I can find her?"

"You're Sharon," he said enthusiastically with a big grin. "We've all been waiting for you. Lynn will be overjoyed. Walk past this row of stables and you'll see a riding arena on the far side. They're working with special riders now, but Lynn won't mind if you watch."

"Thank you," Sharon smiled. "And you are--"

"I'm Jake Bentley. General handyman and in charge of the stables. I do whatever is necessary to keep the horses healthy and happy. I'm looking forward to working with you. Lynn says you're an excellent trainer and very good with children."

"I'm happy to know you, Jake Bentley. I can see you take a lot of pride in keeping this place neat. I'm eager to get involved and work with you and Lynn."

"I do take pride in doing my work well. Lynn makes everyone, who works with her, happy to do their best, and I want everything good for her."

"Sounds like my sister," she smiled. "See you." She walked to where he had directed. Sharon soon found a well equipped riding ring and a busy group. Everyone looked as if they were enjoying the session. Several children were on various sized mounts and three teens were with each rider. Lynn was walking beside a young woman on a tall Thoroughbred. The young woman had lost one arm up to her elbow and one leg just below the knee. Her right hand held reins that were made like a leather ladder. Her artificial leg was held in place with a Velcro belt.

Not wanting to interrupt the class, Sharon quietly walked back to the office and into a comfortable lounge. There was a couch and chairs facing a wall made of a window that overlooked an indoor riding ring. Past the seating arrangement was a soft drink machine, restrooms, a pay phone and a water fountain. At the end was a small classroom with a blackboard. A hallway led to offices, a clinic and a therapy room with a whirlpool bath.

To the right a large office had Lynn's name on the door. In it was a desk with a telephone and file folders on it. At a second L shaped desk sat a lovely young woman in a wheelchair. In front of her was a computer, a telephone, a roll-a-dec and tablets on which she was writing notes. Behind her was an impressive row of filing cabinets.

The woman appeared to be in her mid twenties. Sensing Sharon's presence, she looked up with a bright smile and dimples dancing in both cheeks. Her light brown hair was French braided in one long braid. A heart-shaped face bubbled with joy of life and her amber eyes sparkled with her joy.

"Hi! Is there something I can do for you?" She had a friendly voice, bubbling with a hint of laughter. Sharon immediately felt that she could like this young woman and wanted to know more about her.

"Yes, I'm Sharon--"

"Donnelly," finished the woman with a happy shout. "I'm Sheilah Garrison. We've all been anxious to meet you. Lynn is ecstatic that you'll be here and has sung your praises to anyone that will listen, even the horses."

Both young women laughed. "That's embarrassing. I don't know what Lynn has told you."

"All good stuff. In fact, I could hardly wait to meet the paragon of virtue. Oh, my goodness," she slapped a hand over her mouth. "Me and my big mouth. That didn't come out right. It sounded sarcastic and I meant it to be funny." Sheilah looked so distressed that Sharon had to laugh.

"Don't think anything about it. Remember, I grew up with Lynn. We were raised together as sisters. Truthfully, we've been closer than most siblings. So, I'm aware of how exuberant she can get."

The two young women became instant friends, chatting away when Lynn walked in looking very tired. She spotted Sharon, gave a shout of joy, hugged her and jumped around with tears streaming down her cheeks.

"Hey!" Sharon was finally able to say. "I had my shower before I left the house. Can we tone it down a little and turn off the water works?"

"Oh, shut up," Lynn laughed through tears. "I am so relieved to see you and know that you're okay. I -- let me take a short break and then I'll show you over the place. I would love for us to go for a ride, but I have another class of special children and two private lessons. I also need to exercise the two horses I'm training for the hunt field."

"Take it easy," Sharon chuckled. "I'll be around until you'll want to run me off."

"Not a chance. It's been way too long and I need you here with me."

At that moment the young people who had been walking beside the special riders came in. They were introduced to Sharon. Most of the special riders came in to wait for their families to pick them up. Sharon was so impressed with these youngsters that she almost forgot Lynn. She sat beside a boy in a wheelchair.

"Hello. What's your name?"

"Leland Nesbitt, and I'm nine years old."

"Marvelous. Forgive me, Leland. I hope I won't upset you, but I'd like to know why you're in this riding program."

"Well - my folks say I was born active. When I was four, my mom said I climbed a tree and fell out and hurt my back. I was in the hospital a long time; then the doctor put me in this wheelchair, but I won't always be here. Since I've been riding and exercising, I can walk a little with crutches."

"That's wonderful. Maybe you'll be walking entirely without your crutches soon."

"My doctor said he wouldn't promise anything. He says I might even have to have surgery, but mom and dad say we're hopeful."

"Great. Who suggested this program to you?"

"We saw a special on television. My parents contacted the address given and they wrote and said this stable was the closest to me. And here I am," he finished with a satisfied grin.

"You sure are here, and they're lucky to have you. What do you like about this program?"

"I've always loved horses, and all kinds of sports. By riding I can be as high up as anyone and enjoy the same things others do. I don't feel like people are having to look down at me or hold themselves back because of my chair. You know what I would love to do?"

"What's that?"

"I have my heart set on going on a trail ride."

"I bet you will some day and I would love to go right along with you." Sharon patted his arm and turned to a cute little girl sitting beside them in a wheelchair.

"What's your name?"

"Kara Zeigler and I'm eight years old."

"That's a good age. Why are you in your wheelchair?"

"When I was very little, I had a real high temperature and was in the hospital. After that I was home in bed sick for a long time. Muscles 'er too weak to hold me up and do things other kids do. I love horses. Do you know my horse knows me and loves me. She talks to me when I talk to her. We're good friends."

"I bet you are. I'm glad to know you love horses because I love horses, too. Would it be okay if I ride with you sometimes?"

"Sure! Peanut will love you, too."

"Peanut?"

"Yeah. My horse. You'll love her, but she's too little for you to ride."

"I understand," Sharon smiled and kissed Kara's cheek. *I'm going to become too emotionally involved if I'm not careful. I'll volunteer as often as I can, but first, I need to enroll in USF and earn my degree.* Her thoughts were interrupted by some of the teen volunteers coming in.

"Hi. You must be Sharon. I'm Ashley Odom."

"Hello, Ashley. I'm impressed with the work you're doing here."

"Don't think too highly of me. I'm one of many volunteers, but I'm the one who is blessed. These youngsters rarely complain. They are so brave and exciting to work with. It makes me feel very insignificant. The injured adults are great, too."

"I can understand that feeling. What are your plans for the future. What's going to happen to Ashley Odom?"

"I'm in my freshman year of college, and I'm studying to become a physical therapist and I'm also taking psychology. Hopefully, I'll be able to work in a situation like this. If I'm lucky, maybe I can work with Lynn. She's the most loving and compassionate person I know."

"Hey, I can't take any more of this," Lynn broke in. "I wish I could afford to pay all of my wonderful volunteers. There's no way I could operate without you, and you can certainly take credit for the love and understanding you've given these youngsters."

"Can I get in here?" A girl pushed to the front of the group. "Hi, Sharon. I'm Jardine Willis. Ashley and I have been in 4 H together since we were pups. We're both horse crazy and love children. We talked it over and decided to volunteer here and kill two birds with one stone.

"Please, no killing of birds. I love our birds," Lynn laughed.

"Hi, Jardine. I'm in such awe of you young people. You'll have to get Lynn to tell you about us when we were young and horse crazy. Just be patient with me while I learn what to do."

"Okay volunteers. Start volunteering. The horses should already be ready for the next class. Sharon, I'll have to cut back on the program once school starts. Most of these teens will be in college and can't afford the time." Lynn spoke with some concern.

"That's too bad, but won't you still have classes for the special children on Saturdays? Maybe you'll pick up more volunteers by then."

"Yes, I'll have a few classes on Saturday, and one evening, but not as many as we've had this summer. Come here, please, Sharon. I want you to meet someone."

"Sharon, this is Dr. Jennifer Monroe. Jenni is not only one of the best veterinarians in the business, she finds time to work with a mounted scout troop and a 4 H horse group." Lynn introduced the two young women.

"Hello, Dr. Monroe. I'm delighted to meet you."

"Please call me Jenni. I've been looking forward to meeting you. Lynn tells me you're not only a top notch horse trainer, but you're an excellent equitation instructor. We sure need someone like you.

"Lynn is speaking from the love in her heart and doesn't realize how embarrassing it is for everyone I meet to tell me how she sings my praise. Forgive me for staring, Jenni, but I feel as if I'm looking in a mirror."

"I know," Jenni laughed. "Lynn told me you and I look enough alike to be twins or I would have been as shocked as you seem to be. I'd love to stay and talk, but I have to go to work at other stables. We'll have time later to have a long talk."

"I like her," Sharon smiled at Lynn, "but isn't she young to be a veterinarian?"

"She's twenty-seven and was a straight A student all through school. She has earned a place for herself in Pasco County. Everyone likes her as a person and respects her as a veterinarian."

The time passed too quickly for Sharon and she hated to leave. Lynn had shown her all over the property and they were now in Lynn's apartment over the office. They went downstairs where Sharon said goodbye to everyone and then walked to her car. As she drove out the long driveway, she shivered when a cold chill hit the back of her neck. *What, or who, is it, and why have I been targeted? I don't see anyone, but I get this feeling of danger too often now. But maybe it's just past troubles.*

The next morning Sharon was up early and eagerly prepared to go to church. She met Lynn in the Narthex and was pleased to see that most of the teen volunteers were present. The people at First Baptist, on Fifth Ave., were friendly and greeted her warmly. The music was lively and inspirational.

"Dennis is our music director and works with seniors," Lynn explained. He and his wife, Peggy, are real assets to this church. They truly live their Christian faith."

After church Lynn and Sharon ate at The Village Inn. "Tell me more about Zephyrhills. I'm intrigued with the quaintness of the town, and yet, it's very modern," Sharon observed. "I had not heard of Zephyrhills until you settled here."

"Hmm. Where to start. The Calusa Indians were here between four and five hundred years ago. Many explorers came through, mostly Spanish and some French. In the early 1800s, settlers came in to build homes and clear land for farming and cattle raising. This was finally named Abbott Station after a much loved physician, Dr. J. M. Abbott. Following the War Between the States, the town became a refuge for wounded and homeless veterans, both north and south. The descendents of the settlers built better homes, started businesses, and many are still here."

"That is so interesting. It sounds as of a book should be written about Zephyrhills and all about the people who made it grow."

"Been done. I'll get you a copy. One place you don't want to miss is Neukom's Drug Store. It's more like the old variety stores, except, in addition, there is a pharmacy and a branch of the post office in it. The Neukoms are one of the families that have been here since the beginning of time. Also Peeples Clothing Store has been in the town for scads of time. The Peeples family are early residents."

"What else is special about Neukoms?"

"Besides offering almost anything one needs, the men of the town gather in the restaurant part about six every morning for coffee and fellowship. If you want a pastor, priest, reporter, police, doctor, attorney, plumber or what have you, you'll find them in there. They all gather throughout the day, also.

Sharon laughed. "That more than answers my question. How did the name, Zephyrhills, get in the picture? I love the name."

"Capt. H. B. Jeffries suggested the name. It's an Indian word meaning soft breezes over low hills. The Jeffries home is still here on Fifth Ave. It's supposed to be haunted. I'll take you soon to go through it."

"Thanks for the interesting history lesson. Can you go home with me?" Sharon asked.

"Thank you, but no. I need to check on a couple of horses with minor injuries and catch up on my bookkeeping. Are you coming out later?"

"I don't think so, but I'll be out tomorrow. I know you're closed to the public on Mondays, and it'll give us time to catch up on gossip. Family gossip that is."

"Oh, let me tell you a quicker way out to me. Turn right out of your driveway and come through the Florida Estates Mobile Home Park to Hwy. 54 east. Turn left, west, and come out to cross 301 on to Eiland Blvd. This is a new by-pass around town and is named after a beloved police chief we had. Stay on that and cross 54 west on to Morris Bridge Rd. It'll be simple after that."

"Thanks. I'll try it in the morning."

"Sharon, I wish you'd reconsider and live with me for awhile, but I guess we all do what we think is best for us."

"Yes, I need to be independent and gain some confidence. By the way, this isn't a large business area and yet there's hundreds, if not thousands, of vehicles."

"Boy, are there cars!" Lynn laughed. "During the summer months, we have around twenty thousand people, but during the winter, when the people come down from Canada and northern states, we have an additional hundred thousand, or maybe more. There are over one hundred sixty mobile parks. One of them has over two thousands units in it."

"Holy Toledo! What do you do with everyone?"

"We manage. I personally look forward to people coming down for the winter. I've met some great folks, and you will, too. Well, if you won't come with me, I'll go home to my solitary state and find loads of work to do." Lynn hugged Sharon.

The girls parted in the parking lot. Sharon casually looked around when her neck prickled. *There's no one that I can see. That tall man getting in the dark car looks familiar, but all I can see is his back. I probably have never seen him. He's not even looking this way. I won't tell Lynn about my scary feelings. She worries enough.*

At home Sharon changed into shorts and shirt, leaving her feet bare. Sitting down to read the Sunday paper she jumped when the doorbell rang.

"Greetings. I'm your neighbor across the street. Hope you like Banana Cream pie. I made some and thought I'd bring you half of one to welcome you to the neighborhood.

Call on us any time you need anything. My name is Krystal Torres, and that's my husband, Jose, over there." The woman didn't stop to draw a breath.

Sharon looked across the street to see a man waving at her. "I'm Sharon and I know this is going to be a good neighborhood. I'll be busy with college classes and helping my sister in her stable, so, I won't be home much. Thank you for the pie. I love them."

Two more neighbors came by with goodies and to welcome Sharon. *I appreciate their friendliness, but I hope they don't expect me to be a regular visitor in their homes.*

It's true, I'll be busy, but I also need time and space.

By evening she wasn't hungry enough for a full meal. She made a sandwich and decided to shower and get into bed to watch television, or, if nothing interesting was on, to read. It wasn't long until she drifted into a peaceful sleep.

"Hi Hank. It's me, Duke. She's in her new home in Zephyrhills, Florida and has been to the stables to see her sister, or cousin, or whatever she is."

"Does she seem to be nervous or looking for anything?"

"No. She acts like she don't care about nothing. I'm beginning to think she didn't know nothing about what he was doing."

"Maybe not, but something might trigger a buried memory. Stay low but keep an eye on her."

CHAPTER SIX

Monday morning Sharon called the Zephyrhills News to start weekly delivery and then a local daily paper. She drove around town to do errands; open an account at the bank, introduce herself at the post office and make sure her mail would reach her, found an attorney that had been recommended and finally to the grocery store.

Sharon could hardly wait to get to Lynn's. The stable seemed like a lost person without the bustle of lessons and loads of people milling around. A few of the volunteers were there to clean and mend leathers. They were delighted to teach Sharon the ins and outs of what they were doing. They took her out into the field to meet the boarders' horses.

Coming back to the stable, Sharon saw a van pull into the space for visitors. A side door slid open and a ramp lowered a wheelchair to the ground. She was immediately drawn to the wide, sincere smile of the man. His sandy hair was moving in the light breeze making him look like a young boy. As he wheeled closer to her, she could see dancing green eyes and a tanned complexion. He would be tall when standing.

"Hello. We're closed to the public on Monday. Is there something I can do for you?"

Sharon asked smiling in spite of herself. He exuded happiness. *Such a good looking man, and he doesn't seem to be bothered about being in the chair.*

"I hope you can help. My name is Martin Swanson. I'm an attorney and I've just opened an office in Zephyrhills. My doctor suggested that I talk to you about therapy riding."

"I'm Sharon. You need to talk to my sister, Lynn Yates. She's the owner and is in charge of the riding program. Please come into the lounge and I'll get her."

They talked as if they had known each other before as they made their way into the lounge. Martin was impressed with the indoor ring and the lovely, clean, pleasant surroundings. He was especially interested in the therapy room.

"Excuse me, Mr. Swanson. If you'll wait here, I'll go get Lynn from the stables."

"The name's Martin, and I'll be right here," he grinned.

A few minutes later Sharon and another woman he assumed to be Lynn walked into the lounge. The woman's clothing was rumpled and sweat stained her underarms. He could even smell the odor of the muck from the barn clinging to her boots. Yet, he was awed by her natural beauty. *Now there's an unusual woman. I want to know more about her. She doesn't need cosmetics and doesn't seem to mind.* Lynn made a feeble attempt to smooth her shirt and push her hair back from her face.

"Hello," Lynn smiled. "Sharon says you want to speak to me about therapy lessons. I do hope you'll forgive my appearance. I've been working with our vet."

"You look great to me. I mean - you're fine. My name is Martin Swanson. Last fall, while riding in a hunt show, my brave steed apparently saw the sun shining on the water jump. He decided to be a gentleman and allow me to go over first. As I left his back and started flying through the air with the greatest of unease, he decided to follow me. We crashed on the other side. I had fallen on the back of my neck and shoulders. He fell beside me but his head hit my chest. He jumped up and nickered to me, but I couldn't move. Naturally I thought of Christopher Reeve. It took many weeks in the hospital and more weeks at home with therapy. I was finally able to move from the waist up, but my legs have decided they like the vacation. My doctor thinks your riding program may be just what is needed to wake these ole legs and get them going."

Lynn and Sharon were chuckling at his easy attitude.

"Forgive us. We're not laughing at you, but we are laughing with you. Wow! You have a great attitude! I'm not sure I'd be so quick to joke if I were in your place," Sharon explained.

"Why groan and moan? What's done is done. I need to help myself and cooperate with those who are helping me. A disgruntled attitude never makes any situation better."

"I salute you," Lynn smiled. "I can't just sign you up, though I wish I could. I must have a copy of your medical records and your doctor will have to complete the obligatory papers. Our nurse and therapist will have a talk with you after they peruse your records. Your doctor might feel the riding program is enough or he might recommend the massage therapy and whirlpool along with the riding. If your doctor cooperates, we should be ready to go in about ten days."

"Good enough. I'll take care of my part. Would it be too much trouble for me to see what's around here?"

"Sharon, would you please show Martin round? I need to get back to our veterinarian, but we'll be in touch. Leave your address, phone number and name and phone number of your doctor with Sharon. Thank you for coming." Lynn strode off with Martin looking thoughtfully after her. *Uh oh*, Sharon smiled to herself.

Sharon introduced Martin to the horses and answered his questions about their training. She showed him the special saddles and bridles and related equipment for handicapped riders. They then went to the back ring.

"I've heard of the ramp, but how does it work?" Martin was interested.

"Let's walk over to the ramp and I'll show you. See, there are two ramps about forty inches apart. There is a level place on top and a ramp down the other side. A horse is walked between the ramps and stopped at the level on top. Two side walkers will take the wheelchair up the ramp, or help a person who has trouble walking. The rider is then lifted to the horse's back and all safety equipment is put in place. The leader leads the horse out and the side walkers run down the opposite ramp to walk on either side and be prepared to help wherever needed."

"Ingenious. Whoever came up with that idea deserves an award. Will I start with that?"

"I don't know, Martin. We won't know until we get your medical records and your doctor's recommendations. You might have a backrider to start."

"What's a backrider?"

"A qualified person rides double with the rider. He, or she, will sit behind the rider, giving support until the body adjusts to the motions of the animal."

"I'm impressed, and I can hardly wait to get started. It will be so different for me to have help to ride. Is Lynn's husband involved in the program?"

"She's not married." Sharon turned her back to hide her grin. She had been observing that Martin wanted to know more about Lynn. "This is her life's dream and she's worked night and day to make a success of it. Not that she doesn't date. They're standing in line waiting to be the lucky one. Some day some lucky man will come along that will appreciate her and give her the support she needs." Sharon smiled. *I'm laying it on thick, but I can't resist. Who knows. He may be just the one to fill the bill.*

"Thank you for the tour, Sharon. I'll call and make an appointment as soon as I know that my medical records are in."

Sharon waved as he drove off and then laughed out loud. "My guess is that this is going to be a man who will truly care about Lynn and her work. More power to you, Martin." She quickly looked around to make sure no one was hearing her talk to herself.

After lunch in Lynn's apartment, the two girls saddled two young, feisty Thoroughbred geldings for a ride.

"Lynn, as usual, you've done a wonderful job starting the training on these boys."

They guided their mounts across a hundred acre pasture on the far side of the back ring. They worked the young horses to train them to remain quiet while gates were opened and closed by a rider from their backs. As the horses walked briskly, Sharon told Lynn of Jeremy's violent mood swings and his abuse.

Lynn was furious and hurt for Sharon. "Why didn't you leave him the first time he showed that side of him? Why did you stay around for more ugly treatment?"

"I had the same thoughts that most women do in the same situation. I hoped he would change. I also hoped that he wanted the marriage to work as much as I did." She took a shaky breath. "After he injured me so badly and put me in the hospital, I asked him why he married me. He said, "Little Miss Puritan, you had other people fooled, but I know you for what you really are, and so does mom. She knows you've never backed me as a military wife should."

"Oh, Sharon, how in the world did you react to that?"

"I ask him what he meant that I wasn't backing him and reminded him that I had always been proud of him and supported him. He said, 'Yeah, but you don't treat me like mom always did'."

Lynn laughed. "Poor baby. He finally had to follow rules and think of someone else besides himself."

Sharon continued. "I ask him again why he married me."

"What answer could he possible give to that question?"

"He said, 'because miss goody, goody, pure and proper would not go to bed with me until we were married.' He left in a rage and I cried until I was ashamed of myself. That's when I called Dad Taylor and told him what was happening."

"How did he take it?"

"He cried and was so hurt, but when they came, Agnes Taylor raked me over the coals and blamed me for all that had happened."

"Oh, that witch. I wish I'd been there to take care of her," Lynn spit out through gritted teeth. "She'd better hope she never faces me with any of her filthy comments."

Sharon then told Lynn about being rear-ended and about the murder in the motel where she stopped for the night. "I can't explain it, but I had a weird feeling that I shouldn't have given my Zephyrhills address. I know it must sound crazy, but I can't shake the feeling that I'm being followed."

"Honey, I wish you would go for counseling. I know you have been very brave and you think you're in charge of your feelings, but there were a lot of hurts both physically and emotionally. It sure can't do any harm and it might help to gain some inner peace, especially if you see a Christian counselor."

"I know you care about me, Lynn, and you're probably right about the counselor, but I hesitate to tell anyone else about my personal problems. Can we gallop these beasties now?" Racing until the horses began breathing hard, they then settled down for a quiet walk.

"What a beautiful, peaceful trail through these woods," Sharon sighed. At that moment the young horse she was riding jumped with surprise when a rabbit ran across under his nose. He reared and spun around facing the way they had come. His quick action threw Sharon slightly to one side, but she had a solid seat. She spoke calmly and gently pulled him in. At that split second there was a popping sound. The young horse again reared and screamed. Lynn saw a drop of blood on the tip of one of his ears. At the same time she recognized the sound of a bullet as it struck a tree near Sharon.

"Sharon," she yelled. "Run. Some blasted fool's shooting.

The frightened, young horses ran hard toward home. When the girls got to the pasture, they had to run the horses in circles to slow them down. Sharon had to run her horse in smaller and smaller circles. They then walked the horses to the stable to cool them down.

Lynn told Jake and some of the volunteers that the horses were too hot to be given water and food. "Groom them first, then give them water and some hay. They can have grain later tonight."

Sharon and Lynn went into the office to tell Sheilah about their misadventure.

Sheilah was indignant when she heard of the incident. "Let's go get whoever it was. If we wait, he'll get away."

"How in the world are you going to manage that, my friend," Lynn asked irritably.

"Run him down with your wheelchair?"

Sharon gasped. "Lynn! I can't believe you'd be so callous. Sheilah is concerned and wants to help. She's just as angry as we are. She cares."

Sheilah grinned sheepishly. "Lynn isn't being cruel. I know her well enough to know she couldn't be like that. You see, about three months ago, a drunk driver came up on the sidewalk and ran me down. That's why I'm in this wheelchair. I had a back injury. It's still new and if I get excited, I forget that I'm in the chair." She turned to Lynn "Why don't you take the men and hunt for the shooter."

Lynn shook her head. "He's armed and we're not, Citizens shouldn't try to do what others are trained to do. Sharon, if Jeremy were still alive, I'd wonder about your so-called accidents. It's still fishy to me. I'll call Sheriff Howell and ask for his advice."

The sheriff was deeply concerned. He asked several questions, but realized that Lynn was too upset to talk and make much sense. "Both of you wait at the stable and I'll send a deputy to take your statements and make a report. In the meantime, I'll dispatch a patrol car to check along Morris Bridge Road. Tomorrow morning mounted deputies can ride into the woods and search for clues. Call me if anything else happens or you think of something."

"Thank you, Sheriff." Lynn sighed with relief that he was going to take charge. She was a very independent person and took charge of her affairs successfully, but the threat to their lives, the safety of the young, innocent horses and all that Sharon had endured, made her want to just stand and scream because she felt so helpless.

In a couple of minutes Jake came running into the office. "Lynn, there's a Sheriff's car barreling up the driveway with lights flashing."

"Stay with us, Jake. I had to call the sheriff. You can hear the entire story as I tell it."

Jake opened the door and asked the deputy to come in.

"Evening folks. I'm Deputy Vincent Belasic. The Sheriff sent me out to take a statement and find out what's going on."

"Please come in, Deputy Belasic. I'm Lynn Yates, the owner of this stable and this is my sister, Sharon. Jake Bentley is stable manager and Sheilah is my secretary and my right hand. Have a seat. This is going to be a long story. Would you like some coffee?"

"No, thank you. Can we get started? Who's going to talk to me?"

"I'll tell you what happened to us this afternoon, and then I want my sister to tell you her story," Lynn sat and began a concise statement.

Listening to Lynn, Vincent, in shock and surprise, got so absorbed in her story, he neglected to take complete notes. "Excuse me. I'm sorry, but this is a lot to take in. Would you mind going over that again and allow me to use a tape recorder? There's too much to write down and I want to be sure and get the facts."

"That's fine with me," Lynn answered. "In fact, I'll place my own recorder beside yours. That way we'll both have a record of what is said by everyone."

"It's okay with me," he said politely. "I'm here to help you, if I can."

Lynn carefully reiterated all that had transpired that afternoon.

"Well folks, I'm going to suggest to the sheriff that signs be placed along the highway reminding people that horses and riders are in the woods. My opinion is that it was a careless hunter, or kids just shooting for the heck of it."

"But it isn't hunting season and the majority of young people, in this area, own their own horses. They're very careful and conscientious." Lynn was adamant.

"I still think we'll find that it's kids. Now you said you wanted your sister to tell me something."

"Her name is Sharon, and you *will* need to record her statement."

Sharon was so pale and wide-eyed, Lynn held her hand for encouragement. Sharon gave him the highlights of all that had happened to her since her marriage to Jeremy, then the rear-ending and the murder at the motel. "I'm not psychic, but I've had strong feelings that I'm being watched and followed since I left Texas.

"Ma'am, it sounds like you're writing a book of some kind?" he chuckled. "Forgive me. I do take your statement seriously. In a weak way I'm trying to get you to relax."

Lynn angrily answered him. "Her life was in jeopardy over and over. Oh -- just let Sheriff Howell hear what you've recorded. I'll call him tomorrow. Goodnight Deputy Belasic. Thank you for coming."

Sheilah soothed Lynn. "We know what is the truth, but others don't know Sharon like we do. It might sound - oh, I don't know - really like a story to others."

As the deputy's car left, Sheilah gathered her personal possessions together. "It's late, dear hearts. I hope all of us get a restful night's sleep. Tomorrow is another day, and a busy one at that. Goodnight all." She waved as she wheeled out to her special van.

"Jake, you haven't said anything. What are you thinking?" Lynn placed a hand on her old friend's shoulder.

"Ah, Lynn. My heart aches for Sharon. You never told us what all she'd gone through. I wish she'd come here sooner. By the way, I haven't had a chance to tell you, I hired a new man today. He's worked with me all day though, so, I don't suspect him of being involved in any of this."

"Good. I told you a couple of weeks ago to find someone. What's his name and what do you know about him?"

"Lynn, you'd never guess our luck. He's a qualified riding instructor, he's great with the children and almost hypnotizes the horses. He crooned and whispered to that nervous mare you're boarding and then walked right in the stall with her. She didn't attempt to kick or bite. She acted as if they were old friends. He cleans up after himself and checks on supplies before they get low. We really lucked out."

"Sounds great. You've told me a lot, but what's his name and where has he been working?" Lynn was tired and worried and not in the mood for anything that was not serious.

"His name's David Baughman. He was going to be a career Marine, but his dad died and he came home to take care of his mother and two younger sisters. They're still out in Indiana. He said he had to leave because his mother kept trying to get him married."

"What's happening to his mother and sisters? How could he walk off and leave them?"

"I asked him the same thing, and he explained that his dad had left a huge farm. He knew his mother wasn't capable of overseeing so much farm work, so, he sold all but a few acres around the house. He invested for her. The older sister is now in college and the young one is a senior in high school. He keeps in touch and sees that all of them get a monthly income."

"Did you explain to him that we have a month's trial before offering a contract for a permanent position?"

"Yes, and he's willing to work with us."

Lynn turned as Sharon came in from seeing Sheilah off. "Sharon, why don't you stay with me tonight?"

Sharon hugged her. "Thanks, but I'd rather go on home. I'll be back early tomorrow morning. Goodnight Jake. See you." Lynn walked Sharon to her car. Jake stood where he could see both girls until Sharon pulled away and Lynn came back in.

When Sharon got home, she was surprised to hear a message from Larry Dauber on her answering machine. "I'd like to talk to you. Nothing serious, so don't get excited. It's personal. I'll call another time."

She shrugged her shoulders and prepared for bed. *What in the world can he want with me? I hope he isn't still thinking I know something about that murder. If it's important, he'll call another time, but he said it's personal. Oh, well, there's no need to stand and speculate; he'll let me know what he wants.*

The phone rang. "Oh, Larry, I hope it isn't you. I'm in no mood for a conversation. I'm so tired and I need to go to bed."

"Hello. Hello? Is anyone there?" She hung up. "Well, it's either a wrong number or someone thinking they're cute. A wrong number should be courteous enough to say so. I hope this doesn't continue. I've gotten a few of these calls. This could be bad. Oh, great! I'm talking to myself a lot lately, and I'm even answering myself," she laughed.

Sharon felt the blows as Jeremy hit her. Running out the front door, she fell down the steps and rolled into the yard. When people began to gather around, Jeremy was saying, "Sharon, baby. Did you trip over something?" He leaned over her and she shrieked so loudly that she woke up.

Dear Lord, how stupid I was to lie for him and tell good friends that I had fallen or walked into something. How embarrassing to learn that they knew the truth all along. Thank God, that's all over and will never happen again. Why can't I quit thinking about the unpleasant past and concentrate on a happy future? She got up and took two aspirin with a tall glass of water. *Maybe I can get some rest. Five o'clock will roll around soon. Maybe I should have stayed with Lynn. Stop feeling sorry for yourself, you silly baby. I'm sorry that Jeremy ended the way he did, but I didn't contribute to it. I'm safe now and have family and friends all around me. Go to sleep* she said firmly to herself. She got back in bed and picked up a book from the bedside table.

CHAPTER SEVEN

By five thirty Sharon was at the stable and eager to go to work. She hurried into the lounge where coffee and doughnuts were on a table. Her eyes closed in pleasure as she sipped the fragrant coffee. She put two slices of bread in a toaster.

"Sharon, I didn't hear you come in. Did you sleep well?" Lynn hugged her.

"Fine. Everything's jim dandy. What do you need me to do?" Sharon carefully composed herself because she didn't want Lynn to worry more over her. She buttered the toast and spread blackberry jam on them. Eating quickly she listened to Lynn.

"We've all been up for ages. The horses are fed as are the dogs, cats and fowl. You could muck stalls and groom horses. Check the work chart for today and see what horses will be worked in the classes. When the volunteers get here, they'll check the tack they'll be using and make sure everything is ready to roll." The two girls walked to the stable chatting as they had always done.

"Hi, Jake. What do you want me to do?" Sharon touched his arm and smiled.

"Hope you don't mind getting dirty," he answered and then looked puzzled when both girls burst out laughing. Lynn excused herself and ran to answer a phone summons.

"I see Lynn hasn't told you much about us when we were little. Poor mom is such a lady and we drove her bananas.

We not only were dirty most of the time, we often didn't smell too good, either."

"Oh," he smiled, shrugging his shoulders and running his fingers through his hair.

"Well, horses need grooming and stalls need mucking. Which would you rather do?"

"I don't mind doing either one, but if you don't mind, I'll start grooming."

"Okay by me. Sharon, this is David Baughman. He's our new instructor and jack of all trades. David, I want you to meet Lynn's sister, Sharon."

"Hello, David. I don't remember seeing you before."

"I'm glad to meet you, Sharon. I started yesterday. I understand you had some excitement yesterday. If you have any more trouble of any kind, don't hesitate to call on me." *Hmm six four at least. Great blonde hair and blue eyes. Great body.*

"Thank you, David." She looked puzzled. "Have we met before? There's something about you that seems familiar."

"I would sure remember you if we'd met. You know what they say about doubles." David looked at Sharon with a tender expression. She realized he was still holding her hand and gently pulled away.

"I hope you'll be happy here. Excuse me, but I have to get to work or I'll be fired."

The volunteers began to filter in. Even though they were chatting and laughing, Sharon was pleased to see how carefully each youth inspected each piece of tack and equipment they'd be using. Lynn had trained them well.

"Sharon, would you come here, please?" Matthew Ryder called to her. She remembered he was one who told her he wanted to study law.

"What is it, Matthew?"

"I don't know whether you've been shown the duty chart. Sheilah makes these up by the week. It lists the horses that will be used in each class, the helpers that will be working with that particular horse and the student who will be riding. It's up to us to learn all we can about the rider and the horse."

"Yes, I glanced at the chart. That's good organization. You have to know the temperament of the horse and the rider so that you can match them safely."

"Sure do, but it gets easier with experience."

Andrew Nikobi walked up to read the chart. "We also need to recognize if a horse has an injury or a temperature. We wouldn't want to work a sick or injured animal. It isn't only cruel to the animal, but it could be dangerous to the rider. And they *are* in our care."

"I'm impressed and I do admire all of you young people. You give your own valuable time to help and put your whole heart in it. Dad taught Lynn and me all of this while we were very young. We've always known to be responsible for your horse."

"Working here is a blessing for us - at least for me," Ashley said as she joined the group. "I find that I have more inner peace when I work with others that have so many physical problems and pain, and yet they smile through it and enjoy the life they have. Too, Lynn lets us ride in our free time and she even lets us use a horse to go on an occasional hunt."

"Yeah. She gives us riding tips. My equitation has improved more than you would imagine. I thought I was a good rider, and I was - just a good rider. Lynn put some polish on me and now I compete in a show with the best of them," Jardine told Sharon.

Lynn came into the stable in time to hear the last remarks. "Hi, guys. We may have a new student soon. He's an adult who had a riding accident similar to the one Christopher Reeve had."

"If he's that impaired, I'd be afraid to work with him," Andrew stated.

"He's been in intense therapy for several weeks and can now move from the waist up. His leg muscles and nerves refuse to work. His doctor hopes that riding, coupled with massages, might help him. It certainly can't hurt." Lynn looked seriously at them.

"Okay. Does he get a backrider?" Andrew asked with a worried frown.

"I haven't decided yet. I'll talk to his doctor and let you know. Hope I don't disappoint you, but I am a certified Master Instructor. I'd like to work with him the first few times, but I'll need two side walkers."

"Say the word, Boss, and we'll hop to," Andrew grinned.

"Smarty," Lynn laughed. "You'd better get a doughnut and take a few deep breaths. The day will start and you won't have time to run back. Besides, when those youngsters get here, there won't be any food left."

They hurried off, but they came back soon and began their duties for the day.

Once the teens had left with the horses they were using, Sharon cleaned the stalls as quickly as she could. This task was therapy for her because she didn't have to think much about what she was doing and it gave her great pleasure to see the finished work.

She watched David start building another row of stalls with an extra wide overhang on the front. "Hey, these are great blueprints. Double Dutch doors on each stall will ensure a lower gate being shut, but allow horses to stick their heads out and look around over it. I don't know where Lynn got them, but they sure fill the bill. With the additional space she can board more horses. She sure needs the income."

David grunted and turned to make a notation on the blueprints. Sharon noticed that there was no name of an architect on the bottom. "You drew them, didn't you?" she asked in surprise. "These are great. Where did you learn to do blueprints?"

He shrugged his shoulders. "Around."

When she realized he was engrossed in his work and not interested in talking, she decided to go to the back ring and observe. Too late. The class was just being dismissed, and the teens were leading the horses in to untack and groom them and check the chart for the next class. Sharon picked up two brushes so that she could give each horse a rub-down.

Sharon was delighted to meet the young woman who had lost an arm and a leg. "I'm thrilled to meet you and be able to tell you how much I admire your intestinal fortitude. Did I hear correctly? Did Ashley call you George?"

The young woman laughed. "Yes, she did, but it's a joke. My full name is Georganna Christine Hamilton. During a conversation with these bozos, I said I hated the name Georganna, and ask that they call me Christine or Crissy. Oh, no. Ashley spoke up and said, 'That's okay, George. We won't snitch on you.' They all laughed and the nickname stuck. Grrr!" she laughed as she reached for Ashley pretending to choke her.

"Yeah but you love it, and we love you," Ashley smiled hugging her.

"Truthfully, I don't really mind. These young people have meant so much to me. I was in a car that was struck when a man ran through a red light at an intersection." She explained to Sharon. "My car was thrown up in the air, then it flipped and rolled. I lost part of my arm and later the lower leg had to be removed. For a short time I felt as if life was over for me because I've always been so athletic. Two years later, thanks to Lynn and the encouragement of these wonderful young people, I'm even riding on hunts, taking low jumps and having the time of my life. God bless Lynn for caring and opening such a business. They've all made me feel as if I can do anything. Lynn has been my guardian angel."

"That's me, Angel Lynn," she said grinning at Sharon. "You haven't noticed the outline of my wings under this very tight shirt, have you?"

"Dear, darling, Lynn. Having known you for umpteen years, I think I would have noticed wings. You are an angel though. How blessed I've been to have you in my life."

"Yuck!," Jardine shouted. "I'm glad I have on knee boots, but I'll need a shovel if I stay around here long."

Through the laughing and teasing, Lynn called for their attention. "The next class is in five minutes. Be on time, please."

Sharon walked out with them to observe the students in the class. LeLand and Kara greeted her as if they were old friends.

"Sharon," Lynn hesitated and turned to her sister/cousin. "Jardine is backrider for Kara today, so, could you please be a side walker for Leland? It'll help you learn more quickly if you're part of the team. I know that you're aware that your entire attention must be on the rider and the horse. I'm sorry, but I'm short a worker."

"I'll be thrilled to work any where I'm needed. Yes, I know to stay alert, but sometime I'd love to walk around during a class and observe more closely."

Lynn nodded, and being a good instructor, began to look around to see if everyone was being cared for properly.

"Will Kara need a backrider for the duration of her lessons?" Sharon asked.

"Yes, because her muscles won't support her for more than a couple of minutes. We're hoping and praying for a miracle breakthrough in her treatments. Her team of doctors doesn't give us much hope, but I believe in miracles."

Sharon's heart went out to Kara, but she hurried over as Leland's horse was led in the ramps. Sharon hurried up one side of the ramp ready to help lift him on the horse. She realized that she hadn't yet met the girl being a horse leader or the other side walker.

"Boy! How lucky can you get? Look, Kara. Sharon's with me," Leland bragged loudly.

"That's nice," Kara said, trying to sound grown up.

Sharon watched carefully as the walker across from her fastened the belt around Leland, gave him his helmet and prepared him to ride.

"We haven't met. I'm Lynn's sister, Sharon. Although I've ridden since I started walking, there's a lot I need to learn about this program. I'm eager to work if you'll be patient with me."

"I'm Gabe, short for Gabriel, I've seen you around, but never got a chance to chat. The person leading the horse is responsible for keeping the horse quiet and under control. These horses are well trained, and we haven't had trouble yet with any of them. Just walk and stay alert. If you feel it's necessary, you may walk with one hand on the rider's leg. Try to remain calm regardless of what may happen."

Sharon looked with interest at Gabe who was obviously Native American. She moved to one side to see the leader. Sharon grinned broadly when the beautiful girl stuck her head around the horse and spoke. She was the spitting image of Gabe.

"Hello! You two must be brother and sister. You look so much alike."

"Try twins," the girl smiled. I'm Rebekah Henderson, and yes, we have Biblical names.

"Henderson? That doesn't sound Indian."

93

Gabe laughed aloud. "Our father is a college professor. He didn't want his students calling him Limping Bear."

As Sharon laughed, Rebekah explained. "Gabe's in a silly mood. Our Great Grandfather worked on a cattle ranch in Wyoming. He was such a good and loyal worker that the ranch owner asked him to take his name of Henderson. Grandfather saved his money and bought a little land. As time went on, he bought more land adjoining that which he had. When the owner died, he had deeded enough land to Grandfather so that he then owned eighteen hundred acres. In his old age oil was discovered on one corner of his property in Oklahoma. He was a rich man. His son, our Grandfather, invested well and became richer."

Gabe continued. "When our father was born, Grandfather made sure he got a college education. In fact, Grandfather put three sons and three daughters through college. Becky and I are in college and have a trust fund, but we donate our time here helping Lynn."

Before Sharon could say anything else, Lynn came rushing to them. "Is something wrong? You're holding us up."

"Sorry, it's my fault," Sharon said and reached to place a hand on Leland's leg as they walked down the ramp and into the ring.

"Okay, my man," Gabe turned toward Leland, "while Steamroller is walking, hold your arms out straight from your shoulders and pretend you're a windmill." Leland worked his arms in circles backward and forward several times. "Great. Now sit up straight, lean forward from your waist, and see if you can reach Steamroller's right ear with your left hand. Good! Now reach his left ear with your right hand." Leland did this five times with each hand.

"Do we walk his entire lesson?" Sharon asked.

"No," Leland said loudly, "I can trot."

"Let's show Sharon how much you've learned. Now what do you do?"

Leland looked thoughtful. "I drop my heels a little, keep my knees against the horse and sit up. Oh, yes. I either rest my hands on my thighs or let them drop naturally at my side."

"Very good. Are you ready?" Leland nodded with eyes sparkling and a big grin on his face. Gabe called to Becky. "Okay sis, let's do it." Becky started at a slow trot.

As they completed the second slow trot around the ring, Lynn came to them. They walked and listened.

"Leland, you're doing so well, and we're all proud of you. Would you like to try something new?"

"Gallop?"

"Not yet," Lynn laughed. "See those poles laid on the ground down the middle of the ring?" There were four poles about two feet apart laid beside four more poles that were the same distance. "I walk you to walk over them first. Sharon will tell you how to sit properly. When you feel comfortable doing that, tell her and they'll help you trot a figure eight over the poles. Either of your walkers can explain how your horse will move differently, therefore, you need to sit differently. If it gets uncomfortable at any time, or you begin to hurt, please tell them. Will you promise me that you'll tell them?"

"Yes, ma'am. I promise." The excited little boy almost bounced in his excitement.

"Okay. I'll leave it to your helpers to start you."

Leland was so excited, he kept yelling, "Hey! Look at me!" to the other riders.

Rebekah stopped the horse. Gabe looked sternly at the youngster. "Leland, everyone sees you After all, they're doing things in the ring, too. How can you concentrate and do your best if you're looking around and yelling? Your horse doesn't know that you're bragging on yourself. He hears the yelling and thinks there's danger."

"I'm sorry," he said looking as if he would like to cry. Sharon felt sorry for him and patted his leg.

"The other students are trying to learn, too. They're paying attention to what they're doing. If you learn to do this well, you'll get to do more fun stuff. It's up to you," Gabe finished.

"I'll do it." Leland solemnly nodded his head. It was obvious that he was making a great effort to stay calm and quiet. The three helpers smiled at each other.

Steamroller was led at a walk in a figure eight four times over the poles. Leland grinned the entire time. Sharon showed him how to keep still from the waist down, but to lean slightly forward from his waist while looking up and forward. They then trotted four times over the poles in a figure eight.

Steamroller was then led to the ramp where Leland was lifted off and into his wheelchair. Sharon hugged him and Gabe gently slapped his back while Becky led the horse away.

"Are you hurting any where?" Gabe asked.

"Oh, no," Leland quickly answered.

Sharon smiled. "I bet you'll feel a little pinch in your leg muscles, but a good relaxing, hot bath will help that."

Gabe and Sharon walked to the gate in the ring with Leland sitting in his wheelchair.

"You'll be back in three days and we'll see how much you remember," Gabe told him.

Leland's parents were waiting outside the ring. "Mom! Dad! Did you see me? I trotted in jump position over those poles!"

Both parents hugged him. "We sure did see you, son, and the whole Pasco county heard you," his dad laughed. "That looked like fun."

"I'm so proud of you. You're very brave and you're doing well with your riding. Are you glad now that you enrolled?" his mother asked.

Gabe explained to Sharon. "At first Leland dug in his heels. I thought he might be afraid of horses, but he explained to me that he was tired of people making decisions for him." Gabe looked knowingly at Sharon.

"I love horses," Leland said with a pout and then he beamed. "Mom! Dad! Have you met Sharon? She's my new friend. Isn't she beautiful? And she's so sweet."

"I'm delighted to meet both of you. Your son is quite a boy and I'm happy to be working with him." Sharon hugged Leland and smiled at his parents.

"Are you a new instructor?" Mr. Nesbitt asked.

"Yes and no. I'm Lynn's sister and have moved to Zephyrhills so I can attend USF in Tampa. Lynn and I have ridden since we started to walk. I'm thrilled to be working with her. Lynn has specific training for this program and is certified, but I'm just a horse nut who feels lucky to be part of this world."

"Yea!" Leland yelled again.

"Oh, gee," his father put his hands over his ears. "Let's get you home, son, before you take off like a rocket." He pushed the wheelchair to the van.

Sharon and Gabe walked to where Becky was grooming Steamroller. Sharon gave the horse a kiss on the nose. "You're the best ole boy. How did you get the name Steamroller? You're anything but."

Rebekah giggled. "He was called Fred when he first came to us."

"Fred! What a change. I like Steamroller better. Forgive me, go on with your story."

"It was before students had enrolled. We were trying out different horses determining their suitability and putting them through a training period. You know, bumping them with clinking wheelchairs, leaning crutches against them and letting the crutches fall, anything to get the horse accustomed to handicapped riders. This horse was so calm and good that we were thrilled with him. I brought him in to brush him and he heard Ashley and Jardine scooping out grain and putting it in tubs in each stall. There were ropes across the front until we were ready to bring the horses in. Old Fred here threw up his head, gave a mighty neigh, and charged in. He placed that broad chest against the ropes and they snapped like twine. He ran to his stall, pushed Jardine out of the way with his head, and charged to his feeding tub.

Because of that we changed his name to Steamroller. He's great until he smells feed or hears it being poured, and then he lives up to his name."

Sharon laughed and patted Steamroller's shoulder. "Well, whatever your name is, I think you're one of the best. Becky, I'll clean tack until you finish the next class, and then I'll help muck stalls and give fresh water in all the buckets."

"Sharon, Sharon, Sharon," a demanding voice called. She turned to see Kara rolling her chair while holding the reins of a pony. "I wanted you and Peanut to get acquainted. Isn't she beautiful? And she's so great."

"She sure is beautiful, Kara, and I can see that she likes you and takes good care of you."

"Yeah, she does. I gotta go, but I'll see you in three days."

Sharon leaned over to hug the little girl and then took the reins to lead the pony into the stable.

Later, in the stable alone, Sharon was cleaning tack when she heard a noise in the hay loft overhead. "Hello. Is anyone there?" She waited, but hearing nothing else continued her work. "I guess senility is setting in early," she chuckled and shrugged.

There. The noise came again. She glanced fearfully around. She was alone and the others were too far away to hear even if she could get enough breath to call out. Her mouth was dry and her heart was thumping so hard she was sure it could be heard by anyone who might be nearby. She took a deep breath. "Come on down. I'm armed and I'm not afraid. I can have several men here in seconds. Make it easy on yourself and show me who you are."

She gave a yelp of surprise when a figure dropped from over head to land with a thud in front of her.

CHAPTER EIGHT

"Wh - who are you, and why are you hiding up there?"

"Not afraid, huh? You could sure fool me."

Sharon noticed the twinkle in the black eyes and realized that he was teasing her.

She looked at his coal-black hair, long eyelashes, copper skin and tall, very thin body. "I want to know your name and what you're doing here," she said firmly.

"Well, Sharon," he spoke tauntingly as he swaggered to a barrel and sat down, "call me Keanu. I've been here one day, but no one saw me or heard me. I guess I was sleeping and made a noise waking up or you wouldn't have known I was here."

"How do you know my name?"

"I heard the others talking to you, and about you."

"Keanu what? How old are you?"

"Doesn't matter -- just Keanu, and I'm sixteen, almost seventeen."

"What are you doing up there? This *is* private property."

"Yesterday morning I was hitchhiking and got tired. I came here for the night and found sandwiches and coffee in that room over there." He pointed to the lounge. "I stayed out of sight and just listened."

"Where do you live? Won't your parents be worried about you?"

He snorted. "I live wherever I am, and no, my parents won't even miss me."

"Surely they will. Would you like to call someone and tell them where you are?"

"Nope. Nobody cares."

"Oh, Keanu. I can't believe that there's no one who cares."

"Yeah. I never knew my old man. He was supposed to be from Puerto Rico, but I don't know. My mom is Navajo and lives on a reservation out west. I got tired of being beaten and kicked by drunks that came to see her and give her a little money. I took off weeks ago and here I am. Whoo! I can't stand myself. I'd like to take a bath somewhere besides the horse trough."

"Goodness. And I bet you're hungry, too. Come with me and I'll tell my sister that you're here. She owns this property. I'm just helping her until college classes open this fall."

"You mean Lynn? Is she your sister or your cousin?" He looked sheepish when Sharon whirled and stared. "I heard those two men talking. Jake was telling David."

"It seems you know quite a bit about us, Keanu." As they walked to the back ring, Sharon called, "Lynn, come here, please."

Lynn strolled over keeping an eye on her class. She looked questionable at Sharon who quickly explained about finding Keanu and that he needed food.

"Take him to Sheilah. She'll see that he's fed. Her brother visited us a couple of months ago and left some clothes. You look about the same size." She spoke to Keanu looking thoughtfully at him. "I'll talk to you later."

"You've done what?!" Sheilah was shocked that Keanu had lived in the stable and hadn't been discovered before this. "Peeu! You're right. You do need a bath. Sharon, check in that storage room at the end of the hall and look in the suitcase that's on the top shelf. There's clothing in there that might fit this young man, although he's pretty tall."

Sharon quickly found the clothing and brought them to Keanu. "There's a shower here, and there's everything in it you'll need. While you're cleaning up, I'll prepare some food for you."

"Thanks. Both of you. I won't be long. I'm too hungry."

Sharon shared the story Keanu told her about his family with Sheilah.

"Poor boy. What are we going to do with him, though? He can't stay here and surely someone is looking for him."

"I'll call dad and discuss it with him. He has a detective who works for the agency. Maybe he can find the story of Keanu." *I sure hope so. There's something that I like about that boy.*

"Well, well," Sharon grinned at Keanu as he sauntered into the room. "You clean up real nice, kiddo. Here, all I have is sandwich material and milk. That'll hold you until we can get more stick-to-the-ribs food."

"I appreciate anything," he started eating before he even sat down. The food was quickly wolfed down. The two young women silently observed the young man.

"Keanu, you didn't give me your last name," Sharon frowned.

"Nope."

"Well?"

"Well, what?"

"Keanu, don't try being clever with me. I want to know your last name."

"All right. If you insist. All I can tell you is that some said it is Rodriguez, but I don't have a birth certificate, so, I don't know for sure."

"What reservation is your mother on?"

"Why do you need to know that? Are you going to try to get in touch with her?"

"I give you my word that I won't let anyone know where you are, for the time being.

I would like to know if she's reported you missing?"

"Okay," he said with a deep sigh. "If you promise not to turn me in."

"I promise. You aren't in trouble with the police anywhere, are you?" Sharon asked concerned.

"No ma'am. I've never been in trouble with the law. Okay. The rez is just outside Pine Ridge, South Dakota. But, if anyone tries to make me go back there, I'll just leave as soon as I can and disappear."

Lynn walked in. "All right, young man. Tell me your story. I own this property and you've been trespassing." She sounded a lot tougher than she was. Keanu told her what he had told Sharon. Lynn stood looking thoughtful and concerned.

"I'll call dad and then take him home with me," Sharon said as she stood protectively by Keanu.

"You'll do no such thing," Lynn exploded. "He can stay with the men over the stable.

I can always use another worker," she said with a stern expression.

"I'm not afraid of work. In fact, I'd love it. I love horses and I'd like to get to know some of the kids that take lessons here. I'd sure like to get acquainted with all of those volunteers. I want to help."

Sharon placed a hand on his arm. "Keanu, I've been listening to you. Have you been going to school? You speak well."

"Yes. I love school, and I love learning new things. Mr. Carvelene was a real good, caring teacher, but he had a heart attack and the man that came in his place didn't like us misfits."

"Misfits? Why do you call yourself a misfit?" Sharon and Lynn spoke as one.

"That's what the new principal called us after Mr. Carvelene left. He called all of us half breeds names. He was kind of patient with the Indian children, but he didn't care for us that were not pure."

"What grade are you in?" Lynn asked.

"I finished the eleventh grade, and I had mostly As and a few Bs. Learning comes easy to me. I knew an education would help me get out of the life I was in and into a better one."

"We'll discuss school later after I learn more about you," Sharon told him. "Lynn, I'm going home, and I'll call dad and tell him about this. He'll ask Detective Morrell to check into it, I'm sure. Bye, Sheilah. See you tomorrow, Keanu."

As Sharon drove away, Lynn took Keanu to David and Jake and told them his story.

David clapped him on the shoulder. "I'd love to have a roommate. An extra worker won't be turned away either. Come on. Let me show you where you'll bunk." Jake didn't say a word; he just listened and took it all in.

Lynn thanked David and went back to her office. She and Sheilah had to go over the day's records and prepare for the next day. After Sheilah left, Lynn thankfully went up to her apartment and prepared for bed. *I must be catching whatever Sharon has. I feel as if there's someone watching me.*

Keanu was thrilled with the apartment he and David would share. "I've never had a decent room. My mother was a beautiful girl, but she was young. She got discouraged and started drinking. I had to take care of her most of the time. Sure hope she's okay. I left because the man that came to live with her is also a drunk and he thought I was in the way." Keanu spoke haltingly. David thought he seemed sad, but determined. *I've seen and worked with many people, so I know people pretty well. I have a feeling this young man is going to amount to something. He's good looking but seems to be* humble.

"You're not in the way here," David assured him. "Lynn and Sharon will treat you right if you're straight with them."

"I figured that. Hey, David. While I was in the hay loft, I could look out a window that faced that long driveway. I saw a man in a dark, green car parked on the side and looking this way through binoculars. He seemed to get excited and look more when he spotted Sharon."

"What did he look like?" David asked with interest, but without expression.

"I didn't see him close. He seemed to be tall and thin. I knew he didn't want anyone to see him because of the way he was acting."

"How was he acting?"

"He'd stand outside and beside the car, but when someone came by, he'd jump in the car and act like he was trying to back up. He'd turn to look over his shoulder so his face couldn't be seen as someone passed him."

"Thank you for telling me. Keep an eye out for him, or anyone else who looks suspicious, and let me know." *I wish I could tell this boy what's going on, but I don't dare. I'm not sure who to trust yet.*

As Sharon drove down the long driveway, cold chills tingled up her back and the hairs on the back of her neck stood up. *Stop being so silly. I'm perfectly safe now, and why would anyone want to hurt me anyway?* She drove on home and called her parents.

Her dad listened to the facts about Keanu. "I'll have Steve check the boy's story, and he'll inform you of anything he finds. In the meantime, be very careful. He could have been sent in by whomever has been bothering you."

"Dad! Why would you say that? He's just a harmless boy."

"I don't know, darling. I have a gut level feeling that there's something you're not aware of. Forgive me. I don't mean to frighten you. Chalk it up to daddy wanting to wrap his little girl in cotton and dare the world to do anything to make her unhappy."

Sharon laughed. She talked to her mother for a few minutes and then told them she loved them and said goodbye.

She prepared a quick supper and ate it in front of the television. As she was cleaning the kitchen, the phone rang. Sharon hesitated to answer. She couldn't explain it, but she had a feeling that she would not like the call.

"Hello," she spoke hesitatingly. Although there was no answer she would hear traffic noise as if the call were being made from a pay phone near a highway. "Hello, is someone there?" Still nothing. "Look. I don't know what sick game you think you're playing. If you think you're scaring me, think again." She slammed the receiver down and stamped to her bedroom. Mumbling to herself she prepared for bed. "Maybe I'd better get a guard dog. What for? I'm not here enough and the poor dog would suffer. Maybe I'd better buy a gun. Sure, and shoot myself. It's probably kids dialing phone numbers and being cute. They're probably bored with little to do this summer. Why would anyone want to harm me?"

She crawled into bed knowing tomorrow would be a busy day and she needed her rest. She smiled to herself thinking of Keanu's courage and determination.

Yawning, Sharon made a phone call. "Lynn? It's Sharon. I'll not be coming in today until noon or a little after." It was four days after Sharon had found Keanu.

"Why not? Are you all right? Has something happened?"

"Calm down," Sharon chuckled. "Nothing bad has happened. In fact, everything's fine. I'm driving into Tampa to enroll at USF. I'd like to know what my schedule will be and how I can manage work time with you. I'll see you later. Wish me luck."

"My love and best wishes are always with you. Drive carefully. I'll be waiting anxiously to hear all about your morning. Bye." Lynn started to hang up and heard Sharon call loudly to her. "Yes? I'm still here."

"How do you think Keanu is getting along?"

"He's great. David is impressed with his maturity and the fact that he isn't afraid to work. He fed all the stalled horses and put fresh water in each stall before Jake and David started this morning. He and David have ridden out to check on the boarders and the other horses in the field. David says he's had some excellent training in horsemanship, but he still isn't eager to talk about himself. David, Jake and I discussed it and decided to just be a friend and let him know we're here for him when he gets more comfortable with us."

"Lynn, I think he's been on his own for so long, and at such a young age, that he just automatically keeps everything inside. I'm anxious to hear what dad's detective finds. He's surely had time to find something by now."

"I'm anxious, too. Keanu's a likeable young man, and I hope we can help him."

"We will and he'll learn to trust us. I have faith. Gotta run. See ya,"

"What did Sharon want?" Sheilah asked, as Lynn hung up the phone.

Lynn told her of Sharon's plans for the morning and then about the investigation to learn more about Keanu.

"Oh, Lynn. I'm excited about this and I know we're going to be happy that Keanu chose us. I won't say a word to anyone."

Both young women jumped with guilt feelings when Keanu spoke as he came into the room. He moved so softly without seeming to be what they would call sneaky.

"Hey, Boss. May I stay in the ring near you during this lesson? I'd like to learn how to help the special riders."

"Sure. I'd love to have you and ask all the questions you wish. I have a good feeling that you're going to be a valuable helper and I know you'll love every minute of it. A lot of detailed training is required to work with handicapped riders. There's a great deal of liability involved. I carry extra insurance, but my heart would break if anything unfortunate happened to anyone in my care, or any animal for that matter. That's why helpers need a lot of training, not only in working with horses, but knowing how to work with various disabilities. And my name isn't Boss," she said sternly with a wink.

They walked , without speaking, side by side until Keanu seemed to decide to talk.

"I'm sure you've heard of the man called the Horse Whisperer. I lived with him and worked with him for almost two years, so, I learned how to care for horses, and many different animals. He and his family took in several young people who were having family problems and helped them to know that someone cared about them. He taught me so well that, at one time, I thought of training to be a veterinarian." He gave a short bark of what was supposed to be amusement. "Takes money that I had no opportunity to earn. I truly care about and like all kinds of people, and, if I do say so myself, I'm patient and I do have a lot of compassion."

That's the most I've heard him say at one time. If I'm quiet and show interest, maybe I'll learn more about him.

Lynn stayed quiet as long as she could. "Keanu, I've had to grow up fast, too.

Sharon's folks loved me and have been good to me, but I learned to be independent at an early age. I like people and I've learned to talk to them and observe them for awhile and then discern what kind of person they are. You seem to have done that." She lightly hit her fist against his shoulder. *I'd love to hug you, but I feel you would resent that kind of gesture until you know us better and trust us.*

"Hi, Lynn. Hey, who's he? Am I going to trot over the poles today?" Leland was so excited, he was not waiting for the answer to one question before he fired another.

"Hey, sport," Keanu laughed as he placed his hands on the wheelchair and wheeled Leland into the ring. "My name's Keanu. I'm new, so I sure would appreciate you helping me get acquainted with everything."

"Keanu! That's a strange name. How old are you?"

"My name is strange to you because you've never heard it before now. I'm sixteen, almost seventeen. How old are you?"

"I'm nine. I trotted over those poles in the last lesson. Are you going to work with me? Where is Sharon?"

"I'm observing today, and Sharon is at the college getting ready for fall lessons."

Gabe, Jardine and Rebekah took Leland to the ramp and placed a hard hat on him before they belted him in the special saddle.

Keanu walked over to Lynn. "That little guy is quite a talker," he laughed.

Sharon drove smoothly on 301 to Fowler Ave. and turned right on to the USF campus. She pulled up and stopped at the guard station. "Hi. I'm going to the Administration Building. Can you direct me there, please?"

The guard gave her directions and a visitor's pass to be displayed on her dashboard.

"What a beautiful campus," she breathed in the odors of citrus blossoms. *Here's where I park. Hope I can find my way with little trouble.*

Getting out of the car she suddenly shivered as cold tingles rolled up her spine and up the back of her neck. "What is this?" she spoke aloud without thinking. Looking around surreptitiously to see if anyone heard her, or was looking at her. There was no one that she could see, so she walked on admiring the campus and buildings.

"I knew it. Old age," she giggled to herself and walked purposefully into the Administration building. *I imagine the woman at that desk can direct me to the correct office.* Walking briskly across the beautiful marble floor, she approached the desk.

"Excuse me. I have an appointment with Dean Arlington. Can you tell me how to find him?"

"Yes. May I have your name?"

"Sharon Donnelly."

"Here you are. Three fifteen and it's now three. Very good. Go to the second door down there on the left and his secretary, Myrna Luman, will take care of you."

"Thank you." Sharon smiled and walked to the indicated door. *Do I knock or just walk in?* She took a deep breath and knocked. She pulled at her skirt and lightly brushed her hands across the front of her blouse. Taking a deep, shaky breath, she knocked again.

The door opened abruptly as she was knocking. An angry young man came barreling out. His shoulder hit one of Sharon's shoulders so hard that she gasped and was flung to one side.

"Sorry," he barked, obviously not sorry. He strode down the hall toward the outside door.

"Please come in. I'm sorry about that. Not everyone who enters these hallowed halls is in a happy frame of mind at all times. Are you hurt?" A very attractive middle-aged woman greeted Sharon.

"No. Just surprised and a little annoyed."

"I don't blame you. I'm Myrna Luman. Excuse me while I make some notes before I forget each detail. Please have a seat." She quickly typed some information and then placed it in a file and closed it. "How may I help you?" she smiled at Sharon.

"I'm Sharon Donnelly. I have a three fifteen appointment with Dr. Arlington.

"Yes, and you're right on time. Would you please fill out these papers? You may sit at the table there. It won't take long." She gave Sharon papers and a pen.

Sharon sat and carefully read through the papers before she started filling them out. The first instruction was: 'print legible with black ink.' The information required personal history, medical history and previous education. She read through everything again before she returned the papers to Mrs. Luman.

"This is fine. I'll have the information typed on to permanent record files and you can read it again before it is placed on your disc. Dr. Arlington is waiting for you. Please follow me."

Sharon followed her through a small waiting room. Mrs. Luman knocked lightly on a door of an adjoining room. "Dr. Arlington, Miss Donnelly is here."

Sharon smiled and thanked her. A tall, handsome middle-aged man with pepper and salt hair stood and came to shake hands. Although the day was warm, he was wearing a dark blue suit with a light blue shirt and red and blue striped tie.

"Hello, Sharon. You won't remember me. There was so much going on, I bet you can't tell me half the people that attended your wedding."

She looked astonished at him. "I'm sorry. No, I don't remember you."

"No reason for you to. I was visiting Judge Glen Alicea and he was invited to your wedding. As his house guest, I went along. You were a beautiful, happy bride. But you're using your maiden name." He said perplexed.

"Yes, sir. My husband -uh-was killed in a plane crash and I decided to take my own name back."

Sharon was uncomfortable talking about Jeremy. Her emotional and physical hurts were still too raw, and she didn't want to explain what had happened to people she just met. She sat up straight and smiled while she listened to Dr. Arlington.

CHAPTER NINE

"Hmm. I knew Jeremy and his parents. The judge and I agreed that we felt sorry for you. We knew how spoiled Jeremy was and how difficult his mother could be." He smiled at her. "It's none of my business, but I can guess that Jeremy was no angel to live with.

"We had some problems, but that's all over. I'm starting a new life and you can believe that I'll be better prepared in the event that I meet someone else that I'm attracted to. That'll be way in the future. My education comes first."

"Good for you. After I received your letter asking to enter USF, we contacted the college in Georgia where you had completed the first two years. I'm not surprised to learn that your grades were all As with a few Bs here and there."

"You have my transcript?" Sharon asked surprised.

"We have everything that is needed, and it only remains for you to meet with your guidance counselor and select your studies. What are your plans?"

"I'd like to be a teacher, especially with younger children, but one never knows."

"I'm glad you choose to attend here. Please feel free to come and talk to me any time. I know you'll do well." He smiled and stood up to open the door. "Mrs. Luman, help Miss Donnelly locate her guidance counselor." He turned as Sharon walked through the door. "Good luck."

"Thank you," she smiled and walked to Mrs. Luman.

"Have a seat, Miss Donnelly, and let's see what we have here." She read something in a file. "Good. Your counselor is one of the best in the whole USA," she smiled. "Mr. Troy Sanborn is not only an experienced college professor and a top-notch counselor, but he's had four books published. He's a horse nut also. You'll have a lot in common." She made a phone call.

"Ellie? Myrna. Is Mr. Sanborn in? Great. I'm sending Miss Sharon Donnelly up to talk to him about her course studies. Thank you."

Mrs. Luman wrote a number on a small sheet of paper and handed it to Sharon. "When you walk out this door, turn right and go past the receptionist's desk to the stairs. On the next floor up, turn left. Ellie Martin is waiting for you. Best of luck."

Her heart fluttering in excitement, and a little nervous, she followed the instructions to find her counselor. The note said Room 226. There was no need to wonder whether to knock or enter; the door was open.

"Hello. Come in. I'm Ellie Martin and you must be Sharon Donnelly."

"Yes, I am. I was told that Mr. Sanborn is to be my guidance counselor."

"He sure is, and after reading your transcript, he's very anxious to meet you. He's waiting for you now. Come with me."

Ellie Martin looked as if she might be someone's sweet grandmother. She was brisk, slightly chubby with a sweet smile, beautiful silver hair and a look in her eyes as if she loved life.

"Thank you," Sharon smiled at her. "Everyone is so friendly and helpful."

"We try to be - when students will allow us to be. Mr. Sanborn, this is Sharon Donnelly," she said leading Sharon into an adjoining office.

"Miss Donnelly, come in," he spoke enthusiastically. "I'm delighted to meet you and look forward to helping you with your course of studies. Have a seat, please. Would you like a soft drink, iced tea, coffee --?"

Sharon tried to keep from laughing aloud. Mr. Sanborn looked like a leprechaun or a jockey. He was short, small built and even dressed in a green suit. His blue eyes sparkled and his bright red hair spiked to show that he'd been running his fingers through it. His bright smile made her feel as if he truly wanted to be friendly and helpful.

"Nothing, thank you." Sharon stammered embarrassed, and trying not to grin. "I'm not sure where to start. I've always wanted to be a teacher. You have the information concerning what I've completed. I'm trusting you to tell me what I need to earn the degree that I want."

He had planned a course of studies for her. "Read this and tell me what you think, or what more you need." He handed the papers to her and began to work at his desk. After a few minutes, Sharon looked up to find Mr. Sanborn looking intently at her.

"What do you think of it? Do you feel you can handle the load this semester?"

"It looks great, but may I ask you something?"

"Fire away."

"I would like to have some time to work with my sister at her riding academy. Those special children are truly special. It helps me as much as it helps them to work with them and the horses. I'm reluctant to take on a full load at this time. I realize that you don't know what I've had to deal with for the past two years, but believe me when I say I don't need the pressure."

"Yes, Sharon. I know some of what you've endured. I understand. If you attend the year around and take fewer studies each semester, you'll finish in about the same time you would by taking a full load and leaving the summers free."

"That's just it. I don't know whether I want to work during the summer. Forgive me, but I'm unsure of a lot of things now."

"Why don't you try taking three classes this fall and then make a decision as you progress. You might decide that you can handle a full course load of some subjects, but that others require more concentration time. There's no pressure for you to finish at a specific date. Play it by ear and see how you get along day by day."

"I can accept that. How do I sign up for these classes?"

"I can take care of it for the first time. After this, you'll know where to go and how to do whatever is needed. Always remember that I'm here for you regardless of what you need."

"I can't thank you enough, and I do appreciate your kindness."

"It's my pleasure. There's also a method to my madness," he smiled. "I'd like to meet Lynn. Do you think I might impose and visit sometime? I've ridden most of my life and have shown in pleasure and hunt shows. I miss it, but my work here keeps me too busy to have a horse of my own."

"We'd love to have you visit. Let me give you the phone number and you can call and make arrangements when it's convenient for both of you. Lynn's secretary, Sheilah, might answer. She's a card, but you can't help but love her, and you'll really like my sister."

"I've been under the impression that you're an only child."

"Lynn is actually my first cousin. Her mother was my father's sister. Lynn was five when her parents were killed in a car accident. I was three. We were so young that being raised together seemed more like siblings than cousins. We love each other more than some sisters do. In fact, we're almost like twins. We have feelings of joy or dread about each other when we're separated."

"Then Lynn is settled and has her education."

"Yes, dad invested her money that she inherited and raised her as another daughter.

When she was ready for college, she had plenty of money for education and her dreams of a riding academy for the handicapped. Truthfully, she is more mature than I am and is an excellent business woman."

"I'll try to come for a visit before fall classes get in full swing. Sharon, it has truly been a pleasure meeting you. Don't forget to contact me for help with your classes, or as a friend."

"Thank you again." *I'm thankful for all these people I've met today, but I feel I'm really going to like working with Mr. Sanborn.*

"Ellie." Mr. Sanborn called to his secretary.

"Yes, sir?" She came briskly into his office.

"Give Sharon the papers that are in the folder I made up for her and let her fill out what is necessary. I'll check everything before she, or I, sign them."

Sharon was relieved to see that it was only twelve fifteen as she drove off campus and turned left on Fowler. She drove on until she could turn left on 301 and back to Zephyrhills.

"Hank, it's Duke. She went to the college today. I guess she's really getting ready to go back to school. I was worried for awhile. The police kept coming and going so much, I thought I was going to have to make sure she wouldn't talk."

"Don't panic and do something foolish. Just keep watching."

"Maybe I should try to get a job at the stable."

"Stay away! The less she sees you, the better off you'll be. Did it ever enter your feeble mind that if she sees you, it might jog her memory? Right now she doesn't seem to remember much that happened in Texas. Maybe she really doesn't know anything."

"Yeah, you could be right. It's getting boring, though. I don't feel like I'm earning my money and there's not enough for me to do."

"Why were the police there so much?"

"Uh --I don't know, but I'll find out somehow."

"Stay calm. Stay focused. And do stay in touch. Remember, don't do a thing until you've discussed it with me."

The rain had increased the closer Sharon came to Zephyrhills. As she drove into the stable parking area it was a downpour. . She jumped out of the car and ran into the office just as Lynn was getting ready for a lesson in the indoor ring. A few parents were sitting in comfort in the lounge, sipping hot chocolate, and watching their pride and joy through the glass.

"Hey! How'd it go? Are you all set?" Lynn called excitedly.

"Hi, college girl," Sheilah greeted her.

"You're both sure feeling good for such a gloomy day. But I'm not gloomy." Sharon spread her arms and spun around. "It went well. I'm all set, and yes, I'm a college girl now. Isn't it great? I can't remember when I've felt so light and eager. Oh, it feels good."

"Hey, good. The rain has stopped. Come on to the ring with me and tell me all about it. No, you can't. Those shoes would never make it through the sawdust and dirt," Lynn said looking down at Sharon's sandal heels.

"Stay here and talk to me," Sheilah offered. "You can talk to Lynn after the class.

Besides, this group is learning to jump and there'll be a lot of dust."

Sharon happily settled in to chat with Sheilah. Keanu came in as glad to see Sharon as if she'd been gone for days.

"Hey, Sharon. Guess what. David took me to the training ring out back and let me work with Sleep Easy."

"That big red stallion! What was he thinking of?" Sharon was frightened for Keanu.

"David told me himself that this is the only horse he almost gave up on. He felt he might be too dangerous to keep around, even for breeding. Who would want that temperament coming out in their babies?"

"We've been trying something with him. We've fed him, gave him water and hay and groomed him. Other than that we pretty much ignored him. We would give carrots and tidbits to the other horse, and sometimes to him, but we'd talk to the other horses and make over them. David even sings to them," Keanu laughed. "We learned that Sleep Easy craves the attention and is really just a big old baby. In the past, apparently someone has let him bully them and he's never learned manners."

"That's what frightens me. I would rather you didn't work around him."

"Aw, Sharon. David and I together can handle him."

"Sleep Easy," Sharon snorted. "Why would such an innocent name be given to a brute like that?"

"You'd have to read his papers. His bloodlines read like European royalty."

"No thank you. I don't even want to get close to him, and I've worked with many difficult horses. You might as well go on and give me a heart attack. What have you done with the horse?" Sharon asked reluctantly hating to encourage Keanu.

"We're going slow. We want to build his confidence in us and make him think he's happy if he learns what we're teaching. Today we led him out between us and tied him to the post in the center of the riding ring. Then we let him smell the saddle blanket before we pulled it all over him and under his stomach. David would step back a couple of steps and snap the blanket in the air, then slowly walk back and rub him with it again. We just worked like that. After all, he's only two. We don't want to rush his training and ruin him. Remember, he bullied others and hasn't had good training."

"That sounds good. That's the way I start young horses, but are you sure he'll be manageable?"

"Not any time soon. David says we'll do this for two or three days and then he'll lead him around while I hold the long line. David won't make a sound. My voice will be all Sleep Easy will hear. Later David will step away and I'll be on my own. He'll be trained on the lines for a few weeks. David promised me that I can do all the training."

"I hope I live long enough to see it happen," Sharon said with her hand over her heart.

Keanu thought she was funny. "Why do you say that?" he asked laughing aloud.

"I'll be frightened to death every time you're working with that red devil. Lynn, did you know that Keanu is working with killer red?" Sharon asked as Lynn joined them.

"Not at first. I'm willing to let him try as long as David will stay in the ring with him."

"Yeah!" Keanu jumped up and punched the air with his fist.

"Whoa," Sharon stood and placed an arm around Keanu's shoulders. "There's going to be some conditions to your plans."

"What?" Keanu looked mystified.

"That you go with me tomorrow to Zephyrhills High School and enroll for the coming year. Then we'll shop for school clothes and supplies."

Keanu hung his head. "I have to go to school? Couldn't I just stay here and work, after all, this is what I'm going to be doing all my life."

"Don't you want an education? Anything you plan for the future will be more successful with an education. Why wouldn't you want to go? You're a good student."

"I like school, --but -- I want to work here."

Lynn held up a hand. "You'll still be working and living here. All of us want the best for you, and you're so capable of becoming anything you want to be."

"Suppose I want to train horses? And maybe teach people?"

"David has a college education. I have a very special college degree and Sharon has signed up this morning to go back to college." Lynn said.

"I have a college education," Sheilah broke in.

"Aw," he sighed, "I guess it'll be okay. When do we do all of this --mother?" he asked with a teasing twinkle in his eye.

"Tomorrow, and I have spoken," Sharon said firmly.

"What time? I don't want to hold you up." He answered reluctantly.

"I'll be here by six to help with the work. I'll bring clean clothes to wear after I take a shower. Let's see, we can leave about ten. Our appointment with the principal is at ten thirty. Just be sure you're ready."

"The rain has stopped, but I'll have the next class indoors to stay out of the fresh mud." Lynn decided.

Keanu walked out mumbling to himself. The three young women waited until he got outside and then burst out laughing.

"Yes, mother," Sheilah teased. "What do you have in mind?"

"Just what you heard. Enroll him, buy clothes for him, make an appointment with a dentist and one for a physical, eat lunch in town and back here." Sharon nodded.

"Well, I have to get home if I'm going to be any good for tomorrow." Sheilah smiled and prepared to leave.

"I need to get home, too. Do you have anything you want me to do, Lynn?" Sharon asked.

"No, thank you. All's well here. See you both tomorrow," Lynn answered as she went to the indoor ring.

As Sharon ran in her house, the phone was ringing. "Hi, Dad. What a nice surprise."

"Hello, my darling," her mother greeted her on an extension. "Dad and I have decided that we'll come to see you this week-end. We'll be there on Friday and stay with you, if we may.

"Of course you will. No way would I agree for you to go anywhere else."
"Okay, pumpkin. We want to see you and Lynn. We especially want to meet this young man you've been talking about. I have the report that my detective gave to me.

You'll be anxious to read this."

"Tell me what's in it." Sharon asked excitedly.

"Too much to read. You'll have to be patient. You've waited this long, you can wait a few more days. We'll see you in the early afternoon. Take care. You're loved."

"Love you, sweetheart," her mother finished the conversation.

Sharon stood with bowed head thinking. *Oh, I hope there's no bad news in the report. Keanu has had too much of that in his young life. It must be bad or dad would have told me what's in the report. Silly. Standing here worrying about it isn't going to change the situation.* She phoned and left a message for Lynn about the phone call.

"Boss, it's Hank. I'm getting concerned about Duke. He's trying to do too much on his own."

"What do you mean? What's he been up to?"

"He's getting impatient with watching the young widow and he thinks there should be more action on his part. He's wondering if he shouldn't get a job at the stable to be closer to her."

"Oh, heck. What did you tell him?"

"To forget it; that seeing him might jog her memory."

"Good. We may have to replace him, but I hate to do that because he's been in on this from the first. We'd have to share the information with another person and that would mean more people know what's going on. It's too dangerous." He thought for a minute.

"Let things go as they are for the time being. Ask him to report to you daily. Call me each time he calls and keep me apprised of the situation."

"Keep you -uh - what?"

"Never mind. Good grief. Just call me if there's any important news."

Keanu worked diligently to finish as much as he could before he had to leave with Sharon.

"Hey, pal," David called to Keanu. "Better run take a shower and get into clean duds. You have a little less than twenty-five minutes."

"Oh, gosh. Okay. I'm outta here. See you later," he answered David.

Sharon could tell Keanu was nervous because he hummed softly all the way to the school.

"You have nothing to be frightened about or ashamed of," Sharon assured him. "Your grades are excellent and you're very mature and responsible for your age. My money's on you, kiddo."

CHAPTER TEN

Keanu smiled and rushed to hold the door for her as they entered the building, but he stayed slightly behind her walking down the hall. They walked into the main office.

"Good morning. I'm Sharon Donnelly and this is Keanu Rodriguez. I called to see if Principal Ward could speak to us about enrolling him in school."

"Oh, yes. Dr. Ward is waiting for you now. Please follow me." The woman knocked on an adjoining door and introduced them to the principal.

"Miss Donnelly. I'm delighted to meet you. I've met your sister, and I say she's a real asset to this community. I've also met your father and know what a great man he is."

"I agree," she laughed. "I'd like you to meet Keanu Rodriguez. He is my ward and will be enrolling as a senior. We can get his school records from the Sequoyah Indian Reservation just outside of Pine Ridge, South Dakota. He's an excellent student and a conscientious worker."

"Keanu, I'm certainly pleased to meet you," Dr. Ward said reaching to shake hands. "I was beginning to think Miss Donnelly wouldn't draw another breath," he teased, sensing that Keanu was nervous. "Please. Both of you have a seat."

"I'm, sorry, Dr. Ward. Keanu means so much to me and I want him to have the best opportunities available. I meant it; you'll be pleased to have him for a student."

"I'm sure I shall. We'll make the contacts and his records will be here in a few days.

I see no reason why you can't enroll and start making plans for the school year," he said to Keanu. "Do you mind taking a battery of tests to help us determine where we can be of the most service to you?"

"No, sir. I'll take any test you require."

"Good. Why don't you come in Friday morning at eight thirty and start the testing. It might take a little over an hour. Do you have medical and dental records?"

Sharon spoke. "He will soon. We're making appointments today for a complete physical and dental and for anything that will be necessary. Next week he should have completed everything and be ready to be a top honor student," she said proudly.

Thanking the principal for his time and help, they left to make the appointments.

"Let's go to Peeples Clothing and purchase clothes for you to start. After you see what the others are wearing, you might want to buy something else."

"Sharon, I really do appreciate everything you've done for me, but I can't keep taking. I would rather be able to pay for my own things."

"Keanu, I'm so proud of you. You've been on your own and had every opportunity to be bitter and go downhill, but you've developed self respect and a keen sense of responsibility. I respect your pride, but I want to do this for you. Don't deprive me of my blessing of having you and being able to help you." She spoke with a catch in her voice.

"For goodness sakes, Sharon. Don't cry." Keanu looked around embarrassed that someone might see or overhear.

"These are tears of pride and joy. Okay. That's it. You know how I feel. All of us love you and want the best for you. If you don't feel right because I'm paying, then make a note of all that I spend and in the future you can pay me back as you can."

"Okay, if that's what you want."

"No, but it seems to be what you want. I'm not complaining. I love you and want to help you. But if you feel you want to be independent, I can respect your feelings."

"Sheesh. Now I'm glad I didn't have sisters." Then he hurried to add. "But I'm truly glad to have you and Lynn."

They bought jeans, shirts, dress slacks, a couple of jackets, and much to his disgust, a suit, dress shirts and a couple of ties. He balked at buying dress shoes, but he gave in after Sharon assured him he could wear boots to school until the dress shoes were necessary. Mr. Peeples told him there would be dances, concerts and visits to other schools where he would like to dress differently than he did every day. They left loaded down with bags. Keanu felt so much better because Mr. Peeples had made him feel welcome.

"Now let's go to Barb's Restaurant in Neukom's for lunch. After we eat, I have a couple of short errands and then we can go home." They had a leisure lunch. Keanu was impressed with the friendly people.

"Leave room for dessert," Sharon told Keanu. "That looks like yummy home-made blueberry pie. With ice cream it'll be perfect."

"Sharon," he laughed. "I don't know how you keep from weighing two hundred pounds. You're always hungry and always snacking."

"I'm not that bad," she sputtered indignantly. "I do like food, but I don't eat that much."

"Yeah. Yeah," he teased. "Some day I'm going to follow you with a camcorder and have a record of your snack attacks."

Sharon paid for their lunch and they left in a light-hearted mood. "Don't forget this is the night Lynn is having a cook-out for the volunteers. There's to be a bonfire and all the goodies that go with it. Jake and David are making a giant potato salad. Sheilah is bringing baked beans and Lynn is furnishing wieners and buns."

"Thanks for reminding me, Keanu. I'll get marshmallows and I'll make chili for the dogs. You can furnish cheese and paper products. Who's bringing the beverages?"

"That lawyer, Swanson, said he wanted to come and meet everyone together. He said he'd bring soft drinks and desserts. We all know why he wants to come." Keanu wagged his eyebrows and winked.

"Martin Swanson? How is he doing in his lessons?" Sharon inquired.

"He's doing well. His doctor said that he could ride, but he has to have massages and a whirlpool soaking after the ride. Lynn said he would be welcome to join us tonight."

"Whatever," Sharon threw her hands up. "Let's go to the grocery store and get what you're furnishing."

"But if you buy it, it won't be from me."

"Start your list, buster."

They pulled in front of the stables laughing and in good spirits. Gabe was standing looking dejected.

"Something wrong, Gabe?" Keanu called.

"Take a look at that sky. We might be rained out tonight."

David was loading a horse for one of the boarders and passed them. He called out. "Fear not, my friends. The new set of stalls I'm building has roof and walls and dirt floors, but no dividers. If necessary, we can dig a hole in the center and build a fire in the hole. We'll be under shelter and we'll have a splendid time. There's plenty of room."

Keanu drug in a breath of relief. "Good. This will be my first activity with the group. I've never done anything like this, and I'm looking forward to it."

"As are we all," Gabe answered.

Sharon went to the office to talk to Sheilah and wait for Lynn to finish her last lesson.

"Hi, Jenni," Sharon greeted the popular veterinarian. "I hope you're staying for the cook-out."

"You couldn't run me off. I just hope I don't have an emergency call and have to leave."

"Cross your finger, your eyes, your toes and anything that will cross," Ashley clowned around as she walked in.

"Okay. Okay. They get the idea," Jardine laughed. "What can we do to help?"

Lynn walked in. "Just to be on the safe side, the men folks are digging a huge hole in the middle of the new area to build the fire in. Some girls are out there dragging hay bales to make a circle of seats around where the fire will be. I'm sure there's lots to do.

Find some long sticks to roast the marshmallows."

Lynn hurried to complete her daily records for the special classes. An inspector would come in from the state office usually, when least expected, to check on records and how the stable was being run. The surprise safety checks were important to make sure that everyone was operating a safe, healthy stable according to national guide lines.

"We'll need plenty of sticks because hot dogs will have to be roasted," Jardine said as she and Ashley ran out to find the wood.

"Wow! I thought I was going to be blown in," Martin laughed as he wheeled in to the office. "Can some of the kids get the beverages out of my van? I have two large sheet cakes baked especially for us."

"You're a darling," Sheilah laughed as she rolled her chair from behind the desk. "We'd better make a bee-line for the gathering before we're caught in the rain. Come on; I'll race you," she laughed, knowing that neither could make any speed over the rough ground. Martin and Sheilah wheeled out laughing and talking.

"Sharon, would you mind running up to my apartment and getting the buns that are on the table and the wieners out of the refrigerator? You'd better hurry and get over there before you get caught in the rain. Everyone else should be in the dry by now and all the supplies with them. I'll set the answering machine on." Lynn hurried to close the office.

Sharon hurried to pick up the items from Lynn's apartment and had to run through a few rain drops as she reached the new barn. She was greeted by a cacophony of happy voices and a wonderful blazing fire.

Ashley and Jardine staggered in with both arms loaded with long sticks. "Hey, guys, start helping us strip and clean these sticks." The crowd laughingly joined in.

Lynn ran in with a guitar in one hand and a violin in the other. "Marvelous. This is so comfy."

Plates were soon loaded with chili cheese dogs, some with onions and relish, others with mustard and ketchup. Pickles, sliced carrots, potato salad and baked beans were added. Soft drinks were poured and all waited for David to ask a blessing.

Keanu ate and looked around with shining eyes. He had never in his life had friends his own age that he could enjoy and were not causing trouble. Sharon winked at him when she caught his eye.

"Let's eat the cake and save the marshmallows for later," Lynn suggested. There was quick agreement.

After eating the food and burning the paper products, Lynn handed the violin to Sheilah and picked up the guitar. "What shall we sing? Sharon, would you rather play?" She smiled and shrugged her shoulders when Sharon shook her head.

"This dirt floor is just the ticket," Gabe shouted above the roar of the rain hitting the aluminum roof. "Let's have a square dance." Most of them didn't know how. "It's easy. I'll teach you as we go." They danced a couple of square dances and then Keanu taught them an Indian dance of thanks. They sank breathlessly on the hay bales and clapped in rhythm while the two young women played their instruments.

David reached behind him and brought out a banjo while
Jake got a harmonica out of his pocket. The four of them
played familiar songs that the teens knew and some oldies
but goodies.

Keanu took a deep, satisfied breath. This was the best
time he had known.

During the fun, Jenni's cell phone rang. "Shucks. I knew
it. At least I got to eat and sing awhile, and dance," she said
bowing to the boy who had organized the dancing. "I'll be
right there," she answered and looked concerned. She
quickly explained why she was having to leave. "Lightning
struck a tree near where some horses were standing. One
was hit and the others panicked and ran through a barb wire
fence. Hopefully it isn't as bad as it sounds. Good night all
and thanks for including me."

Jenni ran out into the now pouring rain. Lynn prepared to
ran after her and go to her own apartment. "I won't be
back," she called out. "Make sure the fire is out, and
everyone, please get home safely. I'm glad all of you could
make it. Martin, thank you for coming. There'll be a party
for the student volunteers when we finish summer classes.
Feel welcome to join in. Andrew, would you please see that
Sheilah gets to her van?" She then made a dash for her
apartment. Tired, but happy, she showered and got into bed.
Morning duties would come too soon and she needed the
rest.

Jenni ran back into the barn. "Drat and more drat! My
van won't start. Sharon, could you, please, pretty please,
drive me? It's about half way between Zephyrhills and Dade
City."

136

"Sure, I'll be glad to help you. Get the supplies you'll need and put them in my car. Keanu, tell Lynn where I am, but don't bother her if she's already asleep."

David showed the youths how to put dirt on the fire to make sure it was out and wouldn't start up again. The young people ran to their cars and David, Jake and Keanu went upstairs to their place. Keanu called to tell Lynn that Sharon had driven Jenni to the accident. She didn't answer, so he left a message.

About an hour later Lynn was awakened by persistent knocking on her door. She sleepily looked at the clock. One twenty. In the morning!? Answering the door, she was shocked to see Sheriff Howell.

"May I come in, Lynn?" he asked softly.

"Please do," she hurried to get a housecoat. "What's up, Sheriff?

"Sit down, Lynn. I have something to tell you." They both sat, Lynn looking mystified and worried.

"At twelve thirty-five we received a call to come to an accident about three miles north of Zephyrhills."

Lynn felt as if a fist had hit her in the stomach. "Oh, dear Lord. Sharon drove Jenni to an emergency call for some injured horses. Are you telling me that Sharon wrecked? How is she? Where is she? Is Jenni all right?" Lynn jumped up to get dressed and go to Sharon.

The sheriff stopped her. "Lynn, the car was totally destroyed."

She drew in a deep, shaky breath. "Is Sharon hurt badly? Was Jenni hurt?"

"Lynn, you don't understand. The car blew up. There's no survivor. We have found a few body parts and---"

For the first time in her life, Lynn fainted.

CHAPTER ELEVEN

The sheriff quickly ran to the kitchen and grabbed a dish towel, then got some ice to put in the towel. He hurried back to Lynn and rubbed the towel-wrapped ice over her neck and wrists while he called her name.

David and Keanu ran in. David began to talk as he came in the door.

"What's going on? What happened to Lynn? Why are you here, Sheriff?"

Keanu didn't know what to do, so he stood to one side out of the way.

The sheriff cleared his throat. "I had a sad duty to perform. I came to tell Lynn that Sharon's car was blown up and we can only find body parts."

"Oh, please Lord, No! Keanu moaned and sat down hard on the floor with his back against the wall. He sobbed and grabbed his stomach.

"You just came right out and told her like that?" David was livid. "Couldn't you have gotten some of us to come with you, or better still, brought a woman officer with you?"

"Hindsight is always best. I've known Lynn for many years," the sheriff said sadly.

David picked Lynn up and carried her into her bedroom. He lightly slapped her cheeks and called her name. Lynn began to stir. She sat up abruptly and screamed.

David quickly sat beside her and gathered her in a comforting hug. "It's all right," he kept saying. "It's okay to cry, but we don't know all of the truth yet. We'll know more after the investigation."

"Investigation? What investigation?" Lynn asked as if she were in a trance.

"The police will need to know what caused the explosion, and they'll want to know if it was an accident or intentional."

Keanu walked unsteadily to the door. "Lynn, your parents will be here today. Should we call them and prepare them?"

"No!" David and Lynn both spoke as one.

"There's no need to disturb them right now. Let them sleep. There's nothing they can do. I would recommend not telling them until they get here. They would only drive up grief-stricken and nervous," David explained.

"Yeah. You're right," Keanu staggered around as if in a fog. He didn't seem to know what he was doing. His grief was so great that his eyes glazed over and his mouth partially dropped open.

Sheriff Howell came into the bedroom. "I've called Lynn's doctor. She'll know what to do. This young man looks as if he needs her services, too." He helped the white-faced Keanu to go into the living room and sit down.

David kept hugging Lynn and gently rocking her. "Sheriff, would you please heat some water for tea?" The sheriff stared at David, but did go into the kitchen and turned the heat on under a kettle of water.

By the time the tea was ready, Dr. Melinda Sikes came in. She instructed the men to wait in the living room and shut the bedroom door behind them.

After about twenty minutes, Dr. Sikes came into the living room. "I've given Lynn a shot to help her sleep. She's in shock and needs a lot of rest. Is there a woman that can stay with her for awhile, especially tomorrow?"

"Some of the teen volunteers will be glad to help, in fact, they'd be insulted if they were not asked," David said. "They'll be here by seven. I'll stay until then."

"Would someone please tell me what brought this on. Lynn has the constitution of an elephant." Dr. Sikes looked around. "Whoa here. What's wrong with him?" She walked to stand in front of Keanu.

"He's had a shock, too. We all have. It's a long story, but Lynn's sister, Sharon, is his savior. I'll explain later. Let the sheriff tell you why he's here," David said tiredly.

After Dr. Sikes heard the story, she was horrified. "Are you sure it's Sharon in the wreck -er- explosion, or whatever?"

"It's her car. We traced it by the license plate." Sheriff Howell answered.

"But if Dr. Monroe was also in the car, what happened to her? Good grief. You mean both of them were blown up?" She hesitated. "I can't stand here and let this young man suffer as he is. I'm going to give him the same shot that I gave to Lynn. Can he sleep on the couch here? The injection works quickly."

"Sure, go ahead. He needs to sleep, also." David recognized that the doctor was upset. She and Lynn had been friends, and very close, every since Lynn had come to Zephyrhills.

David lifted Keanu and straightened him out on the couch before rolling up his sleeve. Dr. Sikes gave him a shot and patted his cheek.

"He's already so relaxed, like a piece of wet spaghetti," David commented.

"Yes, but he was in a stupor. I was afraid he'd hurt himself without realizing it. Besides, he's grieving and needs time to get accustomed to being without someone who had become so important to him." Dr. Sikes observed. David had briefly told her part of Keanu's story and how important Sharon, and everyone, had become to him.

Dr. Sikes pager chirped. She had to go to the hospital. "Call me immediately if there's any change or reason to be concerned. They'll both sleep for several hours."

David was alone with the two sleeping people. He looked in a mirror and shook his head at his red, swollen eyes. They felt gritty and his skin felt like sandpaper stretched thin. His heart actually hurt. Taking a deep breath, he went to make coffee. Leaving Lynn's bedroom door open, he sat in a lounge chair where he could keep an eye on both Lynn and Keanu. *One of these days, and soon, I'll have to tell them why I'm here. How I wish I could solve this mystery before I had to explain anything to them. Keanu, little buddy, I've become quite fond of all of these people, too, including you. I had especially grown close to Sharon.* David sighed, wiped his eyes and slumped in the chair.

David was awakened by a harsh knock on the door. Struggling up, and rubbing his eyes, he opened the door. He was surprised to see that it was almost daylight.

"Where in the heck is everybody? What's going on?" Jake came barging in talking loudly.

" Lower that foghorn. Be quiet and I'll tell you," David said. "Sit down. You'll need to be seated to hear this."

Jake looked on in amazement as David tiptoed in to check on Lynn. She and Keanu were both sleeping peacefully. David motioned for Jake to join him in the kitchen and sit down at the table.

"What happened to them?" Jake asked in a whisper. He was shocked and horrified to hear of the explosion and the loss of the two young women. David was just finishing his explanation when Ashley and Jardine came tiptoeing in. Their red faces and red, swollen eyes showed that they now knew what had happened. The two girls rushed to either side of David for a hug.

"We heard the news on television this morning and thought we'd come early to see if we could help Lynn somehow," Ashley explained through gulping sobs.

Jake cleared his throat and wiped his eyes. "Why wasn't I awakened? How did you and Keanu know and not me?"

"We came back down to make sure the fire was out and everything was cleaned up. After the sheriff came up, we heard Lynn scream and ran in to see what was going on."

Jake nodded. "Well, horses still have to be fed and watered. There's always a lot of work to be done." He seemed to be sleep walking.

"We've talked to some of the boys. They're right behind us," Jardine told them. "We can give the regular lessons, but we can't give the special lessons. What do you want us to do?"

Jake answered a knock on the door and admitted Deputy Belasic. "Folks, I'm so sorry. I honestly thought those gunshots were careless shooters or kids in the woods.

This means Sharon was right. Someone *has* been after her. I'll not stop until this is solved." He gulped but didn't hide his red face and the sad expression in his eyes.

They all turned as Lynn staggered into the kitchen. She looked at the girls and started crying. The three hugged and shed tears together. Disturbed by the voices, Keanu began to stir. He groaned, stretched and yawned as he slowly rolled over.

"Wh- what am I doing here?" He sat up shakily and looked around puzzled. As he remembered, his face began to crumple and he sobbed aloud. Lynn went to sit by him. They hugged and cried together.

Deputy Belasic knelt in front of Lynn and Keanu. "I promise that I will not rest until the person responsible for this is found and punished. I just wish I could tell Sharon how sorry I am."

"Go ahead and tell me," a voice spoke from the door. They all stood with mouths open as Sharon walked in. "I just heard the news and thought I'd better get out here before some of you had a heart attack."

Lynn and Keanu both moaned and dropped to the floor.

Ashley and Jardine ran to hug Sharon while David and Jake took care of Lynn and Keanu. David looked mystified, jubilant and angry by turns.

Deputy Belasic finally found his voice. "Where have you been? Were you thrown from the car?"

Lynn's eye fluttered open. "Sharon! Sharon! It's really you?" She burst out sobbing while Sharon knelt and hugged her. Keanu knelt by them, hugging both of them and crying unashamed. He tried to speak and couldn't.

"I think I'm me. After what I heard on the news, I'm not sure. At first, I couldn't believe what I was hearing. Then it dawned on me that it was Jenni that is dead." She sobbed again. "Jenni didn't deserve this. Poor Steamboat. Such a faithful car and there's not a scrap left." Sharon shook so badly she had to lean on a chair back.

"Take your time and tell us how you got out of the car," Deputy Belasic spoke gently. He encouraged Sharon to sit on the couch between Lynn and Keanu. Both of them clung to her and kept touching her as if they were proving she was real. Ashley and Jardine sat on the floor at their feet. Everyone seemed to need to cling to each other.

"When Jenni and I left here last night, I told Keanu to tell Lynn that I was driving Jenni to her call. As I drove to my end of town we talked about how long Jenni would need me. I was very tired and told her I'd get out at my house and let her take my car. I knew David would work on her truck and she could pick it up when she brought my car back to the stable. I intended to call a taxi as I did this morning. It was so late I knew Lynn would be asleep and I saw no reason to disturb anyone. I didn't know what had happened until I saw the news this morning."

Everyone started talking at once to tell her how glad they were she was alive.

Sharon turned to Deputy Belasic. "Have you found how my car was destroyed?"

"A team will be working on it. The last I heard, the speculation was that a remote controlled bomb was on your car and was detonated, possibly from another car."

Several cars were heard driving in. Jake went down to meet whomever was arriving. He came back in a couple of minutes so excited, and angry, that he could hardly talk.

"The vultures have arrived. There's reporters of all kinds out there. They want to know how we feel about Sharon's death. Andrew and Matthew almost came to blows with some cocky guys who came right in taking pictures as they walked. Rebekah, Gabe and three of the boys are seeing to the horses. I couldn't tell any of them in front of the reporters that Sharon is up here. I figured Lynn'd want to tell them." He was breathless because Jake, as a rule, was not a talker.

Deputy Belasic stepped forward. "Lynn, I'd like to handle it. Whoever perpetrated this crime thinks they've killed Sharon. I'd like for them to keep thinking that for awhile. They might get careless and crawl out from under their rock. Will all of you cooperate?"

"We sure will," Lynn nodded, speaking for everyone.

"I know the reporters are doing their job, but it seems cruel and heartless charging in here to wring Lynn out knowing she is grieving. Or at least they think she's grieving. I'll take care of it," Deputy Belasic said firmly as he walked out hitting his heels hard as he walked.

"Just let me look at you," Lynn put a hand on either side of Sharon's face. "Are you sure you're not hurt?"

Sharon wanted to giggle, but the situation was too serious. "You keep forgetting that I wasn't in the car." She turned to see Keanu gazing at her with his heart in his eyes.

She gently put her arms around him. "Oh, Keanu. I had no idea you would take it so hard if something happened to me."

He hugged her hard and then drew back to look her straight in the eyes. "Everyone here has been nice to me, and I do appreciate it. Lynn has given me a job and a place to live. Growing up I can't remember anyone being nice to me except the Horse Whisperer.

When you found me, you were instantly caring and concerned. I feel a closeness with you that I've never felt with anyone else - not even my mother. Aw, I can't explain it."

"I think you did a superb job of explaining," Lynn said. "Sharon is very special to me, too, so, I can understand why you feel as you do. Wait until our parents get here this afternoon. They're going to love you, and you'll love them."

"Oh, no!" Sharon groaned. "I forgot them in the excitement. I hope they don't hear a news broadcast and drive up here grieving. They could wreck. I need to talk to them now."

"No," Lynn said. "Wait. They have to drive in here looking properly upset or the reporters will suspect something. Remember, we need to keep the scum bum, who did this, off balance. Keanu, do me a favor and go ask all of our young people to meet me in the office. Don't tell them anything yet because the reporters will be watching."

Sharon

He hurried out, glad to be doing something. All of the horses had been fed, watered and groomed as well as stalls cleaned. Two of the boys were just getting in a farm truck to ride out and check on the horses in the field.

"Hey, gang. All of our people," Keanu called out. "Lynn would like for everyone to come to the office right now. Not you turkeys," he said angrily to reporters that tried to follow. "This is a private meeting with just our people. When Lynn's ready to talk, she'll let you know."

"Hey, kid, we're just doing our job," a reporter stated.

"Yeah, I know, but you're all ghouls, preying on the misery of other people."

The reporters stood grumbling while the young people walked solemnly into Lynn's office. Keanu gave a start when he saw a tall man at the back of the crowd hurry away to a dark car parked farther out than the rest. *Who is he?* He waited until he was sure the unwanted guests would stay in place before he came in. He would have chased after the stranger, but he wanted to hear what was going on in the office.

Sheilah pulled up just as Keanu was at the office door. He hurried back to the van to help her. She was crying so hard that she had trouble getting out. Keanu felt so sorry for her but did not dare tell her anything for fear she would give their secret away with her joy at hearing Sharon was really alive. The reporters were still around.

"Sheilah, why did you drive here in your condition? You could have had trouble of your own." he gently scolded.

"Don't fuss at me, Keanu. I had to come. These are my people, and I love all of you."

148

"I know the feeling. You'll feel better after you hear what Lynn has to say," he whispered to her. She looked puzzled at him and then at the reporters crowding around.

"Lynn's called a meeting for all of us in the office. You're just in time."

That's strange. He doesn't act as if he is grieving at all. She wheeled into the office as Keanu held the door for her.

Sheilah quickly went to Lynn and reached to hug her, bursting into sobs. The young people were so sad seeing Lynn's red, swollen eyes. Some thought that it was sad that she just got her sister back and had now lost her. All of them loved both Lynn and Sharon.

Rebekah and Allison looked surprised to see Ashley and Jardine grinning. They all gasped and made noises of surprise when Sharon walked in smiling at all of them.

"Was it Mark Twain who said, 'the reports of my death have been greatly exaggerated'? Well, my friends, if you'll get comfortable, I'll tell you what has happened." Sheilah grabbed Sharon's hands and held so tightly that Sharon had to gently work her hands free. Sheilah was gasping like a fish out of water.

They listened as she told how she had avoided being in the car. More tears were shed thinking of Dr. Jenni, who was loved by everyone. "Let the police make the statements to the press and television. They don't want the perpetrator to know that there are clues, or that I'm alive. The more the criminal thinks he's gotten away with it, the more careless he might become."

"Now everyone listen carefully. Our parents will be here soon," Lynn got their attention. "When they pull in, whoever is closest bring them in immediately, but please don't tell them anything until they come inside. We don't know who might be watching. I'm canceling classes today. The public will expect it. I would appreciate it if you could find something to do and stay around here for awhile. Sharon and I will stay upstairs out of sight. Does everyone understand how important it is to keep quiet?"

"Yes, ma'am," Andrew saluted and grinned. "We'll take care of everything. You can count on us." They all agreed and started out to do their jobs.

"Wait up!" Jardine called anxiously. "You're all looking too happy and relieved.

The reporters, or the dirty person, might get suspicious. Can we keep happy expressions off our faces just for today? Try to look sad and unhappy. Think of something that makes you angry. Boys, it wouldn't hurt if you, too, shed some tears."

"We certainly will, and if any suspicious person comes around, we'll make short work of him," one of the boys answered.

"How do we know it's a he? It could be a she," Gabe spoke thoughtfully.

"Yeah. How do we know it's a man?" Ashley asked.

"All we know is that someone is out to kill Sharon, and we'll make sure it doesn't happen when any of us are around. " Matthew spoke firmly with a glare.

"Since we don't know who's responsible, we'll be extra careful about talking to anyone who's around. Don't even talk at home yet. Someone might accidentally let it slip that Sharon is alive." Ashley cautioned.

"Or anyone in town. If you let it slip to anyone off this property, the criminal might talk to them, or to someone they've told, and word will get out that he failed." Andrew warned.

The young people talked among themselves and then left looking suitable solemn and thinking over what had happened, or what could have possibly happened if Sharon had stayed in the car. A couple of the girls even leaned against a boy and hid her face as she was crying. They all grieved for Dr. Jenni.

Sheilah, Lynn and Sharon ate their lunch in the back part of the building behind closed doors. Sheilah stayed alert to come to the front in case someone came in. Her eyes were still red grieving over Jenni and thankful that it wasn't Sharon.

CHAPTER TWELVE

"The reporters won't give up as easily as they've seemed to," Sharon observed. "Watch around all sides of the building. I won't put it past some of them to try to peep in the windows or try to sneak in." She looked nervously at the front windows.

"Hank, ole buddy. I have some bang-up good news."

"Okay, Duke. Lay it on me. I sure could use some good news."

"Our problem has been taken care of. Don't you watch the news?"

"Yeah, but I've been too busy to watch this morning. You might as well tell me."

"Kaboom! A car blew up during the night with our favorite female on board." He laughed hysterically.

"You idiot. Don't tell me you set it up. No, don't tell me. Hooboy. The boss is going to skin you alive."

"Why? I thought he'd breathe easier knowing that he won't be exposed."

"Dumb head. If she knew nothing in the first place, and we don't know that she did, we were never in danger. Now there'll be an investigation and --" he groaned. "I hate to tell him, but he's probably heard the news now. Suppose she did know something and has told others. There'll be more suspicions and, for sure, more investigations."

"I'd call the boss myself if you'd give me his number. Why 'er you the only one with his number?"

"For this very reason. The more who know, the more dangerous it is. Hang up, and let me get enough nerve to call him and tell him. Boy! I'm sure glad I'm not you. I suggest you leave Zephyrhills right now. Go back to Texas and lay low. That's an order."

"Boss. This is one call I hate to make. I should have seen it coming. Duke was getting too antsy and I knew he would try something on his own."

A shrill whistle stopped his prattle. "I don't know what you're blabbering about. Why not just tell me straight out and save a lot of time."

"Oh, I'm glad I'm not Duke. He's really done it this time."

"Spit it out. Now!" the person screamed.

He listened silently as Hank told him the news.

"Are you sure about this?"

"Yes. After he called I watched the news, and there it was, big as life and twice as natural. To make matters worse, her old man is a personal friend of the Florida Governor and there's to be a full scale investigation. This is a high profile family."

"Did you tell him to get lost?"

"Yep. Told him to head to Texas, keep his mouth shut, stay sober and lay low."

"I'll call ahead and there'll be a welcome committee for him. Don't let on to anyone that you even know who the woman is. I'll be in touch."

A little after one a volunteer ran in breathlessly. "Lynn, your folks are here and they look bad. I feel so sorry for them. Tell them as quickly as you can."

"Get them in here quickly and tell everyone to go on as you have been. I'm so thankful for all of you, and I'll make it good for all of you." Lynn was misty-eyed.

"None of us are doing this to be rewarded. We truly care about you and Sharon. Don't insult us or our friendship."

"Please forgive me. You know how upsetting everything has been. I'm not thinking as clearly as I should I guess. True loyalty can never be bought. Hurry. Get my folks in here."

Lynn ran to meet them as they came in the door. "Mom. Oh, Mom, don't cry. There's no reason to cry. Dad, both of you come back here." Lynn walked hugging both of them and pushing them to the back room. Sheilah sat in the front office wiping her eyes.

"Lynn, are you that heartless? No reason to cry," Megan sobbed.

"Hi, Mom, Dad," Sharon smiled as she came to meet them.

Megan shrieked and dropped back against Sean. He was shocked and then angry.

"What's the meaning of this? We heard that your car blew up and only a few body parts have been found. Our hearts have been breaking and you breeze in here as if nothing has happened."

"I was hoping you wouldn't hear about the accident until you got here."

"The news was breaking into every station on television and on the radio." Sean said. "Girls, I don't know whether to cry from happiness or shake you from anger. How could you put us through what we've suffered?" He didn't know whether to be angry or shout for joy.

"Dad," Lynn spoke, "we both decided that neither Sharon, nor I, should call you for fear our phone lines would be bugged."

"Bugged! Why would you think your lines were tapped? I suggest we sit down and give you both a chance to fill me in completely." Sean spoke through tight lips.

Megan tottered on her disgustingly high heels to a couch and sank down as if she could no longer stand on her own. With a quavering voice she said, "You'd better tell us everything. You know dad is a first-rate interrogator. Save time by telling him all of the facts or you'll be grilled through the night."

"Mom," Sharon chuckled. "I don't know whether you mean to be funny or not, but you're great. I mean it sincerely when I say Lynn and I are the two luckiest daughters in the world."

Lynn ran to get coffee for all of them and to check with Sheilah to make sure they wouldn't be disturbed. "Blow a whistle or something to alert us if someone comes in we don't want to see, or rather we don't want them to see Sharon."

Sheilah was on guard like a pit bull. These were her friends who were more like family. Her own family was two states away and she didn't see them often, even though she called them every week. Her love for Lynn and Sharon was as if they were sisters.

Sharon took a deep breath. "You're not going to like what you hear and you're probably going to be mad at me - again - for not telling you while this was going on. But when you hear it, you'll know that I love you with my whole heart and being and didn't want you worried when you could do nothing about it."

"I'll hold further comments until I hear what you have to say," Sean said sitting by Megan with his arm around her.

Lynn sat by Sharon to give her moral support. "Tell them everything from the beginning. We all love you and will be with you all the way."

Sharon smiled shakily. Taking a deep breath she began by reminding her parents of the abusive treatment from Jeremy and of his mood swings. Megan sobbed quietly while Sharon talked. Sean had made a fist and was beating up and down on the arm of the sofa.

"All of you were at the hospital after I was hurt so badly. When dad and mom Taylor came, she continued to scream that everything was my fault."

Megan couldn't keep quiet. "Yes, when Malcolm apologized to Sharon and asked her forgiveness for his son being so cruel, Agnes butted in and called Sharon a little tramp. She said Sharon had a talent for wrapping men around her finger and Malcolm was stupid for being one of them. .She went on to say that women were not fooled by Sharon." Megan told Lynn, who nodded silently.

"Dad had to hold mom off Agnes, and Malcolm forced Agnes to leave. I did get to tell her that Jeremy needed professional help. She left screaming back that it was all me.

You would have been proud of our lady-like mom. If dad had not held her, she would have wiped the floor with Agnes." Sharon explained.

"Does Malcolm know about the latest episode?" Lynn asked Sean and Megan.

"Yes, I talked to him and he's devastated," Sean told them. "Wait until he hears all Sharon's been going through. As far as that goes, why haven't you been telling us about it?"

Sharon quickly filled them in on the strange feeling of being watched and of Keanu seeing a stranger around. She reminded them again that she was trying to protect them and not worry them any more than could be helped.

"We can't solve your problems by sitting here going over and over them. Under the circumstances, why don't we discuss something pleasant that I meant to come tell you in the first place? Where is this Keanu character?" Sean asked, relieved to change the subject.

Lynn jumped up. "I'll get him. I'll also bring David and a couple of volunteers that you haven't met." She hurried after first checking to see if anyone was lurking outside.

"You will love Keanu. He's appointed himself my protector. David has been attentive, too." Sharon looked off and smiled.

"Uh oh. Do I detect romance entering your life after all you've been through so recently?" Sean looked worried. He knew his daughter was young enough that she might find someone else in her future, but he knew the hurt of her previous experiences were still raw and needed time to heal.

She quickly changed the subject. "Is your good news about Keanu?"

"Just hang on. You'll know soon," Sean smiled.

Before Sharon could tell her parents that she wasn't interested in romance with anyone, Lynn came in with Keanu and David.

"David, this is my mom and dad, er uncle and aunt, Sean and Megan Donnelly. This is David Baughman. He has been such a valuable worker and a true friend."

"Mr. And Mrs. Donnelly," David chuckled. "I'm honored to meet you and compliment you on raising two fine daughters. The relationship is a puzzle sometimes."

The two men shook hands. "I'm sure my girls have told you of their relationship. Lynn has always been a daughter to us and she's such a dear. Any family would be blessed to include her." Sean stated while sizing up David.

"Dad," Sharon interrupted. "This is Keanu," she said as proudly as if she were introducing her own child. "You can see for yourself that he's as wonderful as I've told you."

Keanu actually blushed. "Aw, you know how girls are." He looked surprised and then very pleased when Megan jumped up and hugged him. "We've been so eager to meet you. I feel as if I already know you. Both Lynn and Sharon speak highly of you."

Both girls have told us how much help you are and how you fit right in." Megan had a loving heart and was willing to accept the young man if her girls did.

"Keanu," Sean began, "I was coming to talk to you about the report my detective gave to me."

"Report, sir? What kind of report?"

"Sharon, didn't you tell him?"

"I didn't tell him that the detective had actually gone to the reservation."

"To the reservation! What for?" Keanu was curious and a little alarmed.

"It's a complex situation," Sean explained. "Would you rather we talk in private?"

Keanu looked around uncertainly and then shrugged his shoulders. "You can talk here. These people are my friends." He hesitated. "You could say they're my family."

Lynn and Sharon sat down placing Keanu between them on the couch. "Go ahead, Dad," Lynn encouraged Sean.

"Keanu, I have a written report that I'll leave with you to read at leisure, but I'd like to share some things with you now." Keanu nodded at Sean.

"After Sharon told us about you, I had my detective go to the reservation and to the school where you attended. The news is mostly good, but some bad. Did you know that your mother is dead?"

Keanu gasped and turned pale. Each girl took one of his hands and Sharon placed an arm around him.

"A few days after you left, the man that was living with her, came in drunk and beat her severely. A tribal council member happened to pass the house when the man ran out. He was acting suspicious, so the councilman went in and found your mother lying on the floor in need of medical attention. He called the Tribal Police and two of them got her to the hospital. She didn't survive the night. I believe the councilman's name was Charging Buffalo Brighton, better known as Buck. He gave a report to the police and there is now an APB out on Dwayn Brewton for the second degree murder of your mother."

Keanu shuddered and looked at Sean with moist eyes. "Go on."

"The detective talked to school teachers and many people on the reservation. Without exception they all spoke highly of you. He even talked to people in town. You'd probably be surprised at the people who remember you and speak well of you. There is nothing that says you must go back there, unless you wish to go. If you're satisfied here, you might as well stay."

Keanu took a long, shaky breath. "I'd like to stay." He looked questioningly at Lynn.

"You're here until you decide to leave us," Lynn said with tears in her eyes.

"Dad, Keanu has registered in Zephyrhills High and will be preparing for whatever he wants to do in the future." Sharon said with pride.

"Well, I'm proud of you," Megan told him. "You must promise to come to Fort Lauderdale and visit with us. I'll confess, I feel so much better after meeting you." She smiled at Keanu and turned to David. "I feel a little better about my two girls knowing that both of you, and Jake, are with them."

Lynn fixed sandwiches with chips, soft drinks and fresh fruit. They talked and got better acquainted. Keanu quietly went to stand by Sean. He was almost as tall as the six one attorney. "Sir, may I talk to you privately?" Sean nodded and they went out the back door, walking to the fence separating the pasture from the back lawn.

"What's on your mind, son?" Sean spoke gently to show his interest.

Keanu looked as if he might cry. "Do you know that's the first time in my life anyone called me son?"

Sean hugged Keanu. "You'll find that being a part of this family means you're in all our hearts and we care about each other."

"That makes what I'm going to tell you easier. I was concerned when I first saw the man, but after this car incident, I'm really troubled. I don't want to upset Sharon any more than she is."

"Are you saying there's been a suspicious man around?" Sean asked concerned.

Keanu told him of the dark car and the man watching with binoculars. "I can't swear to it, but a tall man was with the reporters this morning. He stood at the back of the crowd and wasn't taking notes or pictures. I've only seen the watching man at a distance, but I'm almost positive it's the same man."

Sean thought a moment. "Didn't Sharon say the men who left the motel in a hurry were in a dark car? Maybe they think she knows something that she doesn't. After hearing about Jeremy, I wouldn't be surprised at any company he kept. Maybe he was into something illegal and his buddies think Sharon might know about them. I'll be here tonight and tomorrow. I tell you I feel much better knowing you're watching over Sharon and Lynn."

David sauntered out to join them. "Am I interrupting anything?"

"No, I was just telling Mr. Donnelly about the watching man."

"My name is Sean." He turned to David. "Did you see this man, too?"

"No, but Keanu has told me about him, and I trust Keanu's judgment."

"Me, too," Sean smiled reaching to give Keanu a friendly slap on the back. "Keanu, do you have any idea what you might like to do in your future?"

"I like working with people, especially youngsters who need special attention, and I like and trust horses. David has taught me a lot and your daughters have been good to me."

"This young man is very observant and quick to learn. He's an asset to have around," David said.

Sean looked long and hard at David. "Forgive me. I don't mean to be rude, but you don't add up."

David's eyes grew darker. "Mind explaining to me what you mean by that?"

"I've been an attorney all of my adult life. I also took the complete training for the Sheriff's department. Before that I was a member of a youth group that was sponsored by our local police. I've learned a lot about reading people. You're better educated than the average person that does the work you're doing. You're well built, and I get the impression that you've worked out a lot in a gym. Your hands don't look as if they've been in outdoor work much. Should I go on?" Sean said solemnly.

David laughed. "No, you're right. I have a Master's degree, and even though I ride and have owned my own horses, I've never worked in a stable for anyone else. I've also had training in law, but I hope you'll trust me when I say I will protect your daughters with my life. I have a good reason for being here. I can't tell you now, but I will soon."

Keanu was astonished. "Aren't you who you say you are?"

"Sure am, good buddy. Will you trust me for a little while longer? Please don't tell the girls yet, but I didn't just happen in. I'm here on an assignment - a lawful one."

Keanu stared at him. "Yes. Okay. You've given me no reason to doubt you. Just remember, I will protect Lynn and Sharon with my life if necessary." He looked to the front and side of the building. "I saw a car pull in. I'd better go see who it is. It might be someone we don't want around today," he said as he trotted away.

"You're very astute," David said to Sean. "I'm not at liberty to divulge information about myself now. Will you trust me a little while longer with your girls, and I meant it when I said I'd protect them with my life."

"I'll back off for the moment. Just know that I'll be keeping in close touch, and I have a good deal of influence with the powers that be. If push comes to shove, I can always ask the Governor to send special forces to investigate and protect."

"Believe me, that won't be necessary."

Keanu came hurrying back. "That weird man." He frowned and made a face.

"What about him?" David asked anxiously.

"He said he wanted his twelve year old daughter to take lessons here. He wanted to see all over the stables and ask a lot of stupid questions."

"Questions? Such as?"

"He wanted to know if she could learn to ride on a stallion because she loves Black Beauty. I explained that geldings were used in movies and stallions were not for beginning riders, especially little girls. Then he wanted to know if we had lessons on holidays or if there were other arrangements made. He just went on and on. I don't think he knows any more than his daughter does about horses. I swear, if brains were made of leather, he wouldn't have enough to make a saddle for a flea."

Everyone, at the stable, had become accustomed to Keanu's derisive or sardonic comments about people, especially those whom he didn't approve of. But this was Sean's first encounter with Keanu and his caustic tongue. He recognized that Keanu had a sharp mind even though he was young. He reasoned that it was because Keanu had been on his own for many years. Sean also recognized that Keanu had a soft spot for animals and youngsters in need, and he felt confident that Keanu would be a loyal friend to Sharon and Lynn.

Sean laughed and put his arm across Keanu's shoulders. "Maybe he's just someone with more money than brains and hasn't been around horses. He probably has a spoiled little girl that he tries to do whatever she asks, however, under the circumstances, it pays to be cautious. Would you recognize this man if you see him again?"

"Sure." Keanu answered with a thoughtful frown.

David started walking toward the back of the office. "We'd better go in. Mrs. Donnelly keeps looking out here as if she's alarmed."

"Well, you know women," Sean chuckled. "They have to know every word that's said and everything that's going on. I guess Megan **is** alarmed. She's the proverbial mother hen. I can't blame her though after all that's happened to Sharon. I hope I won't be the first one to find who's responsible. I'd be in serious trouble because there wouldn't be enough of them left to take to court." He spoke as a father and not as an attorney.

"Not if I find him first," Keanu said.

Megan jerked the door open. "It's about time you men came in. Don't you realize how nervous the girls are? They need assurance that you're close to them."

Sean smiled as he hugged her. "Who's nervous? The girls look fine to me." He winked at them.

Sharon smiled at her parents with her heart in her eyes. *What great people. Dad's forty-five and mom's forty-three, but they look much younger. They've been the best parents to Lynn and me.*

Lynn jumped up. "Sheilah, it's early, but why don't you go on home. You're welcome to stay for supper, but I'm turning in early. The stress has been exhausting."

"Thanks, but I'm going home as fast as I can wriggle. I'm looking forward to a hot shower and an early, lazy time in bed. Tension has been high and I've been on pins and needles all day. Sharon, I can't tell you how relieved and thrilled I am that you're okay."

David knelt beside her wheelchair. "Sheilah, please be careful. We don't know who this nut is. Too, there might be reporters hanging around. Can you look distressed if they try to talk to you?"

"You bet I can. All I have to do is think of Jenni's death and what might have happened to Sharon."

"Would you feel better if I followed you home?" David patted her arm.

"Thanks, but that's not necessary. Reporters will be the worst thing that'll happen now. As far as the killer thinks, he's killed Sharon. He's not going to bother me."

"I don't want you to live in fear, but don't get too cocky. We have to consider that a kook like this might think Sharon knows, or has observed, something, and he might be afraid that she'd tell you." He stood up agitated. "What is it she's supposed to know? It would clear up a lot of things if we knew why he's after her."

"I'm not afraid for me. Even if his thinking is warped concerning Sharon, he thinks he's got her and he surely won't be calling more attention to himself by going after me."

"Don't frighten her," Sharon begged. She knew how Sheilah felt and wouldn't wish that on anyone, especially such a dear friend. And what a dear friend Sheilah had proven to be. *How blessed I am to have so many caring people around me.*

"I'm not scared. Really I'm not. I'll say goodnight to all of you, and again, Sharon, I'm so relieved that you're okay."

Sharon leaned over to hug her as Lynn spoke. "Call me when you get home so we'll know you got that far safely.

"Yes, Mother," Sheilah grinned as she wheeled to the door. David walked with her to her van and came back looking thoughtful.

"David," Lynn called. "Would you get Jake and Keanu and bring them here, please. Why don't the three of you have supper with us while we have a council of war?" She tried to smile. "I'm just fixing spaghetti and a salad with garlic bread. It'll be no trouble, but I meant it when I said I'm going to bed early. I know what Sheilah meant. The stress is exhausting. My brain is whirling with questions and what ifs."

"I think that's a great idea." He walked briskly out still looking as if he were thinking deeply.

As soon as everyone gathered, the phone rang. Lynn touched the speaker phone button. "It's me, chickadees. I'm home safely, but you were right. Reporters were hanging out at the end of the driveway. They wanted to know about Sharon's funeral plans and what all of us had been thinking and talking about." Sheilah told her.

"Oh, Sheilah. I'm so sorry. Are you all right?"

"You betcha. But I'm roaring mad. Some of those buzzards seem to be gleeful at the news. They're looking for sensationalism."

"What did you tell them?"

"I told them arrangements would be decided by Sharon's parents and her sister. I'm not a relative, therefore, I'm not privileged to the information."

"Good for you," David spoke. "You sure think quick on your feet."

Sharon

"In this case, it's quick on my seat. Night all." She hung up laughing.

After supper, as they were cleaning up, the phone rang. Lynn jumped and looked as if she were afraid of an attack. "The phone makes me feel as if I'm going to hear bad news."

"I'll answer it," David stepped to the wall phone in the kitchen. "Soaring Eagle. Oh, hello. Yes, Martin, she's here, but she's been through the wringer. I'll see if she's up to talking right now." He turned from the phone and placed his hand over the receiver.

"Lynn, it's Martin Swanson. He heard the news about Sharon and wants to talk to you."

"Okay," she sighed, drawing a deep breath, and reached for the phone. "Hello, Martin. No, I haven't been doing well. My parents are here, and, of course, all the folks who work here. Thank you. That's kind of you. I'll let you know when I decide to continue lessons. Take care of yourself, and thanks for calling." She shook her head. She hated not being honest with Martin, but they had to make sure Sharon was safe. Someone might, in all innocence, say the wrong thing to the wrong person and give away the secret that Sharon was alive.

CHAPTER THIRTEEN

"I've had calls from most of the students and loads of people in town. I'm grateful that they care and are offering help, but I'm going to feel badly when I have to tell them that Sharon isn't dead and we lied to them."

"Lynn, I'm so sorry. It looks as if I'm going to be an albatross to you all our lives."

"You are not," Lynn said firmly. You're my dear sister and I love you so very much." She burst out crying and she and Sharon stood hugging.

"Shock," Sean explained. "Lynn, darling, you've been so brave and have taken a lot on your young shoulders. I wondered when it would catch up to you." Sean put an arm around each girl. Lynn turned and hid her face on his shoulder.

"Oh, Dad, I'm such a baby, but I keep thinking that horrible person is still out there and will still try to kill Sharon, or any of us that he thinks she has told something to. We can't hide here forever."

"Shhh. I know. We've all had the same thoughts. You'll just have to go about your work as usual and everyone must keep alert and be suspicious of everyone and everything that's either out of the ordinary or around too much."

Jake, moving restlessly, reached for a Kleenex and blew his nose. "We're all going to stay on guard and take care of both of you. That d - uh- person isn't going to get Sharon."

"He won't have another chance," Megan wiped her eyes. "Honey, pack your clothes. You're coming home with us."

"No, Mom. There's no way I'd drag this dirty business in on you. It's bad enough that all of these people have been placed at risk because of me. Besides," she grinned, "I still can't stand to be in the same town with Agnes Taylor."

Sean snorted. "Who can stand her? That reminds me. I need to call Malcolm and let him know about Sharon. He was grieving and in agony when I last spoke to him. I talked to him on the car phone as we drove up."

The call was made and Malcolm insisted on speaking to Sharon. "Honey, I'm coming up there tomorrow. I have to see with my own eyes that you're all right and hug you. I've been so angry remembering what my son did to you and then to think you had gone through what was reported made me forget I'm a gentleman." His grief and anger were palpable over the phone. "Thank goodness Agnes is at her sister's and doesn't know this yet. You can be sure it will come out eventually. Be very careful."

"I'll be glad to see you, Dad Taylor, but don't go to any trouble just for me," she hesitated, "or cause more trouble for yourself."

He knew she meant she didn't want Agnes angry at him. At that moment a voice could be heard screaming in the background.

"You mean that witch isn't dead after all. What will it take to kill her? That proves she's evil. She's protected by her guardian devils."

"I'm so sorry, Sharon. I didn't realize she had come in and was standing behind me. I have to hang up, but rest assured I'll be there and your dad and I will get to the bottom of this."

Sharon was shaking as she told the group of the conversation. Just the thought of Agnes made her skin crawl. Then she felt ashamed. *I should be trying to understand her and feel sorry for her, but she sure makes it hard for anyone to care about her.*

"Did any of you think that woman might have a mental problem?" Keanu asked. "I sure hope I never meet her."

Sean pinched his lower lip and pulled it out with his right hand. It was a habit he'd formed when thinking deeply. "Malcolm and I have discussed that she needs professional help, but she'd fight getting any help. I just hope she doesn't go off completely and hurt Malcolm - or someone else."

"That's enough," Megan spoke. "We need to calm down and think happy thoughts.

It's time to get settled for the night. Like Scarlet, we'll think about this tomorrow."

Keanu ran out to see who had driven in. He came in about ten minutes later spluttering with indignation. "That was another deputy that just wanted to stick his nose into things. He didn't know much about the situation and asked the most stupid questions. I told him Deputy Belasic was handling everything admirably. This man reminds me of Barney Fife, you know - Andy Griffith - Mayberry. This deputy is a bullet short of a load." Keanu's comments helped to relax the others as they chuckled at his reaction. "He needs to take lessons from Deputy Belasic."

David looked thoughtful. "I may be swallowing a camel and choking on a gnat, but we need to be careful, and suspicious. We don't know if there's a rogue cop out there."

There was a quick discussion about what each would do the next morning. Sean said a prayer for the group. David, Keanu and Jake went to their apartments. Megan and Sean slept in Lynn's bedroom and Lynn and Sharon snuggled down on a sleep sofa in the back room downstairs.

It seemed that they had just gotten to sleep when they were awakened by a banging on the outside door and Keanu shouting. "Wake up! Wake up!"

Lynn threw on a robe and raced for the door. She opened it enough for Keanu to slip through in case there were people that she didn't want in or to see in the room. By then Megan and Sean were downstairs.

"What's up?" Sean asked.

"There's a police car coming up the drive and a lot of cars following."

Answering another knock, Lynn let David and a uniformed police officer in.

"Good morning. I'm Deputy Angelo Diaz. Sorry to get you folks up so early, but someone is leaking information to the press, or one of them is mighty enterprising."

Deputy Belasic ran in at that moment followed by a puzzled looking rookie deputy. It was obvious that Belasic was agitated.

"What's being told to the press?" Sean asked with a grim expression. "By the way, I'm Sean Donnelly. I'm Lynn and Sharon's father. This is my wife, Megan."

"Boy am I happy to see you. I'm Deputy Vincent Belasic and this is Deputy Bob Wakefield. It's a relief to know there's a man on the property, especially a relative."

"We're here," Keanu bristled. "We care about these girls and will protect them with our lives."

"I know. I'm sorry. I worded that badly because we're all upset. I just meant the girls probably feel better with their daddy here."

"You must have come for a specific reason," Lynn broke in.

"A reporter came to the sheriff's office this morning and asked if we knew who had planted the remote-controlled bomb on Sharon's car and if we knew why Sharon is targeted. We deliberately kept it quiet that a remote-controlled bomb was used. We were hoping that someone would get careless and give themselves away."

"What was the reporter told?" David asked.

"That an investigation is in progress and nothing will be discussed until there is more information. I reminded them that if the police told everything the criminal might be alerted and get away."

"We'd better get out there and protect those reporters," David chuckled. "Jake has a shotgun across his arms and is daring anyone to come any closer."

"Oh, for heaven's sake," Lynn spluttered. "As if we don't have enough problems. Let me get dressed and I'll be right out." She ran upstairs, Sharon right behind her, mumbling, "They could have at least waited until after we had breakfast."

"Sharon," Deputy Belasic called to her as she came back down. "I think it's time to tell them you're here, but I want to be with you when you speak to them. Don't tell them anything except that you had gotten out of the car and didn't know about the incident until you heard it on the news. Impress upon them that you're still in shock and have no idea why your car was destroyed. It's better that all this information comes from you instead of them getting piecemeal information and arriving at the wrong conclusions."

"I can do that," she said softly.

"I'll be right beside you, Sharon," David said.

"And I'll be on the other side," Keanu stated fiercely.

As soon as everyone was ready, they followed Vincent Belasic to the stable. There was a collected gasp and shouts of excitement when some, who knew Sharon, caught sight of her. The reporters began to run toward Sharon, crowding each other. They were all yelling at once asking questions and making observations.

"Jake! Put that gun down," Lynn yelled as she ran to him. She was too late to stop some of the reporters from taking pictures of Jake aiming the rifle.

"What do you people want? Technically you're trespassing on private property." Lynn demanded that they back up and leave.

"It isn't so private when you have a school for the public to use," one reporter answered Lynn as he took a picture of her.

"It's still private property and I have the right to say who comes on these grounds."

"Deputy Belasic, maybe you'd better take charge and clear the grounds," Sean suggested.

"Who'er you?" a woman pushed a mike in Sean's face.

"This is the father of these two young ladies," Deputy Belasic answered her.

David placed a protective arm around Sharon and pulled her close to his side. She willingly leaned against him. The reporters were so anxious to get a sensational story that they didn't seem to be human for a few moments. They were all yelling at once. Flashbulbs were popping, cameras were whirring and there was a lot of shoving.

Keanu stood slightly in front of Sharon, his feet spread apart and his arms akimbo.

He thrust his chin out and gave the impression that he would welcome a physical confrontation.

"Hey, Sharon, who's your protector?" A man laughed. "Hey, kid, you look Indian. Are you Indian, kid? What'er you doing here?"

"Are you Sharon?" A woman tried to shove a mike in Sharon's face while a man stood behind her and aimed a camera. They couldn't get past the firm, determined body of Keanu. David hugged her closer and turned so that she was slightly behind him.

"We thought you were dead. Why did you let us think you were dead? Who was in the car? Somebody was killed, and it was your car." Several crowded in closer.

Keanu knocked the mike down. "Lady, and I use the term loosely, you need to learn some manners. Didn't anyone ever teach you that it's bad manners to shove something in anyone's face?" he asked belligerently.

"Stop it, kid. Someone needs to teach you manners. Who are you anyway?" The man who had talked to Keanu before came to stand beside the woman reporter.

Sharon

"Well mister, there's no bulb lighting up over your head. It's plain that you're not the sharpest tool in the box or you could see that I *am* an Indian. You would also observe that I will not allow anyone to harass either Lynn or Sharon. Now play nice or leave. Call me the Lone Ranger if you wish." The reporters began to shove in closer.

"Why were we given to believe that you were dead, Sharon?"

"Were you in the car at all?"

"Who was killed in the car and why did he or she have your car?"

"Who wants you dead enough to blow up your car?"

The questions came too fast for Sharon to answer even if she wanted to. She might have been naïve when she married Jeremy, but she had learned to be self-reliant. The trauma of her marriage was still fresh, however, and she shrunk against David at the audacity of the reporters.

Deputy Belasic called for order. "All right everybody. You were told earlier that no information could be given because an investigation is in progress. I'll answer a few questions. No, as you can see, Sharon was not killed. We have some leads, but you folks know they can't be discussed. We'll give you what we can. I appreciate the fact that you have a job to do, well, so do I. Let's respect each other and act like civilized people."

Keanu snorted, then thinking of something, he began to walk slowly and methodically among the reporters and cameramen. He ambled back to stand by David.

"He isn't here," Keanu looked worried.

"Who?"

"That tall, mysterious man I've been seeing. He isn't in this crowd."

"Maybe he hasn't heard the news yet. Stay alert."

"You know I will."

Deputy Belasic brought Megan and Sean forward. He hoped to get the attention off Sharon. "This is Sean and Megan Donnelly, parents of the two young ladies. Naturally they're here because these are their daughters and they love them and want to be with them at this time."

"Mr. Donnelly, did you think your daughter was dead?"

"Yes, I did - we did," he hugged Megan to his side. "How thankful I am that it was a mistake."

"When did you learn that Sharon is alive?"

"Yesterday afternoon as soon as we got here." He half turned and gave a small nod to David. David whispered to Keanu and Jake, and the three men began slowly to move between Sharon and the crowd while they slipped around to the back of the stable. As soon as they were out of sight, they made a run for the back door of the office. Lynn was right on their heels.

"I'm ashamed to run off and leave my folks out there to face the reporters," Sharon said, looking concerned.

"Don't worry," David reassured her. "Your dad signaled me to get you away. Have faith in him. He's an excellent attorney and will talk a circle around them."

"There's a car pulling in. Some big guy just got out and is running toward Sean," Keanu was excited, acting as if he didn't know whether to run out and challenge this new arrival or stay and protect the girls.

Sharon quickly moved to look out the window. "That's Dad Taylor," she said happily. "He'll stand by dad and they'll take care of everything. Deputy Belasic is doing a great job, and I'm so glad he's the one assigned to the case."

The reporters hadn't yet discovered that Sharon was missing. "Who's this man? Is he an attorney? Did Sharon hire him to represent her?"

Sean smiled. "Yes, he's an attorney. He's my partner. We have an office in Fort Lauderdale. This is Malcolm Taylor. He's known Sharon all of her life and has been very concerned at the distressing news we first heard."

"Taylor?" a man said. "Didn't I read that Sharon used to be married to a Taylor? Yeah! He was an alcoholic and killed himself crashing a plane. Does his death have anything to do with Sharon's car being blown up? Hey, I have a photographic memory."

"Too bad he's out of film," Keanu muttered. He was leaning against a window that was opened just a crack so that he could hear what was being said.

"I can't say that the two incidents are related," Malcolm said. "If you'll excuse us, I need to talk to my partner." he got between Sean and Megan and they walked quickly toward the office.

"Where's Sharon? Does she have something to hide?" The reporters milled around.

Deputy Belasic held his hands up for quiet and order. "Thank you for being so understanding," he said diplomatically. "This has been a shock to Sharon and her family. They don't know any more than you do. We'll keep you informed. Please leave in an orderly way and try not to damage the grounds with your tires. I promise you that I'll tell you everything just as soon as I feel it can be told without jeopardizing the case."

"One thing Sharon knows that we don't," a man shouted.

"What's that?" Belasic asked.

"Who was in the car?"

"A beautiful young woman who was a veterinarian, Dr. Jennifer Monroe. She was here for a cookout and was called out during the storm to doctor some horses near Dade City that had been hit by lightning. Her truck wouldn't start, so, she borrowed Sharon's car. That's all we know at this time." He had not wanted to tell that much, but realized that he needed to give the reporters some new facts until the investigation would reveal more.

The questions came fast and furious as they gathered tighter around the deputy.

"I'm sorry, but I've told you all that we know. Thank you again." As he walked toward the office the reporters followed him shouting questions. Suddenly there was silence. He looked around to see why everyone got so quiet. He grinned and walked on to the office.

Jake hadn't said a word, but he stood with the shotgun across his chest in a position that it could be brought in firing position quickly. Mumbling angrily the reporters fled to their cars, each trying to be the first one out.

Sharon ran to hug Malcolm. "How sweet of you to come."

"Why wouldn't I? You're my little girl, too." He turned to hug Lynn. "How are you doing, sugar? It's rough on you, I know."

"Not too bad now. When I first thought Sharon was dead, I was devastated."

"I can well imagine. We all were. Will someone please enlighten me as to what's going on.

They all sat in the back room while Malcolm was brought up-to-date.

"Thank God, you're all right. I'm not going to apologize for Agnes any more. All of you know how she is. Sharon, you know that I love you and will do anything I can for you. You too, Lynn. You're both as dear to me as if you were my own children."

David laughed out loud. "Hey, everyone. Come listen to the news." They all turned to look at the television and burst out laughing.

"Aw," Jake grumbled. "It doesn't take much to amuse some people."

There was a big picture of Jake holding the gun across his chest. The reporter made a joke of Sharon being protected by a modern day Wyatt Earp. Pictures were shown of Sean, Megan, David and Keanu and finally of Malcolm. The reporter congratulated Sharon and her family. He then told a sweet story of Jenni and extended sympathy to her family. It was obvious that he had done some research on Jenni and was honestly sympathetic to Sharon.

The next day Malcolm went home with a promise to come at once if needed.

"Hank, I swear I did what I was supposed to."

"Fool. You've put us all in danger by taking matters in your own hands. You were told to go back to Texas and wait for orders."

"I wanted to clean up loose ends."

"Well, you only pulled them out farther. Where no one was bothering us before, there'll be a detailed investigation now. The Donnellys are friends of people in high political places and can get some mighty important help. I'm sure glad I'm not in your shoes. I pity you when the Boss hears about this."

"I know. You gotta tell him. I wish you'd let me talk to him and explain."

"He doesn't want anyone else talking to him."

"I guess I'll have to wait until I hear from you. I gave you my phone number here."

"Yes, if I get to use it."

"What d'ya mean?"

"When the Boss hears of this, there may be no you around for me to call. Get it? I'll be in touch. Stay out of sight."

"He did what?! I heard the news, but it never entered my mind that the man could be such a fool. Idiot! He was supposed to go back to Texas. Why didn't he?"

"He said he wanted to make you proud of him, so he arranged the blow up. He thought you'd be pleased that he got rid of her."

"If he goes down, he'd better not take any of us with him."

Sharon

"He don't know you. If he got pushed in a corner, he might give my name. I don't know what to think. He'd been dependable up till now."

"I'll take care of this. I'll have someone pay him a visit soon. If anything happens to him now it might cause a few unwelcome questions. Don't worry. I know you're okay. Thanks for calling."

CHAPTER FOURTEEN

The Tampa Tribune and the St. Pete Times, as well as local papers all carried about the same news. The front page of each paper was filled with the story of Sharon and all the happenings. There was a big picture of Jake holding the shotgun with the caption, HOLD OFF AT THE OLD SOARING EAGLE CORRAL. This was followed with pictures of all the people from the stable who had been there the day before. There was a nice article on Jenni and her work. One newspaper had finished with a picture of Deputy Belasic holding both hands up with the statement, "Deputy Belasic gave the benediction and sent us on our way".

The phone rang while Sharon had started reading the paper.

"Please, dear God, Sharon, believe me, I had nothing to do with it. Oh, what can I do?" From the tone of his voice, she could tell that Malcolm was crying.

"Dad Taylor, what are you talking about?" She was shocked. She'd never seen him cry. It must be something terrible.

"You haven't read the paper yet?"

"I'm just reading it now."

"One of those reporters got smart yesterday and connected the name Taylor. He got hold of Agnes and she regurgitated all kinds of trash. Sharon, I'm so sorry."

"You can't help it. We all know about Agnes."

"You won't feel kindly toward her when you read this article. This has made up my mind for me. I've contacted a dear friend, a psychiatrist, who attends our church, and he has agreed to commit her to the mental ward of a hospital where he works. The damage is done in the paper, however, when the news gets out that she is mentally ill, it might help some. There will always be people who want to believe the worst and glory in other people's troubles."

"Oh, Dad Taylor, I'm so sorry. Sorry for you; never mind me. I can imagine what you're going through. Mom and dad are still here. I'll tell dad that you need him."

"No. Don't bother him. He's too worried about you."

"But you're like a brother to him. He'll want to be with you and I have loads of friends gathering around me. The editor of the Zephyrhills News is a personal friend of Lynn's. When we tell him the true story, he'll be glad to print an article clearing Agnes' statements."

"Oh, that witch, OH!" Lynn screamed.

"Lynn must be reading the article you're talking about. I hear her screaming. I'll talk to you later, and Dad Taylor, remember how much I love you and trust you. Take care of yourself. I'll need you around for my grandchildren, if I ever have any. You're always welcome wherever I am. If it will help to get away awhile, come on up."

"Thank you, sweetheart, but I need to be here, for a few days at least."

"Where is Agnes now?"

"I called her sister and explained everything to her. She agreed with me and came to take Agnes to her house until I can make arrangements. Her sister is afraid that she might try to hurt me if she catches on that she is being taken to the hospital. The psychiatrist, Dr. Wilber Miller, is going to personally pick her up at her sister's. They both think I should not be present when she is taken and she realizes she is to be committed."

"I think they're right. Hang in there. Everyone here is your friend and I'm sure there are hundreds where you are."

"After I hang up, I'm calling our minister. He'll want to know, and I'm sure he'll want to be with Agnes when she is taken."

"Okay. I love you."

"What was that about," Sean asked as Sharon hung up looking thoughtful, anxious and a little angry.

Sharon quickly told them. "Lynn, why don't you read the article to us."

"I can't," she said with tears in her eyes. Her hands were in fists and her teeth were clinched. "I hope they bury Agnes alive and forget where they've buried her."

"Lynn, you were not taught to give way to those kinds of feelings. Never let anything keep you from being a lady," Megan scolded.

"You haven't read this, Mom."

David burst in followed closely by Keanu, Jake and five of the teen volunteers. "Have you read this?" David shouted, clenching the paper in his fist and shaking it in the air.

"We're getting ready to read it now. Dad Taylor just called and told me about it.

Lynn isn't in any shape to read it aloud, so why don't you read it, David."

"Okay. Sit down or you'll throw yourself to the floor when you hear it." Everyone found seats and waited anxiously for David to read aloud.

He read, "This reporter remembered that Sharon Donnelly was married to a Taylor a couple of years ago. He was in the Air Force stationed in Austin, Texas where he and Sharon lived. Checking with sources at the air base, I discovered that he was very abusive to Sharon and one time beat her, breaking bones and putting her in the hospital.

Taylor later took a plane, without permission, and crashed, killing himself and the woman with him. The widow, Sharon Donnelly Taylor, took her maiden name back and moved to Zephyrhills, Fl. To be with Lynn Yates, owner of the Soaring Eagle Riding School for the Handicapped. Yates is Donnelly's cousin, however, when Yates was five, her parents were killed in an automobile accident. Her mother was a sister to Sean Donnelly, so, he took Yates and raised her as another daughter. I recognized Mr. Malcolm Taylor at the stable as Donnelly's father-in-law.

Taylor is partners with Sean Donnelly in a very honorable law firm in Fort Lauderdale, Fl. Traveling to Fort Lauderdale, I located and interviewed Taylor's wife, Mrs. Agnes Taylor. In Taylor's own words she said; "Sharon is evil, a witch. She has some supernatural force guarding her. How else could she keep avoiding death? Everyone knows what a hypocrite she is and very few people like her. She made life hell on earth for my son. He was miserable while married to her. I guess he felt the only way he could be rid of her was through his own death. She murdered my son just as surely as if she had been piloting that plane. She was going to divorce him telling lies about how he had mistreated her, but he died before the divorce was final. She got all of his money and everything. She was so gleeful about his death that she didn't even cry."

This reporter reminded Mrs. Taylor that I had checked at the air base and the hospital and found lots of records about her son's abuse to Sharon and to himself through drugs and alcohol. Taylor said that was all lies that Donnelly had told and if she was ever hurt, she had done it to herself.

I would be remiss if I didn't further report that while Taylor was working herself up and talking to me, spittle was flying from her mouth and her eyes were wild. A neighbor heard Taylor screaming and came over. The neighbor explained that Taylor was very nervous.

My sincere sympathy to the family of Dr. Jennifer Monroe. She was young, but she had made a remarkable name for herself through her veterinary work and through her work with youngsters in the community. She will be missed by many. A mixture of sympathy and congratulations to Sharon Donnelly and her family.

We will bring you news up-to-date as we know what the police investigation reveals.

"It's a good thing Malcolm is having her committed, or I'd go down and choke her with my own hands," Lynn jumped up and yelled the last six words.

"Only after I got to her," Megan said.

Sean hung his head and slowly stood up. His face showed sorrow and inner strife.

"Sharon, your safety is precious to me, but I hope you'll understand. I need to be with Malcolm and give him the support that he needs. It can't be easy. He's lost his only child and didn't even get to grieve properly for him because of Agnes. And now his wife is worse than dead."

"I want you to go, Dad. There's plenty of people here and I'll be just fine. Bring him back with you so he can recuperate from his misery and be at peace." Sharon wrung her hands and had tears in her eyes.

"He won't come, but I'll encourage him to get away for awhile." Sean went to his wife. "Honey, are you going with me, or do you want to stay here with our girls?"

"I'm torn," she sighed. "I guess I'd better go with you, but I'll feel much better if Sharon would come with us."

"Please don't worry, Mrs. Donnelly," Keanu hugged her and comforted her. "You can rest assured that all of us will be protecting both Sharon and Lynn and loving them."

"I need to go to my own home and take care of my personal affairs," Sharon said.

There was a cacophony of voices as everyone tried to talk at once protesting Sharon going to her home, especially alone. Sharon sat and smiled while they all decided her future - or thought they were.

David gave a shrill whistle. "Quiet. We're getting nowhere this way. Sharon, I know you're mature enough to know how frightened we all are, thinking of what is possible to happen to you. If you leave here, you won't have the protection that you have with all of us. If you want to go and get clothes, or anything, I'll drive in with you and bring you back."

"Indeed you won't. I refuse to be a prisoner for any sicko. I have good neighbors and they'll ---"

The phone ringing caused most of them to jump. Lynn answered and turned with a puzzled look at Sharon. "It's for you. Somebody who claims to be a detective. Larry somebody."

Sharon frowned and then perked up. "Oh! Lt. Dauber. He's the detective who talked to me at the motel about the murder."

"Murder!" Keanu repeated surprised. "What does he want with you?"

"If you'll give me a chance to get to the phone, I'll find out." She patted Keanu's cheek in a teasing manner. "Hello, Lieutenant. Okay, Larry."

She listened a few seconds. "That'll be fine. Yes, it will be nice to see you, too. Thank you for calling." She hung up and turned to meet several pairs of eyes having a variety of expressions.

Impervious to their attitudes, she gave a tiny smile and started to go upstairs.

"Stop right there, young lady," Sean demanded. Sean spoke firmly. "First, who is this man and why is he coming here? Does it have anything to do with the car explosion?"

"As I told you - this man - is the lieutenant, a detective in the state's attorney's office, who was in charge of the murder investigation at the motel. He said he read about me in the papers and wanted to come for a visit."

"Why" David asked with a stern expression

"He said he wanted to see for himself that I'm all right." Sharon explained.

"Couldn't he take your word for it?" Keanu asked.

"Settle down, guys. He's just an acquaintance. He might be in the area on business and just wanted to visit. I don't know, and I'm not going to let it bother me. There are too many things happening in my life that's frightening; why should I get all in an uproar about some man wanting to see me?"

"When's he coming?" Sean pulled his lower lip showing his annoyance.

"Go home with my blessings. I'll be fine and Dad Taylor needs you."

Sean and Megan prepared to leave after making everyone promise that they'd be called at the slightest suspicion of trouble or danger.

The phone rang again and Sean grabbed it to answer. He listened and asked the person to wait a minute, please. "Sharon, do you know a Troy Sanborn?"

"Troy Sanborn," she puzzled. "Oh, yes. He's my advisor at USF." Taking the phone she talked a few minutes assuring the speaker that she was fine and yes he would be welcome to visit. Thanking him for calling she turned and explained that Mr. Sanborn had read the newspaper accounts and was concerned about her. Too, he admired Lynn for her work and wanted to meet her.

David and Keanu just looked at each other thoughtfully. They realized that no one could be trusted until the situation was cleared and the crime solved.

"Mom, I'm fine, and I will be," Sharon reassured her parents as they got in the car.

"I give up. David will go with me to my house and I'll get clothes and things I need.

I'll ask a neighbor to keep my mail until I, or someone from here, can pick it up. I promise that I'll stay here with Lynn - for a few days, at least."

"That's a relief," Sean sighed. "You know how we hate to leave you."

"I know, Dad. I love you both, and I know you love me. If it'll help, I'll call you daily."

"Let me call you. I can use my business phone and it won't run up Lynn's phone bill."

"You forget. She has a business phone, too."

Sean grunted as Jake drove up in a farm station wagon with Keanu in the back seat. They made it clear that they would be escorting Sharon to get her possessions.

"See," Sharon laughed. "I'll be well guarded. Call me when you get home and after you've talked to Dad Taylor."

As they turned to drive down the driveway, Sharon saw an unfamiliar van parked at the stable. "Who's that?"

David looked at the van. "Oh, that's Dr. Gordon Mason. Jake called him to see a boarder's mare that is late foaling. We'll probably be using him now."

The drive took less time than Sharon anticipated. Keanu walked over her house admiring it while Sharon was across the street asking Krystal to keep her mail.

"Lordy, Sharon. I nearly had a heart attack when you got out of that wagon. I heard on television, and read in the paper, that you were dead. Then there's a rumor that you're all right. How can this be?"

Sharon briefly told the tearful Krystal how she escaped the car bombing.

"Who's trying to kill you, Sharon?" Jose stood with dark brows lowered and a stern expression.

"I don't know that anyone's trying to kill me. I don't know any more than you do. The police haven't finished the investigation, and it's all a mystery to me. I'm going to stay with my sister for awhile. Would you mind keeping my mail for me, please?"

"Honey, I'll do anything for you that will help," Krystal assured her.

"I'll give you the number at the stable. Call me if you feel I need to know anything."

Sharon walked back across the street to her house and started in the door just as Keanu burst out. "There!" he shouted David whirled around. "What?"

"That looks like the dark car that I saw the other day. I can't see who's driving for the tinted windows."

Krystal and Jose came hurrying over to them. "That looks like the same car that pulled on your driveway a couple of nights ago. A tall, slender man got out and walked all around the house. He tried to look in the side window. Jose was going to come over and ask if we could help him, but when Jose stepped out our door, the man hurried to his car and left."

"What kind of car is it? Did you see a license plate?"

"It was too dark even with the streetlight. I don't know how to tell cars apart and Jose didn't get to see that much."

"I thought it looked suspicious because the license plate had something smeared on it so the letters couldn't be read," Jose explained.

David thanked them for the information. "We need to get back to the stable. Sharon will be in touch with you."

Sharon hugged Krystal and Jose. "Thank you so much. I'm sorry I haven't had a chance to get better acquainted, but we will. Take care of yourselves. I'll either come or send someone to get my mail. Don't give it to anyone unless they have a note from me. I'll call you and tell you I'm sending who ever comes. Thanks again."

Keanu took Sharon's bag to the wagon. "I guess we'll not catch him. He's had too much of a head start, besides, we can't really identify the car. Doggone. I wish I'd been outside so I could have seen better."

"If he had seen you outside, he wouldn't have driven by. We know now that he hasn't given up. He's keeping track of Sharon. At least he knows she isn't alone." David spoke angrily as he started the car and backed out to go to the stable.

Sharon was frightened but determined to not show how disturbed she was. *Lynn and all the rest of these people care about me and are so good to be concerned. I must not be a big baby and give them more to worry about. Lord, as usual, I'm praising you and leaving it in your hands.*

Sharon smiled broadly when they pulled in front of the office. "See that new van over there? That's Martin Swanson. He's been here so often that I think he'd like to have a closer relationship with Lynn."

"I agree," David smiled. "You should see the expression on his face when he's watching Lynn and doesn't know he's being observed. They're both great people." Sharon got out and walked toward the office.

Sharon

Keanu gave a snort of disgust. "Why do people think a man, or a woman, has to be interested in each other just because they're friendly?"

"Men and women do get interested in each other, as you put it," David answered.

"Can you truthfully tell me you've never been interested in a girl, or wanted to know her better?"

"I've been on the move too much. Yeah, I like girls, but nothing goofy."

"Goofy! The day will come, my man, when you'll fall as hard as the best of them."

"Like you're doing? I see how you look at Sharon." They watched Sharon walk in the door of the office. David smiled at Keanu, gave him a little push, and followed with Sharon's bag.

Lynn and Martin were sitting facing each other knee to knee talking quietly when Sharon walked in. Lynn jumped up and ran to Sharon, "I'm so relieved that you're back. Andrew and Matthew said they saw a dark car pull out of some bushes at the end of the driveway and follow you when you left here."

David had come in. "I'm slipping," he said with disgust. "I didn't notice anyone following."

"He kept a couple of cars between you. I've been telling Martin about all that's happened. Martin, tell them your idea."

"Sharon, were you ever suspicious of your husband's activities, or of his friends?"

"Not really," she said slowly, "but what does that have to do with this?"

"Maybe he was involved in something illegal and whoever associated with him might think you know what he was doing. They might think he was drinking and told you something he shouldn't. Or maybe they think you saw them with him at some time."

"No," she said thoughtfully, shaking her head. "I only noticed when he was drinking heavily. His mood swings were frightening, and as time went on, he was never in a good mood, at least not around me. I don't know what else to tell you."

"Don't let it upset you," Martin reassured her. "I'm only thinking out loud, as the ole saying goes. I've been racking my brain trying to imagine what this person, or persons, is after. We're butting into a brick wall until we know more about Jeremy's past."

"We know one thing," Keanu spoke. "We know he wasn't the brightest bulb in the chandelier to not appreciate Sharon. In fact, he was down right stupid."

"Please. Let's not talk about anything sad or upsetting," Lynn quickly broke in. "I have ice tea and I baked a cake this afternoon. Let's relax, visit and enjoy being together."

Jake joined them and reported on the veterinarian's visit. "I'm pleased with him, and I think he's going to work out fine."

"Good." David handed Jake a paper plate with a piece of cake on it. "Wrap yourself around that. It's delicious. Lynn made it."

"Then I know it's delicious," Jake grinned. He ate as all the rest did; as if he hadn't eaten for awhile.

"Gang," Lynn began. "The stable will be open for regular business tomorrow. All of the volunteers are on the alert. I know all of you will be, too. Sharon, promise me you won't be anywhere alone, in fact, try to have two others with you."

"I don't like it, but I understand. Yes, I promise." *How I hate worrying them. I wish I knew who is after me and why? Please, God. Let this be over soon.*

"I have an idea," Keanu jumped up and walked quickly into Lynn's office. He came back with a cell phone. "Carry this with you at all times. You might need to call for emergency help, or to report a suspicious happening."

"It's a good thing I'm not a scardy-cat," Sharon smiled weakly. "If I listened to all of you, I'd be afraid of my own shadow. I know you're concerned about my safety and happiness, and I'm grateful to have so many good, close friends. Thank you. I love you all."

"Oh, Lynn, I'm so glad you need me again. I'm getting cabin fever cooped up in this apartment and not knowing everything that's going on at the stable. I'm concerned about Sharon, and -- I'm nosy," she laughed. Lynn had called Sheilah.

"Sheilah, you wouldn't believe what all we've been through. Mom and dad have been scared stiff and needed reassurance. We've had countless phone calls and more media coverage than we needed. Thoughtless people just won't leave us alone. I'll be doubly glad when whoever this is, is caught. I'm frightened for Sharon and afraid that the publicity will hurt my business. We'll all welcome your bright, smiling face tomorrow morning. Okay. See ya. By the way, did you read what Sharon's ex mother-in-law said about her? Wasn't that nauseating?"

"Anyone with good, common sense, that read the trash, and then reads the reporter's statement, will know she is mentally unstable."

"Thank you Sheilah. I knew you'd understand. See you tomorrow. Be careful. Stay alert while you're driving out here. This sicko might think Sharon has told you whatever it is he's trying to shut her up about. Poor grammar, but you get my drift."

Twenty-one excited young people greeted Lynn and Sharon with a lot of admiration and respect the following morning.

"Hello, you two," Gabe said. "Am I glad we're back at work. Oh, I know, we came out to help, but it isn't like working with the youngsters and having happy, lively students around. I actually missed all those little - er - leprechauns." They all laughed at Gabe.

"All joking aside. I enjoy helping these youngsters. It's a double pleasure that I can help them, and with horses." Ashley smiled as she reached for a brush to groom a horse.

"Heads up, gang. I hope everyone has had vitamins and a good breakfast. Here they come," Andrew called as he came in to lead a saddled horse out.

CHAPTER FIFTEEN

LeLand wheeled his chair so fast that he almost turned over. "Sharon! Sharon! Boy, I cried buckets of tears. I thought you were in that car. Mom said she and dad were afraid they were going to have to take me to the hospital I got so sad. When we were watching the news and saw you standing with David, my whole family shouted for joy. Tell me all about it."

"Not without me you won't," shrieked Kara. "I want to hear all about it, too." Four other younger students also expressed their interest in hearing.

Lynn blew a whistle. "You're here for riding lessons, and that's serious business. We don't have time for gossip and socializing."

"Yeah," Marcella Berring scolded them. "We have our lesson first and then we'll ALL talk to Sharon. Hi, Sharon. I am sooo glad you're okay."

"Thank you, Marcella. I'm glad, too. Now let's all go to the ring."

"Who's that coming here?" Gabe asked with a frown. "Oh, it's Martin. Wow! A new car. I didn't recognize him."

Lynn blushed and walked to meet Martin. "What are you doing here? You don't have a lesson scheduled."

"I can visit, can't I? When I looked at my appointment calendar, I saw that I didn't have pressing business until late this afternoon, so, I told my secretary where I'd be. Hi everybody," he greeted the volunteers.

The young people had grown fond of the charismatic lawyer. Each one greeted him warmly, some even coming to him to shake hands or slap him on the shoulder.

Martin wheeled to the ring and listened to the lesson. *I'm glad that Sharon has a strong backbone and has taken charge of her life. Lynn will feel easier about her, and I'll help any way that I can. I sure would love to know who is after her and why.*

"Martin." He looked quickly to see who had spoken to him. Jake was behind him holding a horse by the reins. "Lynn says, if you want to, you can practice and warm-up in the training ring."

Martin looked back at the activities in the outdoor ring, and then back at Jake. "I'd like that. Thank you." He wheeled his chair to the stable, talking to Jake as they went along. "How am I going to mount without the ramp?"

Jake took his cap off and ran his hand through his hair. "I wasn't thinking of that.

Will it be all right if Gordon and I lift you on the horse?"

Martin drew a deep breath with a slight red flush moving across his face. "No one hates to be helpless more than I do. I have always been an athlete and very independent. Yes. I'll accept your help with gratitude. We'll try it."

He checked to make sure his brakes were set on his wheelchair and reached down to lift his leg from the chair. He suddenly stopped, gasped, and gave a strangled noise. Jake jerked around frightened that something was wrong.

"What happened? Are you hurting?"

"No. No. I'm not hurting. Did you see that?" Martin asked in an awed whisper.

"See what?"

Martin answered in a strained low voice. "My leg moved." He said with a little more volume and excitement. "My leg moved."

"Yeah?" Jake looked confused. Of course he moved his leg. Jake saw him reach down and take hold of it.

"Jake, what I'm saying, and badly, is that my leg moved and I didn't lift it. I even had a tiny bit of feeling."

"Really!" Jake was excited with him. "Do you want me to get Lynn so you can tell her?"

"No," Martin said hurriedly. "Let's not tell Lynn yet. Wait until I have my doctor check me out. I don't want to build her hopes and find that it was just a fluke."

Jake grinned knowingly. "No, we don't want to give Lynn false hopes. This'll be our secret. I promise." He turned toward the stable and called. "Gordon. Yo Gordon. Could you come here, please?"

"Yes, sir," Gordon came walking rapidly to them.

"Would you help me lift Martin on Banjo's back?"

Keanu walked to them out of curiosity. "What are you doing?"

"Lynn said Martin could practice and exercise on Banjo, but we don't have a ramp back here. Gordon and I are going to lift him on to Banjo's back."

"Good idea. You two lift him on this side and I'll stand on the other side to balance him." Keanu walked around to be on the horse's right side.

"Fellows," Keanu began, "did you ever hear why we mount on the left side?" All three men shook their heads. "Well, during the Middle Ages, the knights wore their swords on their left side. If they mounted from the right side, the sword would slap the side of the horse as they mounted. By getting on the left side, the sword hung down and didn't get in the way. I don't know whether that is the whole truth or not, but it makes a good story," he grinned.

"Sounds logical to me," Martin said. Jake and Gordon just looked at each other and shrugged. Not being educated like Martin, and not interested in learning new things as Keanu did, they were not enthused with the story.

The three men helped a grateful Martin on the horse, and then Keanu fastened the belt around him. Next he fastened the Velcro straps around each ankle and handed Martin the reins. "Let's walk to the exercise ring. I'd like to work with you today, if it's okay with you." Keanu opened the gate to the training ring which was behind the stables.

"I'll feel better if you're with me. I've ridden for many years, but the accident took the starch out of me. Okay, teacher, what do you want me to do first?" he asked Keanu.

"Walk to the right and I'll check your equitation. There's no excuse for you to fall back and become a sloppy rider."

Keanu watched Martin like a hawk eyeing its prey. He called for a walk both directions, and finally a slow trot both directions. "Let's stand here for a few minutes and let your leg muscles rest while you do some simple exercises. Hold your arms straight out from the shoulders and twist from side to side as far back as you can reach. Work your waist."

"That's ten times. I seem to be moving much better, and I don't hurt," Martin was excited. Keanu released the Velcro straps around Martin's ankles. He took one step away.

"Don't do anything that's going to hurt you, but try to lift your right leg away from the horse's side." Martin struggled with no results. "Try the left leg."

Martin gave a gasp of surprise and pleasure when his leg moved about one inch. "See! Did you see that?"

"I sure did. There seems to be some life returning. Don't hurt yourself but try it again."

Martin grunted with the effort and laboriously moved his leg slightly. He gave a sigh of exhaustion and slumped in the saddle. "Keanu, do you think I'm going to have the use of my legs again?"

"I'm not a doctor, and I'm not sure a doctor could answer that question at this time. Tell your doctor what happened. In the meantime be faithful to your therapy sessions and don't get discouraged. You knew it was going to be a slow process. You don't want to try to force movement and hinder your progress."

"I know. Please don't tell anyone yet. Can I trust you to keep this between us until we see if it's repeated or if that was all she wrote?"

"Sure." Keanu patted Martin's leg. "I'm going to let you walk Banjo down to the ring so you can dismount at the ramp. I'll push your chair down with us."

Martin's legs swung uselessly by the horse's side as Keanu pushed the chair and walked beside him. Just as they started down the slight grade leading from the stable to the outdoor ring, a red sports car came swooping around the circle and stopped with a flourish, throwing gravel. The sudden noise and quick movement caused Banjo to jump and take off at a gallop to the ring.

"Heads up," Lynn called to everyone in the ring. She almost screamed when she saw Banjo barreling down on them. These horses were so well trained to be safe for helpless riders, Banjo's actions were a surprise. Lynn opened the gate to the ring. "Get out of the way," she yelled at the volunteers who were leading horses toward her. *Oh, please dear God, don't let him get hurt.*

Banjo roared into the ring and gave a short hop over a pole on the ground before he galloped around the ring. Lynn quickly closed the gate and turned toward her volunteers. "Keep your eyes and hands on those horses and students. Everyone stay calm."

Sharon had quietly and quickly stepped in front of Banjo. She was talking softly and calmly. "Ho, Banjo. Ho, pretty boy. Easy. Easy. Ho, now." Banjo dropped to a walk and stopped obediently in front of Sharon. She took the reins and soothed the horse while running a quick eye over Martin to assess his condition.

"Martin, are you all right?" Lynn was shaking as she walked to his side. When she saw his sparkling eyes and flushed face, she felt a spurt of anger.

"I'm fine," he spoke loudly and excitedly. "Did you see him hop over the pole and I stayed right here." He babbled in his joy and excitement.

"Stop it," Lynn almost shouted. "Are you crazy? You could have been hurt worse - and I'd be liable. How could you do this? How could you do this *to me*? Who is the idiot that allowed you to come charging down that bank. And without ankle straps," she was almost screaming again. Her heart was beating double time, and she surprised herself because of her worry, and - yes - anger. She realized that she was being unreasonable, but couldn't help herself.

A wild-eyed, pale-faced Keanu came to them too frightened to speak at first. "I--I--I was bringing him down so that he could dismount at the ramp when some jerk raced in here and stopped on a dime throwing gravels and running right at the horse. It scared Banjo and he did what comes naturally - - he ran."

"That doesn't excuse the fact that you did not fasten the ankle straps. At least he has the belt around his hips. You certainly know better," she sputtered in anger and fright.

Martin recognized that Lynn wasn't as angry as she was frightened. *She's worried about me. I do believe the lady actually cares*, he grinned. "All's well that ends well," he said trying to relieve the tension. Lynn was too shaky to smile. *What is wrong with me? I want to grab Martin and hug him hard, but I don't dare in front of the others. What would Martin think of me anyway?*

"Get him off there," she glared at Keanu and demanded as she went to open the gate again. Leaving Gabe and Amanda to help Martin, Keanu followed Lynn and Sharon out of the ring.

"Hello, Sharon."

She looked shocked. "Lt. Dauber!"

"Larry, please." He turned to speak to Lynn. "I take it you're Sharon's sister. I see the family resemblance. I'm Larry Dauber. Sharon and I met some time ago and I decided to come see her after all the newspaper and television news." He turned to smile at Sharon but recoiled in surprise when Keanu walked right up in his face.

"Mister, you're either one stupid dude or careless and don't care. Any idiot knows to keep slow, calm and quiet around horses, or as far as that goes, any animal. What did you have in mind coming in here as if you're on a race track?"

Sharon was appalled. "Keanu, shut up. This is police Lt. Larry Dauber from the state's attorney's office that I told you about." She looked apologetically at Larry.

"I don't care if he's head of the F.B.I. He's got loose boards in his attic to drive in here that way." Keanu was his usual antagonistic self. With all of his worry about Sharon, he would welcome a chance to hit someone.

As Larry apologized and explained to Keanu that he didn't ride and wasn't aware of doing anything wrong, Lynn was puzzled at David's attitude. He had looked startled when Larry introduced himself and then had quickly turned and walked briskly into the stable.

"Lt. Dauber, I'm sorry you didn't receive a warmer welcome, but you did drive in too fast. There are handicapped children on the grounds in wheelchairs and on crutches. It so happens that they were on horseback in the ring with older people walking beside them. There is no damage done, but the man that was on that runaway horse is also in a wheelchair. He could have been hurt badly." Lynn took a deep breath and forced herself to calm down. *I must be gracious to this man because of Sharon.* "Please excuse me. Sharon can visit with you, but the rest of us have work to do. She nodded slightly, without smiling, and walked away.

Sharon was embarrassed. "I'm sorry, Larry. Of course you didn't know to drive slowly through the parking area. The horses are well trained to deal with all kinds of noises, but roaring cars is not part of their training," she smiled.

"I'm embarrassed. I truly had no idea that I was driving irresponsibly. Is it possible to talk to you somewhere that all these people won't be glaring at me?"

Sharon laughed. "I can't imagine the big, brave police lieutenant being afraid of a few people. Keanu was scared and spoke harshly. He really isn't as nasty as he sounded."

"He had a right to be upset. Can I drag my red face inside where we can talk privately?"

"Let's go in the office. I want you to meet Lynn's secretary. She's a hoot. You'll like her. Then I'll show you around the place."

Before they could walk toward the office another sport convertible drove in with Troy Sanborn at the wheel. Sharon welcomed him and introduced him to Larry. She excused herself to take him to the ring to meet Lynn. Larry walked with them looking around with great interest. Troy stayed with Lynn and Sharon brought Larry to the office.

"I'm happy to meet you. Sharon told us of the mess at the motel. We're all relieved that she got away from there safely," Sheilah told him.

"Mess?" Larry raised his eyebrows.

"Oh, I hate to say the word, murder." Sheilah shuddered.

"That's all right. I hate the word myself. Larry smiled at her.

Sharon took Larry over the building showing him the indoor ring, the medical area and office. Then they went to the stables to meet some of the volunteers and see the horses.

"I'm impressed. I had no idea that this type of work involved so much time, effort, training and so many people needed to work. This is a beautiful place." Larry looked over the pasture back of the stable at the horses that were boarded. "Are those horses used, too?"

"No, we don't work them," Sharon answered. "They belong to boarders. Each of our animals have to have special training and is carefully selected to make sure they'll be patient with clinking crutches, wheelchairs bumping them and excited kids. Those are good saddle horses out there, but they're not trained for the main work here."

"What do you mean by boarders?"

"People own horses but don't have property of their own where they can keep them. They pay someone else to keep their horse and care for it. They're called boarders."

"Wow. I'm learning a lot. Can you get away to have dinner with me?" Larry asked.

"I have to help with the work before I can leave," Sharon answered.

"I'll cover for you," Andrew offered. "Go on home, get prettied up and have a great evening."

Sharon gave a start not aware that anyone was near and listening.

"She's pretty enough. She doesn't need extras," Keanu snapped and glowered.

Uh oh. I didn't realize Keanu had come in. I must be losing it not hearing others around. I know it isn't because Larry is here. I don't care about him as a male interest.

Sharon

"Ooo," Larry whispered. "Let's leave before I get scalped, quartered, hung and burned at the stake. Is that young man Indian?" Larry leaned close, placed an arm around Sharon and whispered to her.

"Yes. Half at least. I doubt seriously that all those horrendous cruelties would happen to you. Remember, I told you Keanu's bark is worse than his bite." Sharon answered Larry after Keanu had walked down the aisle of the stable.

"I don't want to stand around and tempt fate," he laughed.

Larry followed Sharon's car to her house and followed her inside. While Sharon was showering and dressing, Larry played her piano. He played classics and popular songs of the day. His touch sounded professional.

"I love your house," Larry told Sharon as she entered the room. "Did you do the decorating?"

"Lynn purchased it for me and had it furnished before I got here. I did a little decorating and planting flowers after I moved in. Are you ready to leave?"

Larry smiled and put an arm around her waist as they walked toward the door. He looked with appreciation at the lovely flowers and flowering shrubs. "Did you plant all these flowers? Did you do all this work?"

"Most of it. I'm glad you like my house. I do, too," she laughed. "Lynn did a good job selecting it for me before I came here from Texas."

"That's right. You did live in Texas. Did you like it in the west?"

"I sure did and I met so many wonderful people. I hated to leave."

"Why did you feel it necessary to move here from Texas?"

"I was there with my husband who was in military service. We were stationed in The San Antonio Air Base. After he -- died, I came back east because all my relatives are here."

"But why Zephyrhills?"

"Lynn is here. We have always been very close, and too, I wanted to attend classes at USF in Tampa. Here we are. Turn right here into John's Steak and Seafood. The acoustics leave a lot to be desired, but the food is excellent and the service is very good. I think you'll approve."

That's good enough recommendation for me." Larry got out of his car and hurried to open the door for Sharon.

Larry was impressed that so many people, men and women, greeted Sharon. She felt uncomfortable because Larry kept putting his arm around her and hugging her closer to him. *There's no way he could be jealous. We hardly know each other.*

Sitting back with a satisfied sigh and patting his stomach, Larry said sheepishly, "I made a pig of myself. You're right. The food is excellent."

Sharon smiled and looked around because people were still calling to her and trying to get her attention. *Do I really like this man? No. I don't know him well enough. He's trying so hard to be nice to me and he does show that he's interested in me. I don't want to encourage him unless I decide that he's someone I want to know better. He isn't too bad looking, but his eyes don't show warmth and caring. He looks calculating and suspicious. Maybe that's his occupation causing him to look --- Stop it. I'm not interested and I don't want to give him the idea that there's a future for us.*

"I don't eat out much, but when I do, this is one of the places I love to come."

"Did you live in Zephyrhills previous to Texas?"

"No. Lynn settled here because she could buy the land necessary for her business. Zephyrhills is close to all the main tourist attractions and yet it's not right in the heavily populated area." She giggled. "Or at least it didn't use to be. Lynn says the traffic increases three fold during the winter with all the people coming down from the north."

"Do you know the police chief?" Larry broke in.

"I've never met him. Lynn is outside the city limits, so the county sheriff is called if police are needed."

"Did the sheriff investigate your car - uh - bombing, or did city police handle it?"

"The sheriff did. I never thought about it, but it happened on the Dade City, Zephyrhills line. Oh, well. It doesn't matter. Just as long as it's covered. Why do you want to know?"

"No reason. I'm just interested. Business curiosity - law work. I see you have a new car. Are you afraid to drive? Are you afraid that the same thing, or something similar will happen again?"

"Why would it happen again? It could have been that I was mistaken for someone else." *Why is he asking so many questions about why I came here and what police I know? Gracious. I'm being silly. He's being a policeman and making small talk.*

"Larry, thank you for coming down to see me. I truly enjoyed the evening and thank you for dinner. By the way, I thoroughly enjoyed your playing. How is it that a big, bad policeman plays so beautifully? You could have another career."

"My mother insisted that I study music. She's a concert pianist and lives for it. She was away from home so much while I was growing up. She held concerts all over the U. S. and many overseas. Dad was a doctor and far too busy to spend much time with me, even if he'd been interested. I was raised by nannies and tutors. I thought about teaching school, but knew I could not be satisfied with the sameness day after day. We work many hours, sometimes around the clock, but police work is never boring. One wonderful housekeeper, who took care of me, had a son who was a detective. I thought he was the great American hero."

"Ah ha. Did you want to emulate him?"

"Not really. I was impressed with him and what he did. I love the work. There's not enough income for a man to raise a family. I guess that's why I've never married. I want a wife to stay at home with children, so I'd need to earn enough to support a family. I'm due a promotion soon, and I have something in mind for the future that will give me a better income. Maybe I'd better start thinking of marriage," he rambled nervously.

He pulled onto her driveway and got out of the car to go around and open her door.

"Good night and take care of yourself. Maybe I can even win the friendship of Geronimo."

"Geronimo? Who --" Sharon responded surprised.

"Your young Indian protector. It's obvious that he doesn't like me. He probably doesn't trust me either,"

"Keanu?! He's a teen who's been forced to grow up too soon. We've developed a very close friendship. I feel toward him as I would a younger brother."

"That's well and good, but he's very protective of you. He gave me the impression that he thinks I'm bad for you."

"He is protective, but it's because I'm the one who found him and have given him complete support."

"Found him? Why? Was he lost?" Larry asked with interest.

"It's a long story and not germane to this subject." She clamped her lips tightly.

"No need to get testy. I was just making an observation." He tried to lighten the moment.

"I'm sorry, but I'm protective of Keanu, too. He's had a rough time and now he's happy. I want him to have good reasons for being happy and for him to lead a productive life."

"Forgive me for bringing a sour note to the ending of our night out. I enjoyed every minute of being with you and sincerely hope this is not the last of it."

"Nothing to forgive, and no, I don't think this is the last. We're miles apart, but you'll probably be in the area with your work. I'm sure there'll be an opportunity to get together again. Now, good night and thank you again."

"The pleasure is all mine." He leaned toward her but she deftly moved aside as if she were unaware of his movement to kiss her. She quickly stepped inside her house, waved at him and shut the door He waited until he heard Sharon lock the door and then walked to his car. He looked over the neighborhood as he opened his door. His eyes half closed when he discovered a car, in the next block, sitting with lights off. He could see the shape of someone in it. While he was looking, the car slowly moved out. The lights were not turned on until the driver turned the corner.

Curious. I wonder why that person was sitting there. Was he watching Sharon? I didn't notice a tail as we drove home, but then, I wasn't expecting one. He got in and started his car. Backing out of the driveway, he turned to follow the car that had pulled out. He drove around a couple of blocks in all directions but could not find the car.

It could have been a coincidence, but somehow I doubt it. As Larry drove back to Tallahassee, he kept as eye out for a dark sedan, but no luck.

Sharon prepared for bed and thought about the evening. *I don't know why Keanu and Larry seem to rub against each other when Keanu gets along so well with everyone else. Keanu is very good at sizing people up. Maybe I should pay attention to his feelings about Larry. On the other hand, Keanu could just be resentful of anyone who might show a personal interest in me,* she smiled to herself. The phone interrupted her thoughts.

"Hello." Silence. "Hello." There was a sound of breathing and movement. She hung up thinking it might have been a wrong number.

As Sharon was getting into bed, the phone rang again. "Hello." Silence. "Look, if you have the wrong number, why don't you check with the operator."

Sharon

A hoarse whisper answered. "Not wrong number. Just want you to know I'm keeping an eye on you, and I'll know what you say to everybody."

"What business is it of yours what I say to people? I think you have the wrong number. There's no reason for anyone to be concerned about me." She slammed the phone down.

The phone immediately rang again. She grabbed it up. "All right. I've had enough. The police will be checking all calls that I have and you'd better be might sure that you have the right number."

"Sharon, what's wrong?" Lynn's frightened voice implored. "Tell me, honey, did Larry do something to you?"

"Oh, Lynn," she answered relieved. "No, Larry was a gentleman. I've gotten strange phone calls, mostly deep-breathing and hang-ups. I thought it was a teen having fun or a sicko and paid no attention, but the caller just now threatened me."

"What! Did he give you a clue as to who it might be? Did you recognize the voice?"

"No, and no. He disguised his voice."

"What did he say?" Lynn's voice was shaky with concern.

Sharon told Lynn of the call. "Lynn, what could he have meant? What could I say to anyone that would hurt someone else?"

"Sharon," Lynn said thoughtfully. "There's more to this. In the past, probably in Texas, you've observed something that didn't register with you, but it was important to someone else. Or you might have passed close to people who were talking and they thought you might have overheard them. Think! Could you have seen something at that motel where the murder was committed? Maybe it didn't mean doodily-squat to you, but the person might think you'd be a dangerous witness against him."

"Lynn, we went over this same line of thinking after my car was bombed. I've thought until I keep a headache and I can't remember a thing that would cause someone to try to kill me, or to threaten me. Lynn, I'm so tired of this - tired in mind and body. I just want all of this over and don't want any of my family and friends hurt because of me. Losing Jennifer nearly killed me. I wish I could think of a solution and get this over with, whatever it is."

"I'm coming in to stay with you for the rest of the night. Tomorrow you're moving back in with me. No arguments, or I'm calling mom and dad," Lynn said firmly as Sharon started to argue with her.

"Oh, please don't worry our parents. Stay where you are. You have too many responsibilities on your property. Sure you have good employees, but it isn't like taking care of your own affairs. I would feel badly to take you away."

They talked a few more minutes and hung up after Sharon made Lynn promise not to tell their parents.

Twenty minutes later, Sharon's doorbell rang. Her heart leaped and she felt as if she were choking. She jumped with racing pulse and thumping heart as the doorbell rang with determination. She tiptoed to the front and threw on the outside lights.

She shrieked.

CHAPTER SIXTEEN

"Keanu!" She jerked the door open. "You scared me to death. What are you doing here? Is something wrong at the farm?"

"Everything's fine," he said as he walked in. "We were all in the office when Lynn called you. Everybody wanted to come, but I won. Truthfully, I out-ran them." he laughed as he crossed the living room and headed for the first door on the right. "I'll be here in your guest room. I'm a light sleeper, so, have a good restful sleep and know that I'm on the job. No yo yo is going to get to you if I can help it."

She stared speechlessly as he walked into the room and firmly shut the door cutting off any chance of an argument. Anger washed over her and then she almost giggled. *It doesn't matter what I say, they're going to try to protect me whether I want it or not.* She shook her head and smiled as she went on to her own room.

"Pon my honor," Sharon exploded. "The whole gang's standing in a row, like birds on a fence, to see me arrive." Keanu brought her car to a stop in front of the stables. She burst out of the car with the intention of telling them off. As she looked at their anxious faces, she realized it was their love and caring that made them hover. Her heart leaped knowing that each of these people would do whatever possible to keep her safe. They would be just as concerned about any of the others.

"Hey, gang. You folks look as if you're waiting for something exciting or important. What's the occasion?" she teased.

David strode toward her. "We just want to be sure you're okay."

Sharon was startled when she saw the expression in his eyes. *He really cares.* She had to look up so far at him that the back of her neck felt the pressure.

"I'm fine," she stammered, stepping back so that she would not be looking straight up at him. "It would take a mighty stupid person to try to get to me past all of you."

"He hasn't been too smart so far," Jake explained. "The thing is, we have no clue who this bozo is or if he's even sane. Until we have a clue as to who it is and what he - or she - wants, you need to be extra careful and let us watch your back."

"I'll get your case and take it in." Keanu turned to get her suitcase from the car. "One of you will have to drive me back later. I left the stable car at Sharon's and drove her here. I'll need to go back and get the car." He didn't add that it would give him a chance to see if anyone was hanging around.

The teen volunteers gathered around, concerned, but not knowing what to do or say.

"I'm truly grateful, folks, but business needs to go on as usual. Are we going to let this unknown person run our lives?" They looked at each other and shook their heads. Lynn blew her whistle with a catch in her throat. "Okay, group, time to roll."

Sharon

Volunteers led horses to the ring and gave a last safety check. Gabe walked the ring and checked all of the equipment. Lynn released a sigh of satisfaction as she watched the organized manner in which all of them proceeded with the day's work.

Martin no longer needed a leader or side walkers. With his therapy, massages and riding, he was rapidly gaining strength. He continued use of the wheelchair on the open, grounds, but depended on leg braces and special canes indoors.

"Lynn, Martin looks at you as if he could eat you with a spoon. Has he talked to you about his feelings toward you?" Sharon asked, concerned and pleased at the same time.

Lynn blushed. "Hush, Sharon. Others will hear you."

"Darling, it's no secret. All of us have eyes, and we hear the softness in his voice when he says your name."

"Well, he hasn't actually said it aloud, but his actions and, yes, his expressions, let me know he's interested." Lynn looked as if she wanted to say more but was unsure.

"Do you return his feelings? How do you feel about him?" Sharon was pleased for Lynn and wanted the best for her.

"I don't really know. I've concentrated so long on realizing my dream of this school that I haven't even given it a thought to have a relationship other than as a friend with anyone. I know he's a gentleman and a gentle man. He's intelligent, compassionate, kind to all those around him and we do have a lot of the same interests."

"But you haven't given it much thought," Sharon laughed.

"Talking about feelings, little sister, how do you feel about David? It's obvious to everyone how he feels about you."

"I guess I feel about him like you do about Martin. I think David cares about me, but we've never had a chance to discuss our feelings. My priority is my education for the present. If we're meant to be together, then it will happen in time."

Martin rode up behind them. His face was actually shining as he looked at Lynn. His eyes were so full of love that it was no secret how he felt. "Is this a private discussion or can a poor slob join in?"

"Poor slob," Sharon jeered. "Are you digging for compliments or giving a character reference?"

"Neither. I was lonely and thought I might find stimulating company over here." He smiled at Lynn and winked. She immediately blushed which brought a hearty laugh from Martin.

"Lynn, you've blushed more since Martin came here than I can remember," Sharon wisely excused herself to go help with some of the students. She looked back to see Lynn leaning against Martin's leg and talking seriously with him. She smiled to herself when Martin leaned down and gave Lynn a quick kiss. *Hooray! I hope they let each other know completely how they each feel, and soon.*

"Hey, Hank. It's me, Duke. Nothing interesting going on. The whole stupid gang is circling around the little witch like a herd of wild cattle guarding their calves."

"You know you're not supposed to be there. You were told to leave and go back to Texas after the bombing. You're lucky you're still alive. The Boss is really mad about you taking things in your own hands. You were told to watch, not to do. Get away from there before you're discovered."

"Okay. Okay. One more day. I'll be in touch."

On the following morning, Lynn and Sharon, with some of the girl volunteers, were stacking hay bales in the loft and cleaning in the storage barn. The men were riding fences, checking and mending breaks as well as any chores that needed doing. Lynn had been teasing Sharon because David had made several trips back to the barn. Each time he called Sharon to him and whispered to her.

"It's so romantic," Rebekah sighed.

Jardine grinned at Lynn. "On the subject of romance, Martin wasn't letting your lips get cold last night."

"Oh, ho," Sharon sighed. "Tell all." She was thankful for the change of subject.

"There's nothing to tell," Lynn said blushing.

The girls started teasing each other and wrestling in the stacks of hay. Suddenly Amelia Reardon screamed. "I've been bitten. A snake bit me. Is it poisonous?"

Lynn and Sharon, alarmed and frightened, grabbed a shovel and a hoe to find the snake while Ashley and Betsy helped Amelia down from the hay loft. They all laughed nervously when Sharon called, "Never fear. I've found the - um - snake." Laughing she held up a short length of barb wire. "I don't know how this got here, but someone was very careless."

David had raced his horse to the barn when he heard the scream. He looked at Amelia's wound. "Ouch. That must hurt," he sympathized. "Sharon, go to my car and get the bottle of peroxide in the glove compartment. I had to buy some yesterday for myself."

Sharon ran outside the barn to David's car while he checked Amelia's wound. "How long has it been since you had a tetanus shot?"

"I don't know," Amelia sobbed. "I don't remember having one."

"Hold it." Lynn spoke with authority. "That's a requirement for working here, and you told me that you had a tetanus shot."

"Oh, I remember. I had one when I went for my physical for school."

"Thank goodness. Gang, this is why I insist on all of us having up-to-date shots. On property like this, there'll be splinters, barb wire, scrapes of all kinds and sometimes animal bites. What's keeping Sharon?"

Sharon stumbled in looking pale and shaky. She handed the peroxide to Lynn without looking at anyone.

"Poor dear. Don't tell me you're squeamish," David teased her.

"All right, I won't tell you," she snapped and wobbled out to go to the office.

After David had treated and wrapped Amelia's hand, Lynn advised her to ask her mother if she wanted their doctor to check the wound. Lynn then excused herself and went to see about Sharon. *I hope she isn't sick. What can be troubling her other than the usual irritants that she's lived with for a time?*

"Sheilah, did you see Sharon come in?" Lynn asked as she stepped worriedly into the office. There was an unnatural silence in the building.

"Yeah. She was acting funny. I ask her if she was sick, but she said she wasn't and went to your apartment walking like a zombie."

Worried, Lynn went quickly up the stairs with her heart aching for Sharon. Lynn's breath was short and fast in her anxiety. "Sharon, where are you?" Lynn walked into her living room area to see Sharon sitting on the sleep sofa looking as if she might pass out.

Her arms were wrapped around her stomach and she was rocking back and forth staring into space.

"Sweetie, when did you become so wimpy? I've never known you to be so sensitive about a small wound, especially when you found it wasn't a snake after all."

"It wasn't that," Sharon sighed deeply and got up to pace while wringing her hands. "Lynn, do you remember me telling you about the murder at the motel and the man who accidentally knocked me down?"

"Sure, and you said you wished you could have had the opportunity to get acquainted with him." Lynn waited patiently for Sharon to continue.

"Well, I've gotten to know him, and now I wish I never had."

"What!? Who? Where?" Lynn squeaked anxiously.

"Let me finish. I didn't tell you something else because I kind of forgot it in the excitement of learning there was a dead man in the room beside mine. The man who ran into me was polite and reached his hand to me to help me up. I noticed that he had an unusual gold ring looking like a coiled snake with ruby eyes. It was obvious that it was an expensive piece of jewelry." Sharon looked as if she had lost a loved one in death.

Lynn was curious, but waited to hear Sharon explain her behavior.

"No. You never mentioned the ring. You just said he had a deep, sexy voice and was obviously a gentleman in spite of the circumstances. What do you mean you now know him?"

"I saw that ring today."

"Good grief. Who had it? Where did you see it?"

"Remember when I went to David's car to get the peroxide?" Lynn nodded but wisely said nothing. "I found that ring in David's glove compartment."

"Sharon, that doesn't mean it's the same ring. There might be others like it. Besides, David never has let on that he knew you or anything about your accident, even though he has heard the story of the motel murder."

"I hope and pray that he'll have a good story of his own, but the more I listen to his voice, he sounds like that man. When he ran toward his car to go with Keanu, I had a memory jog because he ran just like the man ran to that car that night."

Lynn started to answer when a buzzer sounded. "Sheilah is signaling that one of us has a phone call on the business line." She answered the phone in her apartment and turned, with a puzzled expression, to Sharon. "It's Larry wanting to speak to you, Sharon."

"Larry, I'm so glad you called. You must be a mind reader. I need to talk to you. I think I have some news you'd like to hear."

Lynn hissed. "Careful, Sharon. You don't know that David is the mystery man."

"What? I'm sorry. Lynn was talking to me. Do you remember when we met at the motel and you wanted to question me about the murder?" She listened for a few seconds.

"Do you remember me telling you about the two men that ran after one accidentally knocked me down? He was wearing an odd ring made of a gold coiled snake with ruby eyes. Yes, I know I didn't tell you about it before, because I forgot it in all the excitement. I found a ring just like that today in David's glove compartment. That made me remember it. Too, David has a deep voice as that man did and is about the same height and size of that man."

Lynn could hear his raised voice over the phone. She was standing by Sharon shaking her head. Sharon said, "Okay, I'll do that. See you then." She hung up and sat down quickly because her legs were trembling.

"Sharon," Lynn was disapproving, "I have a bad feeling that you've done the wrong thing. You owe it to David to let him explain first before you mentioned it to anyone else. You know how kind and helpful he's been. Besides, he loves you. It's as clear as the nose on your face, and we've all recognized it."

"Then why haven't we seen that ring before now?"

"He doesn't wear any rings. Neither does Jake. A lot of men who work in the open or with dangerous equipment will not wear rings."

"Larry said for us to sit tight and say nothing to anyone else. He's coming down here tomorrow morning and he'll question David.

The men were concerned because Lynn went about with a serious face, not smiling at anyone and looking as if she was upset. They were also concerned because Sharon was staying inside and talking to no one. There was no explanation except that Sharon didn't feel well. When David said he wanted to talk to her, Lynn advised him to let her rest and wait until the next day.

Neither young woman rested well that night. The next morning Lynn skipped breakfast feeling nauseous. She felt sorry for Sharon knowing the frightening things that had happened in her life. Lynn also felt sorry for David and felt that he didn't deserve this kind of treatment. She wanted to talk to him herself, but she had promised Sharon that she wouldn't.

Sharon stayed in Lynn's apartment and wouldn't even come down to the office for fear she'd have to face David and talk to him. David was upset and worried about her.

"Lynn, what's wrong with Sharon? I need to see her and see for myself that she's all right." David said anxiously.

"She has a personal problem that she's trying to solve, David. I'm sure she'll tell you all about it soon." Lynn's heart was so heavy thinking of Sharon's fright and the accusation against David.

"Lynn, maybe I could help. I'm worried about her."

"I know David, but she has asked to be let alone. She didn't even want me to stay with her."

David looked crest-fallen. "I do hope she'll talk to me soon. You know how much she means to me."

"I know, David." Lynn turned away quickly so that David would not see the tears that she couldn't keep from her eyes. *I'm ashamed that Sharon didn't trust David and let him explain first before she told Larry. I don't know why, but I don't feel comfortable with Larry knowing.*

With a heavy heart, David doctored two young male horses that had gotten into a fight. He helped groom and tack a few horses and gave a jumping lesson out in the field over natural obstacles. *I can't put it into words, but I feel as if a thick blanket has been dropped over my head making it hard to breathe.*

Just as all work began to slow around eleven thirty, Larry pulled in - carefully this time. He didn't speak to anyone; just jumped out of his car and walked rapidly toward the office.

"What is his highness doing here?" Jake asked while David stood beside him looking bewildered. David felt anger washing over him. *Is Sharon in more trouble? I'll tear anyone apart with my bare hands that causes her more grief.*

Lynn felt guilty, but she had promised Sharon not to discuss her business even though she didn't agree with her. She continued to feel that Sharon was making a mistake.

Keanu, Andrew and Gabe came to stand by David and Jake. The rest of the young people were not far behind. None of them liked Larry and did not approve of him.

After about half an hour, Larry and Sharon walked to the stable. It was obvious from Sharon's red eyes that she had been crying. David started to walk to her giving a hard, angry look at Larry. Larry stalked to meet him and stood close in front of David.

"All right Baughman. I have some questions for you. First, let's go to your car and you can show me a ring that you have in your glove compartment." The two tall men were standing eye to eye; one blonde and one dark.

David's jaw dropped and he looked at Sharon like a wounded animal, much as a kicked dog might. Sharon sobbed aloud. Jake became belligerent to Larry, and all the male volunteers gathered around looking angry. The girls looked worried and horrified.

"Who do you think you are coming in here demanding anything of David?" Jake barked. "Lynn, are you going to condone this?" Keanu clinched his fists and stepped closer to Larry.

"David deserves a chance to explain the ring and certainly deserves respectful attention. Larry Dauber, you may be an officer of the law and feel you're within your rights, but you're on my property and I've not seen a warrant. David is not only a valued employee, but he's a trusted friend." She glared at Sharon who hung her head, sobbed harder and turned her back to them. Lynn continued. "If David chooses to answer you, that's his business, otherwise, get off my property and don't return unless you have a warrant."

The crowd cheered and moved threateningly toward Larry. Sharon gasped, "Lynn!"

"Not a word, Sharon. Not one word. I'm so disgusted with you right now that I don't trust myself to speak. David, what do you want to do?"

"Sharon?" David spoke with deep hurt in his voice, looking imploringly at her.

"Sharon, what *have* you done?" Jake barked.

Matthew Ryder ran to them breathlessly. "I've called Martin, and he's on his way."

"Who's Martin?" Larry sneered.

CHAPTER SEVENTEEN

"He's a top-notch attorney," Gabe answered. "I suggest that everybody just hang loose until Mr. Swanson gets here," he said.

"Oh, him," Larry smiled a lop-sided smile. "He won't make a bit of difference. Baughman, are you going to show me the ring, or am I going to have to arrest you and let you spend time in a cell where scum like you belongs?"

David drew himself up. "You're making a major mistake and you'd better think twice before you try to arrest anyone."

Larry rushed toward David and reached to grab his arm. Matthew, Keanu, Gabe and Andrew all rushed to attack Larry. Before they could reach him, David had swung and knocked Larry flat on his back.

"Stand back. Please don't get involved. I appreciate your friendship, but I'll handle this." David told them.

Larry came up swearing and swinging. It was a short fight and David had him on the ground again sitting on him when Martin drove in.

"Hey, hey, what's going on?" Martin yelled almost falling as he hurried as fast as he could on his metal crutches.

The boys all tried to talk at once in their anger. Jake put his fingers to his mouth and gave a shrill whistle.

"Get off of him, David," Martin ordered. "All right, buddy. This is private property and I understand you came threatening and causing trouble without just cause. You'd better have a good reason for your actions, and show a warrant signed by a judge, that gives you the authority to question people on this property."

"Let Sharon tell you," Larry blustered. "This man," he pointed at David, "was present at the motel where Sharon stayed when Arnold Millhouse was killed. I have reason to suspect that Baughman is either the murderer or knows who is. I intend to take him in for questioning."

"David, would you like to say something now? I think it's time you cleared the air," Martin smiled.

"Do you know about this?" Lynn asked Martin with surprise.

"Yes. David confided long ago and swore me to secrecy. He has been deeply concerned for the safety of both of you young women, especially about Sharon since he has confessed that she is the love of his life."

Sharon sobbed louder, but this time the girls did not go to her and offer comfort. She felt very uncomfortable as the group just looked at her with no expression.

"David told me," Keanu spoke with importance. "He doesn't have to give an account of himself to anybody." he glared at Larry.

"Excuse me a minute," David said and then went up to his apartment. He returned with a small, black leather folder. "I've been working undercover because we have not been sure who is involved. As you can see, I'm an officer in the DEA. We learned Jeremy was transporting drugs for someone from Texas to Florida and to various areas in the west." He looked sadly at Sharon. "I'm sorry. Yes, I knew who you were at the motel as soon as I saw you. It was a coincidence that we met at the motel. I didn't know you would be traveling on that day although I did know you were preparing to leave Texas. For your safety I had to keep quiet."

Sharon turned red, swollen eyes to him. He wanted to take her in his arms, but she had turned against him without trusting their friendship. She gulped. "What were you doing there -- and why didn't you let me know that you knew me? Why haven't you told me since you came here to the stables?"

"I couldn't tell you. Being undercover means you tell no one for fear of the wrong person catching on. Millhouse was an assumed name. He was working undercover with my partner and me. We were supposed to rendezvous at that motel because we had received tips that drugs were going through there. Millhouse was already dead when we arrived. My partner felt that we should leave and protect our identity. I came here to protect you and try to locate whomever was threatening you. We had already ascertained that you knew nothing about the operation."

Larry Dauber clapped and sneeringly laughed. "Great story, Baughman, if your name really is Baughman. It's easy to counterfeit identities and licenses. I'm taking you in until an investigation can be made. How do we know that you didn't kill Millhouse?" he stepped aggressively toward David.

"Keanu!" Lynn yelped as he swung his fist and knocked Larry to the ground. David and Jake held Keanu to keep him from beating Larry. Keanu said nothing; just looked as if he could eat glass and smile. "David is a decent law-abiding man and I trust him."

David placed an arm around Keanu's shoulders. "Son, I do appreciate your confidence in me, but violence never solved anything. I appreciate all of you believing in me even though you don't know the entire story," David gave a small, tight smile at the group, and looked sadly at Sharon.

Keanu had to be restrained to keep him off Larry. "How do we know *he's* for real? He may be carrying fake identity or he may even be one of the drug dealers. Maybe that's why he's so insistent in bringing David in. To throw suspicion off himself."

"I don't think he's an imposter," Martin said, "but I do have a strange feeling about the situation. Something's fishy. I just can't put a finger on it at this moment." He faced Larry. "Lt. Dauber, I'm wondering why you are such a "Johnny on the spot" and why you're getting so emotionally involved in this."

"Well," Larry stammered, "I told you I care about Sharon, and she did call me to ask for my help. She was afraid after she found the ring in Baughman's car."

Keanu snorted. "Sharon's not afraid of David. He's our friend and she knows he loves her. I have no idea why she thought she should call you, but you're not needed, or wanted, so LEAVE."

Larry opened his mouth to plead with Sharon but Martin spoke before he could say anything. "As an officer of the court, my word is good. If David needs representation, I'll work with him. He'll be my responsibility until answers can be given to the proper authorities. Besides, as far as

authority is concerned, I would guess that David outranks
you. Now I suggest you leave. We'll see you when we go
back to talk to Chief Warren."

All the male volunteers formed a solid front and moved
purposefully toward Larry.

Larry started to speak but decided that he should leave
when Keanu and Jake walked stiffly toward him. He spoke
loudly as he hurried to his car. "Sharon, don't let these
people intimidate you. They're not your friends. I am. Call
me anytime." He garbled the last words as he jumped in his
car and slammed his door, locking it, just as Keanu reached
him. He quickly gunned the car and left in a shower of
gravels.

"Goodbye to bad rubbish," Keanu chuckled. He turned to
give Sharon a long, thoughtful look; one full of sadness and
hurt.

Sharon sobbed harder. "Keanu, please try to understand.
I've been so afraid. I have had no idea who was threatening
me or why. The man, who was a stranger, and running in a
suspicious manner at the time, ran into me and I saw the
ring. When I saw the ring again in David's glove
compartment, the fright and uncertainty came flooding back,
and I could only think of talking to Larry who was the
investigating officer at the motel."

Keanu shook his head and slowly walked away. The
volunteers silently went about their business, leaving,
Sharon, Lynn, Martin, Jake and David standing. Sharon felt
as she had when she was a small child and her parents only
stared at her when she had disappointed them. *I know now*

why people say they feel as if their heart is breaking. Why do I feel so bad if I feel I've done the right thing?

"David, why didn't you tell us who you are?" Sharon asked in a trembling voice.

"I couldn't. I told you I've been undercover and I needed to discover all that I could about the drug running and who might be involved in bringing drugs from South America into Texas and across to Florida. If I had told you, then you might have unknowingly exposed me to someone that you thought was trustworthy but who might be a criminal."

"Did you think Sharon might be one of them since she was married to one?" Lynn asked worriedly.

"No," he answered hurriedly. "We had observed her enough in Texas to know that she was innocent. My guess is that Jeremy started using the drugs as well as alcohol. That's probably why he had such violent mood swings. Too, he had more than likely been warned that if Sharon learned about what he was doing, that they would both be killed."

"I can understand your need for secrecy," Keanu observed. "The tribal police had to pretend to trust some of our own people once to catch the ones bringing drugs on the reservation. If people know who you are they certainly aren't going to operate where you can see them. They'll just go on doing their dirt in secret and breaking hearts as well as taking lives and costing people a lot of money they really can't afford. Do you think you know who the guilty people are now?"

"You're a wise man," David said, placing an arm around Keanu's shoulders. "I wanted to tell you, but I didn't want to place you in danger. If they thought you knew anything, your life wouldn't have been worth a wooden nickel. Besides, when we're undercover, it means just that. I know I keep saying that. And no, I have some clues and suspicions, but nothing that will stand up in court - yet."

"Wow! I've always thought you are cool, but now I know you're better than any of the plastic characters in the movies. You could make 007 look like Mickey Mouse."

David placed an arm around Keanu's shoulder, turned him and walked to the stairs leading to their apartment. The volunteers looked uncomfortable and kept glancing at Sharon but saying nothing. The air actually felt as if there had been a death and everyone was grieving. Jake, Gordon and two temporary men went on about their business and saying nothing.

Sharon sobbed so hard that she trembled. Her legs almost didn't hold her as Lynn put an arm around her waist and half carried her to the office. Sheilah was curious as to why there was so much crying and discord. Lynn motioned to Sheilah that she was taking Sharon upstairs and would then be down to talk to her.

"Sharon did what?" Sheilah shouted. "I can't believe it. She and David love each other. She would never turn on David like this." Lynn patiently told Sheilah all that she knew and had heard. They discussed the situation until it was time for Sheilah to go home.

Sheilah shook her head sadly, "Sharon has been through more than any of us know about. She didn't act as wisely as we thought she should at this time, but we have to understand her situation. We'll have to let her know that we still love her and are standing by her."

"Of course we love her and will stand by her. I still feel like shaking her until her teeth rattle though for treating David as she did. Tomorrow, when she's settled and the air clears, maybe she can give us a satisfactory explanation." Lynn sunk into a chair with slumped shoulders and looking very worried. She contemplated calling Sean and discussing it with him but then decided not to get him upset until she knew more to share.

In the stable David, Keanu, Jake and Gordon talked. The men all had questions to ask David. He patiently explained that he was in the Marines, he had obtained a law degree, and he did have to leave the service and come home to care for his mother and sisters. That much was facts. The nature of his assignment kept him from divulging anything to anyone.

David had two partners, one being the murdered man at the motel. People, who had been caught with drugs, had told enough until, after a period of several months, they were able to learn how the drugs were coming into the United States. A variety of guilty persons had told enough until each bit of information had fitted together like a puzzle. Another undercover agent had discovered Jeremy's part in the operation and Sharon, too, had been observed and found innocent. David explained that the D E A had sent him here for this very purpose; in the event that someone thought Sharon knew more than she did and would cause trouble for her. Experience had taught the law men that these things did happen.

Keanu struggled with his thoughts and feelings as long as he could hold them in.

"David, you do love Sharon, don't you? That wasn't just part of your cover-up, was it?"

"Friend, I do love her, and as badly as I was hurt, I do understand how she feels. After all she's been through, she doesn't know whom she can trust."

"That's no excuse for turning to that reptile," Jake muttered.

David had to laugh. "Fellows, I sure do appreciate your vote of confidence, and I hope I never get on the bad side of either of you, but try to calm down and give Sharon some credit. She's no fool."

Grumbling to himself, Keanu got ready for bed as Jake and Gordon went off to their apartment. There was a good-sized kitchen and dining area in the center between the two apartments with a small sitting room on either side which included a television in each sitting room. Twin beds and a full bath were in each sleeping area. Lynn had provided thoughtfully and well for workers.

"Hey, Hank. It's me, Duke. Still hanging in there. That female still doesn't go anywhere alone. She don't even drive."

"Stupid! Stupid! Will you never learn? You're going to get caught yet and we'll all suffer. You're lucky you're still alive. The Boss is roaring mad at you, and I wouldn't be surprised if he sends someone after you. Please, do as you're told and get away from there; get out of the city. You might leave feet first if you're not careful."

"Okay. Okay. Don't get your drawers in a knot. I'll be in touch in a few days."

"No! Go now."

It was too late. Duke had already hung up.

The next day everyone was going about their duties, but not laughing and lighthearted as they usually were. David and Jake were finishing the new stalls; Gordon was on horseback checking the fencing around the pasture for the boarders; the volunteers were going about their duties and Keanu was in the loft checking the last hay shipment. He looked out the door where the big loading pulley was ready to lift a load. Casually he glanced down the driveway where he could see the entrance over the trees. Suddenly he took a hard look and then ran to the ladder and practically fell down it.

"David," Keanu yelled. He ran toward David's car as Jake and David ran from the stable. "Let's go man. Right now. I just saw someone drop from a tree at the end of the driveway and take off running. If it's that crazy man, we might catch him."

David ran to his car while Keanu was talking. Jake ran toward the office to tell Sheilah. Unlike his usual, careful driving, David took off in a shower of gravels and shot down the driveway. His adrenaline was bursting through his system. They reached the main road but could see no one.

"Let's drive toward town. If he had a car nearby, he might drive that way and we'll catch him." Keanu was so excited that he was bouncing and felt as if he could run faster than the car. His skin felt itchy.

"Easy." David cautioned. "We'll have to be careful to not accuse anyone or do anything that might help a smart lawyer to give the guilty man a loop hole to slip through. We need concrete proof so we can take him to trial and get him put away so Sharon won't be in any more danger. He's more than likely just a small cog in the wheel. We need to play it carefully so that we can get all the big boys involved." David tried to reason with Keanu and calm him down as he pushed the accelerator down harder.

Hearing a siren, David look in the rearview mirror. "Now we're in for it," he said with disgust and slapped the steering wheel with his open hand. He put on the right turn signal and carefully pulled over to the side.

Deputy Vincent Belasic pulled in behind them, got out and ran to David's car. "What's up, guys? I was coming to see you and saw you take off like a scalded dog."

"Why couldn't you have been a little later?" Keanu started to scold the deputy. David reached over and placed a hand on Keanu's arm. He quickly explained what Keanu had seen and why they were driving so fast.

"Gee, I'm sorry. Let's go," Vincent yelled running back to his car. He called the Zephyrhills City Police Department asking to speak to the chief. He told them briefly of the situation and asked them to be on the lookout for a dark car being driven fast or in a suspicious manner. He told them he was following David in and would be patrolling the streets when they arrived in town.

Driving down Fifth Avenue, which was Main Street, they looked for a man meeting the description that Keanu gave. Not seeing anyone, on the second trip David parked, nose to curb, in front of Neukom's. Deputy Belasic stood on the sidewalk. Chief Larry Warren joined them. Daniel introduced him to David and Keanu. "Who's this you're looking for?" the Chief asked.

Belasic told him the bare facts and David filled in with the incidents that had brought him here as well as the phone calls Sharon had been getting. "She lives in Zephyrhills and needs your protection," David finished.

Chief Warren was within rights as he scolded them for not involving his earlier.

Keanu walked to a nearby intersection to look in different directions. As he neared Eighth St., he saw a tall man hurry down a side street.

"Hey, you," Keanu yelled running after the man. He saw the man running toward a dark sedan parked, in of all places, on the City Hall lot. "Hey, wait. Hey, mister, I want to talk to you."

Keanu came close enough to see the man look back over his shoulder and snarl at him as the man came closer to his car. Just as the man was ready to reach for the car door, Chief Warren roared up in a car he had driven around the block. David and Belasic jumped out of the Chief's car just as Keanu launched himself through the air and hit the man in the back, knocking him to the ground with Keanu falling on him.

Keanu quickly shifted around and sat on the man with his fist drawn back. Belasic shouted at him and ducked under Keanu's arm to place handcuffs on the man. When Keanu stood and helped Belasic raise the man to his feet, he saw that two uniformed police and two plain-clothes men had joined the Chief. The Chief stepped forward looking pretty grim. "Okay boy. He's mine since he's in the city limits. Let's get him to the jail and booked, then we can question him."

Belasic picked his hat up off the ground where it had dropped when he helped wrestle the man into the handcuffs. "I'm going to give him the Miranda so he can't say he was not given a fair chance or arrested in a proper manner."

"I'll do it," Chief Warren spoke. Facing the man he quoted, "You have the right to remain silent. Should you decide to give up that right, anything you say can, and will, be used against you in a court of law. You have the right to an attorney. If you can't afford an attorney, one will be appointed for you by the court. Do you understand these rights?"

"Go to the devil," the man answered. "You got nothing against me. Enjoy yourselves because I'll be out of here so fast all you dummies will see will be my coat tail flying in your face," he laughed maniacally.

"Whoooopeeee!" Belasic cheered. "You just told the wrong man off. This is the Chief of Police."

"I don't care if he's the President of the United States. I'm right."

Seeing Keanu was ready to explode, David put an arm around his shoulders and spoke in a low voice. "You heard Belasic. We have to be careful from now on what we say or do. Remember, we don't want to give some slick attorney an opportunity to get this slime ball off because we goofed. Let the police handle it properly. Our turn will come in court when we give testimony. It's more important to keep Sharon safe."

"Can I call Sharon and tell her we got him? She'll be so relieved." Keanu ask eagerly. He was still shaking and red-faced. David was reluctant to let Keanu out of his reach for fear he would forget himself and do or say something that would be destructive to the case.

"Let's see what happens first," David suggested. "We're pretty sure this is the right man, but we don't have positive proof that would hold up in court."

"You suckers can't charge me with anything cause you got nothing on me," the man laughed. His weird-looking reddish-brown eyes were almost glowing. His thin, pinched face actually looked like a demon possessed person. His dirty, thinning dark brown hair hung in wisps that needed trimming. The brown suit, brown shirt and brown shoes blended in to make it difficult to see him if he choose to stay out of sight. Surprising he had straight, white teeth, but thin, angry lips.

"You know," Belasic spoke slowly standing taller than the tall man. "It's interesting that you haven't asked what you're being charged with. I guess you already know though."

"Oh, yeah," the man sneered, "prove something on me."

"We'll know more when we get your fingerprints," Vincent smiled in an irritating manner to the man.

"Why? What'll that prove?"

"We'll see if you have a record, or if the prints found at the crime scene match yours."

"On what? What crime scene?"

"What if I told you we found prints on pieces of the bomb?"

"It would be a set-up. I was no where near that car."

Keanu couldn't keep from jumping and punching the air with his fist. "What car? No one said it was a car that was bombed. What made you think of it?"

"Hush," David whispered, placing a hand on Keanu's shoulder. "Don't give anything away. Please allow the police to do their job."

The man sneered. "Never you mind. Just let me have my call for a mouth piece."

CHAPTER EIGHTEEN

"I see you've been in jail before. You know all the process," Chief Warren told the man. Turning to two uniformed officers standing nearby the Chief ordered, "Book him. Print him and put him in a cell by himself."

"What will we book him on?"

"Murder, attempted murder, stalking, harassment, having an ugly face, smelling bad, anything you can think of. Be sure he's put where no one can get to him unless I say so."

"Prove it," the man kept yelling as he was led away, but he wasn't as blustering as he had been when he was challenging them to charge him.

"Get him out of here," the Chief was disgusted. He turned to the others. "I need your statements about all that's happened. Are there other witnesses who need to make a statement? If what I suspect is true, I want to see that he's put away for many a year and anyone who's been working with him."

"There's several more who would like to give testimony," Keanu said excitedly. "I'd like to call the woman he's been trying to kill. She can tell you more than anyone about what has been happening."

"Easy son," David soothed Keanu. "We haven't proven yet that he is the guilty one. I honestly think he is guilty, but it still has to be proven according to law. I don't want to build Sharon's hopes and then let her down."

Chief Warren listened to Keanu's plea and then agreed that he could call Sharon. Just don't say this is absolutely the man. Tell her we have someone in custody that can't, or won't, account for himself at times that he might be in possession of knowledge about her case. I agree, there's no need to build her hopes yet."

Sheilah answered Keanu's call. When he blurted out that they thought they had the man who had threatened Sharon, he had to hold the phone away from his ears. Her shriek brought Lynn, Jake and several of the teen volunteers. Each one tried to talk into the phone and ask questions.

"Put a lid on it," Keanu finally shouted, then looked around in embarrassment when he realized that several police were looking curiously at him. "I can't hear all of you at once and I don't know any more than I told you. Just get Sharon down here to see if she can identify this man. Too, the Chief wants a statement from her."

Sharon stood in shook while the others babbled around her. Lynn reached for her in concern because she had gotten pale and was weaving. "Come on, honey. We have to go down to the city police station. Jake, I'm going with Sharon. Can you and Gabe take the three remaining individual riders rather than cancel? One is jumping."

Jake and Gabe spoke as one. "Go. Don't worry." They stopped and grinned at each other. "Go on," Gabe urged. "We'll be fine here. I'd love to go, too, and I will if you really need me, but David and Keanu are already there. You'll be fine with them."

"I know," Lynn said. "All of you would love to be present, but we can't have thirty of us tromping in. Besides, someone is needed here to give lessons, watch the stable and property and take care of the animals after the lessons. We don't know for sure that this is the man. Even if it is, he may have buddies. Stay alert."

Lynn grabbed her purse and car keys with one hand and reached to take Sharon's arm. "Sharon, is something wrong?" she asked concerned.

Sharon turned a perplexed, dazed look at Lynn. "I can't believe it. It doesn't seem real. At last I might be going to see the person who wants me dead and find out why all this nightmare started."

Jardine and Ashley moved to either side of Sharon. Ashley put a loving arm around her while Jardine patted her hand. "Are you sure you're up to this?" Ashley asked. "It doesn't have to be done today."

"I'll be fine," Sharon smiled weakly and straightened her shoulders. "I have to face this person and find the answer to a lot of questions. If he isn't guilty, why is he hanging around?"

Martin hobbled in the front door on his two special canes. He was beaming and looking pleased with himself. "Lynn, look who I found in the stables."

Lynn looked in astonished at the tall, ultra-groomed woman with white hair expertly coifed. "Dr. Zimmerman! Were you due today? Oh, I'm sorry. Forgive me, but we've had some unpleasant things happening around here and it's thrown us in a tailspin. Are you here to inspect?"

"No, my dear. I was near here, at another stable, and thought I'd come by and meet the delightful sister of yours I've heard so much about."

"I'm sorry. Sharon, this is Dr. Zimmerman. She's head of the medical group that inspects therapeutic riding stables to make sure we're abiding by rules and regulations and running a safe, healthy riding program. Dr. Zimmerman, this is my sister, Sharon."

"How delightful," Dr. Zimmerman gushed. "I've heard so much about you and your - er - charmed life." She gave a tiny, artificial laugh. "I shall apologize if I've come at a bad time. I was hoping we could visit and chat awhile."

Everyone was quiet until Lynn finally said, "We just had a call from the Zephyrhills City Police to come identify a man that might be the one who has been giving Sharon trouble. It's possible that he might be the one who bombed her car and killed Dr. Monroe."

Dr. Zimmerman whirled to face Lynn, no longer cool, smooth, polished society matron. "Who? What's his name? Have they proven he's the guilty person?"

Lynn and Sharon looked in astonishment at her while Martin narrowed his eyes and scrutinized her thoughtfully. He moved closer to Lynn. "Dr. Zimmerman, do you know something about the situation, or about the man?"

"No, no," she stammered. "I'm just surprised that the police have enough evidence to arrest someone. There's been nothing about it in the news."

As Jake passed her going out of the door, he hesitated. "Dr. Zimmerman, the police are too smart to give away all they know. It would alert the criminals and they would disappear, or go into hiding for awhile. No, it hasn't been on the news because things just started breaking today. I think, here in America, we tell too much in the papers and on television. The whole world knows our business before most of our citizens do." He walked on out with a firm stride.

While Jake had been talking, Lynn took advantage and dashed out dragging Sharon with her. *Martin can deal with Dr. Zimmerman. She acted strangely, but maybe it was just because she's surprised.* Lynn concentrated on driving carefully and keeping Sharon calm as they went into town.

David and Keanu were standing outside the station waiting on them. Keanu was still red-faced and shaking from excitement and anger. His precious Sharon had been threatened and he couldn't do anything about it, but maybe now her life would improve.

David hugged Sharon and asked tenderly, "Do you feel like doing this now? It can wait a day or two if you would rather."

"She's ready," Keanu announced. "Come on, Sharon. Let's go in and nail this dirty b- uh, dirty scum."

Sharon had to smile as she hugged Keanu. "How lucky I am to have all of you. Lead on MacDuff. It might as well be now. Nothing is going to get easier by waiting."

Keanu walked ahead with long, eager strides while David followed walking between Sharon and Lynn, an arm around each.

After Chief Warren had been introduced to Sharon and Lynn he said kindly, "Thank you for coming in so promptly. I have been told, Miss Donnelly, you have had a traumatic time for several months. I'll help all I can, and it looks as if you have strong support." He smiled at the others with a twinkle in his eye. "Come with me, please. All of you can come." He led them through a security door and down a short hall.

Two uniformed officers came with the Chief as he led them into a room with the one door and no windows. There was a glass wall where they could see into a room that had a table and two chairs in it. At the far side of the room was a raised section with lines drawn on the wall to show measurements of height.

The Chief gestured to several chairs. "Have a seat. Please speak softly if you have anything to say. I would rather you look and try not to talk unless it is necessary. Miss Donnelly, take your time. We're going to bring the man in to that room. Look at him carefully and observe his movements, tone of voice and anything that jars your memory.

If you want him to say something, or move a certain way, tell these officers and they'll see that your wishes are carried out. Do you have any question before we bring him in?"

"Won't he see us and wonder why we're here?"

"No. He only sees a mirror on his side. If he has the record, I suspect he has, he'll probably know what the mirror is."

As she nodded, gulping past the knot in her throat, a door opened and a uniformed officer escorted a tall man in and had him sit facing the mirror. "Sit down and let's talk," the officer instructed.

"You're wasting your time, sucker. You don't have to bring me in here to talk." The man looked at the mirror. "Who's sitting behind that mirror gawking at me?" He jumped up and walked to the mirror. He started to put his hands on the mirror, on either side of his face, so that he could peer in. The officer quickly caught him by one arm and turned him around ordering him to sit.

"You can't make me talk, and I get to have a lawyer. I know my rights." The man shouted and swung his arms around as if he'd like to hit the officer.

The officer spoke firmly and softly. "Calm down. I just need to get your name and address."

"What's the matter, smart guy? You haven't figured out my name yet?"

"Why don't you have a wallet or a driver's license with you? What did you do with it or didn't you ever have one? You were driving without a license and that's against the law. Of course, if you're hiding something ----"

"Hey, hey, watta ya' say, the man don't know nothing."

Sharon looked and listened intently. She sat back and slowly shook her head. "I don't know for sure," she whispered. "I don't think I've seen him, although there's something about him ---"

A young woman uniformed officer hurried into the room and handed a folder to Chief Warren. He quickly scanned through the papers, began to smile, and puckered his lips.

"Well, well," he chuckled. Leaning forward, he flipped a switch that would open communication between the rooms.

"You're full of it, Mr. Cassidy. Mr. John Wayne Cassidy, also known as Duke. We sure don't welcome your kind in Florida. I bet Texas is relieved that you're not there. We sent your picture and prints through our system to all the states and Texas has informed us that you have a record that would equal a Steven King novel. I'm surprised that you're not still in prison. You really are going to need a good attorney."

Duke jumped up throwing his arms around and yelling, "Yeah, I'm from Texas and served my time for stuff I done. You got nothing to pin on me."

Sharon stood, staggered and turned pale. David caught her before she could collapse. "Oh, it's him. It *is* him."

Sharon slumped against David, her head on his shoulder and her face turned to his chest. She was trembling and quietly shedding tears.

"Take it easy, sweetheart. You're okay. He can't see you or get to you. Take your time." David rubbed her back and comforted her. Keanu stood with his dark eyes blazing and his fists clenched.

"Miss Donnelly, can you now identify this man?" Chief Warren asked gently.

Sharon trembling faced him. "Yes and no," she said softly.

"What kind of answer is that?" one of the officers asked getting anxious to wrap up the case.

"It's all right, officer," the Chief said. "Miss Donnelly, when you're ready we'll take your statement. Or if you'd rather, we can wait until another day."

"She's ready now," Keanu spat through gritted teeth. "She's one of the bravest most put together person you'll ever meet."

Lynn took a tissue from her purse to wipe Sharon's face and hold her trembling hand. "Honey, you don't have to do a thing today. If you'd rather wait until you're calmer, and can think more clearly, you can. It's your decision." Lynn was worried and as nervous as Sharon. She knew how much Sharon had been through, and although Sharon was basically a strong person, she was, after all, human and could stand just so much.

Still shaking and gulping for breath, Sharon sat down heavily and nodded to the officer who sat with a denograph machine ready to record her statement. She drew one more shuddering breath and began.

"When Jeremy was alive, and we were living in San Antonio, I thought he had gone to work one day, so, I drove into town to find a birthday present for him. I did some sightseeing and then went down St. Mary's St. to go through a historical home. As I crossed the street I saw Jeremy with three men, one short and two tall men. One taller than Jeremy. He was shocked to see me and unreasonably angry that I was in town."

Sharon paused finding it hard to breathe again. The memories were painful. Lynn saw that Sharon was suffering and began saying a silent prayer for God to hold her up and give her the emotional and physical strength to go through with this.

Sharon looked at David and smiled weakly. *He looks as if he's praying. How can I let all these people down who have believed in me and stood by me even when they didn't understand my feelings or actions?*

Sharon continued. "When Jeremy shook me and yelled at me, the two tall men walked away, but the short man stood glaring at me pulling his hat lower on his forehead before he finally sauntered off. The tallest man was this one, what's his name, John Wayne Cassidy. He walked off throwing his arms around and quarreling just as he did here. I never heard his name, but I thought I saw him a few times after that."

Chief Warren spoke kindly to Sharon. "Did your husband explain why he was in town when he was supposed to be working?"

"No. That was the night he came home drunk and beat me. I had to be taken to the hospital. I was so embarrassed when I learned that others on the base had known all the time what was going on. I had lied and covered up for him, but--"

David put an arm around her and allowed her to get control of her emotions. "Do you remember anything else about the men?"

"Not really. The short man has been nudging at my memory," Sharon sighed.

Chief Warren gave her a fatherly pat on the back. She looked at his white, wavy hair and beautiful aquamarine eyes. He wasn't fat, but stocky, about five eleven.

"Thank you, Miss Donnelly. Now that you're beginning to remember, it's possible that your memory will return completely, a little at a time, or maybe in bursts. Things that have been in the back of your mind will become fresh. Don't force it, but if you think of something, write it down while it's still fresh in your mind. You might think whatever you're remembering is of small importance, but you'd be surprised what we can do with the smallest clues. I'm so sorry that your friend, Dr. Monroe, was killed, but I know your friends are thankful you're still with them."

"We sure are," Keanu stated firmly. "Chief, if you need help getting that bum to talk, I'll sure be glad to help."

Chief Warren chuckled. "I know where to find you if I need you, but thanks anyway." He slapped Keanu on the shoulder, thanked them all for coming and went to his office to mull over what he had learned. Too, he needed to make some calls to Texas.

In the parking lot, David hugged Sharon to his side and faced Keanu. "Please keep in mind that nothing has been proven against this man except that he has a record. He may be the one guilty of causing all of Sharon's heartache, or he may be a friend of the guilty one and knows a lot. Be very careful and watch your back, Keanu. Be especially careful about talking to just anyone. If he is part of a gang, they might get antsy when they discover Cassidy has been arrested and they could get real nasty. It isn't over yet. We don't know who all is involved or where they are located. I'm not deliberately trying to frighten you, well, yes I am - in a way. Keanu, you've got to keep your cool because Sharon might need you at any time.

Keanu rode back to the stable with Lynn so they could stop at a feed store on Chancey Rd. and order supplies. Sharon rode with David. He was worried because she sat like a rag doll. She slumped in the seat, pale, hollow eyed, not speaking and looking lost.

David pulled off the road and parked under a big oak tree. He sat quietly for awhile and then turned to Sharon. "Honey, I hope by now you realize how much you mean to me. I want to keep you safe for the rest of our lives, together. I'm trying to say, and very badly, that I love you."

Although Sharon stared at him saying nothing, he was relieved to see that she was getting some color back. Finally, drawing several deep, shuddering breaths, she said, "David, I feel very close to you, but because of what I've been through, I'm not ready for a serious relationship. You're very dear and there would be an aching hole in my heart if you left, but I can't commit to you, or anyone, just now. I'm not saying no, just give me time, please. I can't imagine why you would still care for me or trust me."

"Darling, I do understand. I'll be happy if you promise to think about it, talk to Lynn, if you wish, and we'll discuss it again later. I hope you'll let me take you to choose an engagement ring." When she gave a start, and turned wide eyes toward him, he placed a gentle hand on her arm. "I know how important your education is, and I respect that. I'll support you all the way if you won't write me off immediately."

"David, I do care, but I don't know what to say. I'll be hard to live with until this mystery is solved. Why was I chosen to be frightened and threatened? Did Cassidy follow me from Texas? Who else is working with him and are they near, too, or are they somewhere else? I have so many questions running through my brain that I'm dizzy from thinking."

He understood how confused she had been and how frightened, but he wanted to try to take her mind off the troubles. They were real, and she was going to face much more before all of the answers could be found, if ever. He did love her and wanted to make a family with her for the rest of their lives. He would see that she got the education she wanted and back her in whatever she attempted to accomplish.

"I meant it when I said I understand and will support you fully. Don't give up on us." He gently and tenderly kissed her cheek and gave her a hug. "I shouldn't rush you into giving me an answer because you've had a shock today, but I want to make your life happy and comforting so badly that I can't wait to tell you how I feel." He put a finger under her chin and tipped her face up for a kiss.

"Umm. That was nice. We'll see what happens. I need to know for a fact that all of the threats are over and I can live as a human being likes to live. I feel safe and protected when you're with me, but I have to face my own problems."

Two mornings later, Lynn, Sharon and some of the volunteers were stacking the hay bales that had been delivered and piling bags of feed in the storage barn. Several of the men were loading fence posts and wire on a large flatbed pulled by a tractor. They were preparing to fence in a new area for some yearlings.

The girls had been teasing Sharon because David had made several trips on horseback to the barn. Each time he returned he leaned Sharon over and kissed her.

"He's so romantic," Rebekah sighed. Sharon had told the girls about David's proposal and her answer. They all felt she should accept immediately. Lynn finally spoke up and reminded them that Sharon had been through a war, so to speak, and needed time to recuperate and settle down.

Later Lynn was preparing sandwiches for her crew when David joined her and offered to help. She was pleased with his attitude and that he had understood Sharon's fears and ridiculous behavior when she found his ring. She was thinking that Sharon would be so fortunate to accept David and have a family of her own. Lynn smiled to herself thinking she would love to have David for a big brother. In -

law, that is. She wondered if she could ever find the same happiness with Martin. She had worked hard through school and for the stable which kept her from dating much and having a social life. *Martin is wonderful and a real gentleman. We have the same likes and dislikes about our work and how a family should be. Life with Martin is looking better every day.*

CHAPTER NINETEEN

"How long will it be before we know what they find?"
Lynn asked worriedly. "We still don't know who all is
involved. Someone might still come after Sharon for fear she
knows something that she'll tell on them."

"I'm aware of that," David said. "Please keep Sharon
with you and don't let her go anywhere alone. The more she
can stay indoors, the better, at least until we get some
concrete evidence on this gang."

Keanu and Jake came in and were told of the happenings.
Keanu was eager to go out and play Lone Ranger. David had
to remind him that he really wouldn't know where to go or
who to find. He told him to guard Sharon and stay alert until
he was told differently.

"I'll have to go to Tallahassee, but I'll return as quickly
as I can. I'll call you if I learn anything of importance or
interest." He looked longingly at the stairs to Lynn's
apartment then walked out with slumped shoulders and a
dejected expression.

"I could cry," Sheilah moaned, sorry for David and
Sharon. Lynn smiled and patted her shoulder then went up to
give Sharon the additional news. Lynn prayed all the way up
the stairs for God to give her the right words to say to
Sharon. Lord, she is my sister and I do love her. Mom and
dad would be horrified if we didn't stand together. I need to
stay in control of my own emotions and encourage Sharon.

I know what people mean by hearts breaking, Lynn
thought. She looked lovingly at Sharon crumpled on the

couch and sobbing her heart out. She seemed to cry so much.

"Sharon, honey, I have some good news. David is on his way to Tallahassee to meet with his superiors. They'll be bringing in Herman Morrison from Texas."

"Who?" Sharon asked shocked and puzzled. She sat up suddenly with a catch in her voice. "The Herman Morrison at the motel?" she asked in shock.

"The very one," Lynn answered and then proceeded to tell her about Cassidy ratting on Morrison. "He's either the top dog or he knows who is. David will call as soon as he has news for us. David has been assigned to pick him up. Cassidy ratted on him and Florida state police picked him up."

"I'm so ashamed," Sharon hiccupped. "David must be thinking horrible thoughts about me. I might as well have taken a knife and stabbed him in the back."

Lynn struggled to keep a straight face. "David loves you, Sharon, and I know for a fact that you love him. You were just frightened and didn't take time to think things through before you acted. David came here purposely to protect you, but, of course, none of us knew what David's connections were. Honey, you were just being human. Believe me, David understands. When he returns you can ask his forgiveness."

"I will. I will. I wonder if he'll ever speak to me again. Oh, I acted like such a child - no a fool."

Lynn gave Sharon a sleeping pill and a glass of water. "Lynn, do you think I'm a hopeless jerk?" Sharon asked through sobs and hiccups.

Sharon

"No more than you've been all your life," Lynn chuckled and rubbed Sharon's back until she relaxed and drifted into much needed sleep. Lynn pulled a light cover over Sharon and tiptoed down the stairs and out to the stable.

Even the horses seemed to sense the sadness and quietness and were subdued and cooperative. The students took their lessons and quietly went on their way. The volunteers groomed horses, mucked stalls, washed water buckets in each stall and put them back clean and filled. Hay was placed in the racks in each stall. Tack was cleaned and placed in proper places. Two volunteers took big bamboo rakes and went over the floor down the main aisle. Each one asked Lynn to call them if she needed help before they left.

Jake and Keanu made the rounds giving a last check to animals and property as well as the boarders in the field. Lynn asked them to come in and eat supper with her. They gladly accepted for none of them wanted to be alone and all of them were on edge waiting for news. Lynn asked Sheilah to stay for supper but she refused with thanks.

"Sheilah it isn't time for you to clock out, but why don't you leave early. I'll let you know just as soon as we hear anything."

"Lynn, I'm so sorry that I added to Sharon's troubles. I had no right to voice my opinion of her actions. I'm doubly glad that she's been staying here with you, and, I assume, will continue to do so."

"You bet. That little girl isn't going anywhere even if I have to call our parents and ask for their help. I'm not telling them everything just yet because I want to be able to include encouraging news." Lynn hesitated and went to hug Sheilah.

"Sheilah, don't beat yourself up over what you said. You weren't any worse than the rest of us. Go home and try to rest. Stay alert though and keep your phone at hand in case you need to call for assistance. On second thought, I doubt any of us will rest tonight."

After Sheilah left, Lynn cooked cheeseburgers for Jake, Keanu and herself. Gordon had gone into town to meet an old buddy. She placed lettuce, tomato slices, pickles and sliced mushrooms on a platter. Mustard, ketchup and relish were in jars on the table. She put potatoes in the microwave to bake and then remembered to put out butter and sour cream. Sharon had made maple nut muffins earlier which would serve as dessert. She checked the refrigerator for ice tea or soft drinks.

The three of them ate quietly. Neither one seemed to feel like talking. Keanu stood and began to clean the kitchen when he finished eating. "Has Sharon eaten?" he asked.

"No, she needed sleep more than food. I'll be here in case she wakes and is hungry."

Lynn stood so still that Keanu put his arms around her and hugged her then kissed her cheek and walked out. Jake followed after looking several seconds at Lynn and giving her a salute.

Lynn sat in a chair and watched Sharon until a little after ten. Sharon stirred and fluttered her eyelids. She stretched and groggily tried to sit up.

"Sharon, are you getting up?" Lynn hurried to her.

"I need to go to the bathroom. Why am I on the couch? Why do I feel so heavy-headed?" She struggled to get up, but kept falling back down on the couch until Lynn helped her up. Sharon sagged against Lynn for a few seconds and finally straightened up still with Lynn holding her made her slow way to the bathroom and back.

"Are you hungry?" Lynn asked.

"No, just awfully tired."

Lynn helped Sharon walk back into the bedroom to her bed. "Lie down then and sleep all that you need to. Rest. I'll have food for you when you're ready."

Sharon grunted. She took a couple of deep breaths and dropped off to sleep. Lynn sat on her bed, watching Sharon and praying. She finally got up, brushed her teeth, cleaned up for bed and tried to rest.

When Sharon awoke, the bright light was coming in through the windows. She heard several voices and held her aching head trying to get her thoughts to make sense. *I feel awful. Oh, yes, I remember. Lynn gave me a sleeping pill. Boy, it sure knocked me for a loop. It's lucky Lynn and I wear the same size clothes or I would have no clean clothes to wear.* She dressed in a white shirt and tan jeans with her own boots. Pulling her hair back in a ponytail and tying it with a shoe string, she was ready to face the day.

Lynn had heard Sharon showering and moving around upstairs and came up to make sure she ate breakfast.

"Lynn, it's all coming back. What a dope I am."

"Don't you dare start crying again. Sure it has been rough. Do you think you're the only one in the world that has made a mistake or had something unpleasant happen in their life? I'm not heartless, and I so love you, but it won't gain you a thing to fall apart.

Be stronger than that - stronger than the bad guys. You have loads of loyal friends and innumerable blessings. David will call as soon as he has news for us. Now you can sit here in the apartment and feel sorry for yourself and feel worse, or you can come work with me and keep busy."

"Okay," Sharon answered meekly. I'll come with you, but I'll work in the stable. Please don't ask me to deal with students or the public."

"I wouldn't allow you to deal with the public. David warned us that someone might show up that we don't suspect." She hugged Sharon and they went downstairs.

Sharon hugged Sheilah who was already hard at work. "Not a word, Sheilah. I deserve all you said and more. You should hear the lecture Lynn just gave me," she chuckled. "Please, let's not talk about anything in the past for awhile."

"Okay," Sheilah said with a relieved grin. "Keanu has picked up the schedule for today and the volunteers are in place. Have a donut and coffee. You need the energy."

"No, thanks. Lynn made me eat bacon and eggs. If there's something left, I might get it later." Sharon followed Lynn out to the stables.

Sharon kept her head down as she walked in and found people moving around and leading horses out. *How I wish I were invisible. Father, you've been so good and patient with me, and I've been so willful. I need you desperately now.*

She got grooming supplies, checked the chart and went to the stalls of the horses that were designated to work next. She had Cutler's Dandy in cross ties grooming him when Gabe walked by to take Fleetwood out of his stall. He didn't say anything, but he did stop and hug Sharon before he walked on.

When the horses were brought in from the lesson just finished, Sharon took charge to groom them and put them in their stalls. While the class had been going on she had groomed five horses and thoroughly mucked two stalls. The volunteers were grateful for her help. Having the horses ready meant they could prepare for the next class without pressure.

Lynn came racing into the stable closely followed by Ashley. "Sharon, I need a big favor. The chestnut colt that I lunged yesterday is coming two. I'm training him for a man who wants him for a hunter. I hope he keeps this horse for breeding. He's one of the best I've seen of the Three Bars line. Would you be willing to take him into the indoor ring and work with him?"

"I'd love to. You know how much I love training the little ones from the beginning."

"Yes, I know and you're so good at it."

Sharon perked up and went to get the colt. Ashley grinned at Lynn and held her thumb up. Lynn nodded and went out for the next lesson. This was a good way to keep Sharon inside and busy without her feeling as if she was being manipulated.

"Sharon, may I stay with you and watch? I want to learn to train like you do."

"It's okay with me, Ashley. Just save questions and comments until after the lesson."

"Before you get started would you please tell me what you're doing now?"

"First I'm rubbing small circles between his eyes and up between and back of his ears.

This is a form of massage that relaxes an animal. Lynn has been working with him, so, you won't get to see the training from the beginning."

Ashley watched carefully as Sharon went through the process of preparing the young horse for a work-out. She did want to learn, but she mainly wanted to help keep an eye on Sharon and protect her. She knew it wouldn't do to let Sharon catch on. She would feel badly that even the teens were watching over her. Sharon placed her hand on the line about six inches below the young colt's chin and turned him away from her to take him to the center of the ring.

"I know why you turned him away from you. In the event a horses gets startled it will be facing away from you and won't climb on your back like it might if it's facing you."

"That's right," Sharon said. "Now I'm going to turn him sideways to me and I'll stand about where my leg would be if I were on his back." She then played out the long line until the colt was about eight feet from her. She lifted the training whip and held it where it would be even with the stirrup. "Walk on," she said quietly but firmly.

After he had walked for several minutes, Sharon called, "trot," with emphasis on the t and then the r. After awhile she had him, "ho," or stop, staying sideways to her. She called, "reverse," and flipped the long line around. The colt turned the opposite direction to follow the same commands.

As Sharon finished and praised the young horse, Ashley walked to them. "That's so great, Sharon."

Sharon smiled and hugged her. "Would you like for me to ask Lynn if you can work with me and learn how to train young horses?"

"I would be so grateful. Thanks, Sharon."

Sharon had just finished grooming the colt and placed him in his stall again, when the volunteers came in from the class. They had one more to go for the morning. Although none of them said much to Sharon and none spoke of her troubles, she was painfully aware that all of them knew what had happened.

CHAPTER TWENTY

Sharon, Lynn and Sheilah had finished lunch and were cleaning up after themselves when the phone rang. Sheilah picked it up. "Soaring Eagle. Sheilah speaking." She listened and then stiffened. "Yes, David, we've been on pins and needles waiting to hear from you. Yes. She's right here."

Sheilah held the phone to Sharon but she shook her head and backed away. Sheilah sighed. "David, she doesn't feel well and can't come to the phone. Please tell me you got your man." She listened and then said, "Thanks a million, David."

She hung up and turned to the eager, curious duo. "Well, this Morrison character is safely stored in Tallahassee. Federal agents will come with David to bring him down tomorrow to confront Cassidy." She laughed. "David says Morrison is denying everything and threatening to sue for false arrest and slander to his character."

Lynn reached and grabbed Sharon in time to help her sit down. Keanu had walked in just at that moment. He tenderly gathered Sharon in his arms and carried her to the back room where he deposited her gently on the couch. She lay down and closed her eyes.

"What's wrong with Sharon?" a concerned, quavering voice demanded.

Everyone spun around to see Leland balancing precariously on two metal crutches.

"Leland! You're walking," Lynn exclaimed reaching to hug him.

Jacob Nesbitt, Leland's father, chuckled. "He's flying you mean. I could almost swear that his feet don't touch the ground half the time. He could hardly wait to show all of you, especially Sharon."

"What I really want to show Sharon is this picture." The beaming boy held a picture for Lynn to see. It was one that Mr. Nesbitt had taken of Sharon standing beside Leland on his horse. "I had it enlarged and framed so Sharon won't forget me," he said.

"Leland, my man, how could she forget you?" Keanu grinned and lightly punched him on the shoulder. "You're the best, ole boy."

They all turned as Sharon moaned and tried to sit up. Leland couldn't wait and swung in front of Sharon. "See!" he yelled, "I'm walking."

"Wh --what?" Sharon spoke groggily.

"Son, give her time. She just woke up. She'll be glad to see you and listen to you in a few minutes." his father cautioned him.

"Aw, Sharon, I'm sorry. I'm so glad to see you and share my good news with you."

"I am thrilled to see you, Leland, and know that you can walk with the crutches. It won't be long until you will be riding by yourself and we can go on that trail ride. I'm looking forward to that." Sharon said weakly but trying to appear strong for Leland.

"Oh, me, too," Leland bellowed. "I can hardly wait and I know we'll have a great time. You know, you all helped me to do this good. I won't let you down."

"We have to go, son. You'll be back again soon. Goodbye all." Mr. Nesbitt called.

"I'm so embarrassed," Sharon moaned, "why did I sort of pass out like that? It isn't like me."

Jake cleared his throat gruffly and said, "It's the body's and mind's way of resting when you've been under pressure or tension."

Lynn told Jake and Keanu of David's call about bringing Morrison down to Pasco County to be questioned and for him to confront Cassidy.

"Will David bring him here?" Keanu asked eagerly.

"Not with you ready to tear him apart," Lynn laughed. "There's no reason to bring him here. Morrison will be taken to Dade City to the sheriff's facilities where we will go when they're ready for us." She turned to Sharon. "And you, little girl, will feel better if you go upstairs, take a relaxing shower and lie down for awhile."

"This is one time I'm not debating the issue. I feel tired and plain yucky. I'm so sweaty I know I'm not pleasant to be around."

"To see, or rather to smell, ourselves as others do," Keanu joked holding his nose.

"A poor quote on a good Scottish phrase," Lynn giggled.

"You know I'm teasing Sharon. Do you want me to help you upstairs?"

"No, thank you, Keanu, but I agree. God bless you all. I'm rich with family and friends."

Three hours later Sharon had come downstairs and was talking to Sheilah and helping her with the stable records when Lynn came in followed by David.

"Hey! The conquering hero," Sheilah called out.

"No hero. Just a humble guy doing his job," David said smiling at Sharon.

"David, can you ever forgive me? I'm so ashamed of myself. There's no excuse except my fear caused me not to think, and ---"

"Sharon, hush. I do understand. Let's drop it. The most important thing to do now is to break this drug ring and find who is responsible. Hopefully we'll find the one responsible for threatening you. Do you feel up to facing Morrison and seeing what his reaction will be?"

"No!," Lynn spoke firmly. "Sharon's been through too much. She shouldn't be expected to face that monster."

"Lynn," Sharon said gently, "I have to face him some time and find out the truth. Are we going now, David?"

"No. We'll wait until tomorrow. The officers have a lot of paper work to do and procedures to follow to make sure he doesn't slip through any cracks. They won't want us around until tomorrow."

"I'm going with you," Keanu shuffled his feet and was fidgeting around. "I don't want any arguments. You girls are going to be my sisters and I insist on being with you. You need your brother."

"Sisters," Sheilah yelped. "How do you figure that?" David grinned. Keanu had already told him the good news.

"Sean and Megan have been talking to me and they want to adopt me. Sean wants to send me through college because I told him I was interested in being an attorney."

"Lynn, Sharon, why wasn't I told anything about this?" Sheilah demanded.

"Don't be hurt, Sheilah. No one outside the family knew. Dad wasn't sure Keanu would agree to it. Too, he didn't think it was a good idea for the information to get out to the wrong people and maybe have Keanu attacked because he would be in Sharon's family." " Lynn soothed Sheilah while Sharon was hugging Keanu.

"It's okay with me if you want to come, but you have to promise me something." Sharon looked Keanu straight in the eyes.

"What's that?"

"You must promise that you won't jump on Morrison or Cassidy and beat them up. Will you promise to keep quiet and allow the police to do their duty and handle questioning? David has an on going investigation and we mustn't interfere with his work."

"I promise I won't touch them unless they make a move toward either of you girls. I can't promise that I won't say anything because I want to tear them apart with my bare hands."

David laughed and slapped Keanu on the back. "We're together on that, my friend, but common sense must prevail."

The next morning, after chores were done and Lynn had made arrangements for trained volunteers to take the classes, David drove them to Dade City. Keanu sat up front with David and Lynn and Sharon rode in the back. David parked in the lot outside the Sheriff's offices. He turned to talk to the young women. "Sharon, I don't know how the Sheriff will handle this, but I do know he'll want you to identify the man as the same Herman Morrison that you saw at the Rest Best Motel in Midway. Are you sure you're ready for this?"

"I sure am. I'm getting more angry by the moment thinking of how they manipulated Jeremy and ruined our lives, and no telling how many hundreds of other people's lives. I wondered why Morrison was glaring at me that day at the motel. I had never heard of him, but he probably thought I knew all about his criminal behavior and was afraid that I had come to spy on him. Maybe in his twisted mind he thought I might blackmail him. I want him taken off the face of the earth, but first I want him to tell me how he knew Jeremy."

"That's my girl. Go get 'em, bulldog," Keanu laughed.

Walking inside they stood in front of a bullet-proof window to tell the dispatcher why they were there. She called for a deputy to take them through a security door to an interrogation room.

On the way down the hall Sharon felt prickles of icy shivers tap dancing on her spine. She glanced around to see Morrison at the end of the hall glaring at her. She began to tremble so violently that Keanu looked to see what she was looking at. She buried her face against his shoulder and whimpered. David quickly stepped between Sharon and Morrison reaching out to pull Lynn to his side thus effectively blocking Morrison's view of Sharon. Morrison laughed as if he hadn't a care in the world.

"Hello, folks," a deep voice welcomed them. Sharon looked to see a man as tall as David and a bit heavier standing by them wearing a business suit and tie. His steel-gray eyes and pepper and salt hair gave him a distinguished appearance. He exuded a warmth and friendliness that immediately assured Sharon that he was in charge.

"Sharon, this is Sheriff Howell. Sheriff, this is Sharon Donnelly, and Keanu Rodiquez. You know Lynn." They shook hands and exchanged comments.

"What do you want us to do, Sheriff?" David asked.

"I would like for Sharon to identify Herman Morrison, if she can."

"I sure can. I saw him glaring at me in the hall, and he's the same man that was manager at the Rest Best Motel in Midway. What a scary coincidence that I'd stop there for the night and just a few minutes after the murder."

"He must have had quite a scare himself when he realized who you were. He didn't know whether you knew anything about their business or not and probably thought his goose was cooked," the sheriff grinned.

"I told Chief Warren about seeing my husband on the street one working day with three men, one short and two tall. I now know that one of the tall men was Cassidy and I recognize Morrison as the short man. He had a hat pulled low on his forehead and the sun was in my eyes or I might have gotten a better look at him. Of course he didn't know that I couldn't identify him then. Too, my husband was so angry that I looked at him more than I did the men with him. I remember that Jeremy ran after him calling his name."

"I can tie him in but the noose will be tighter if I can get Morrison and Cassidy to acknowledge each other," Sheriff Howell explained.

"Yes, Morrison is a cool customer. Cassidy is getting real nervous and might break with the right push," Vincent

Belasic spoke softly behind them. He had joined them so quietly that they had not heard him come in. Sharon felt that her neck was cracking as she smiled up at the tall, handsome deputy. Standing well over six feet, blonde wavy hair, sea blue eyes and deep dimples, he looked like a teddy bear, but they all knew what a diligent worker he had been. In fact, the sheriff had commented that Belasic was making a first class detective.

The sheriff placed a hand on Sharon's shoulder and explained, "I'm going to have John Wayne Cassidy brought in a room adjacent to this one. When the light is on in that room, this one will appear dark. The window you see here is a mirror on the other side."

Sharon nodded. "Then I'll have Morrison brought in with Cassidy. They haven't seen each other since Cassidy's arrest, and I don't think Cassidy knows we have Morrison in custody. We can observe them and hear what they're saying without them knowing we're listening."

Sharon looked over her shoulder when Keanu got up from where he was seated and stood near the door leaning one shoulder against the wall and crossing his ankles. "Are you okay, Keanu?" she whispered. "Remember, be quiet."

"Everything's copasetic." Sharon looked suspiciously at him because he had acquiesced too easily. She turned around because Cassidy was led into the room and seated at a long, metal table.

Cassidy stared at the mirror but finally shrugged his shoulders, leaned back in the chair, put his feet up on the table and his hands behind his head. He looked mighty sure of himself but they could see a nerve twitch at the corner of his mouth. Satisfied he was alone, Cassidy began to hum to himself. He hadn't shaved and his thin, ferret face looked even more like an animal.

The door opened and Morrison was led in and made to sit down. The officer quickly left. Cassidy's mouth was open.

"Hank! When did you get here? Why and how did they get you? Oh, Lordy, huh oh the jigs up ain't it?"

"Shut up, you fool. I told them I didn't know you. They're probably listening to us."

"You said you didn't know me?! Well listen good, old friend, old buddy, old pal. I'm not going down on this alone when you're the one that told me what to do. That is you told me after the Boss gave you the orders."

"I didn't tell you to bomb that car. All I told you to do was follow Jeremy's wife to be sure she didn't know about us or what was going on. Neither did I tell you to shoot at her."

"Yeah. I did follow her and tried to protect us by making sure she wouldn't talk."

"How could she tell anything she didn't know, you idiot?"

"Stop calling me names. I've only done what you told me to do like I took care of the spy at the motel after you figured out who he was. I just followed your orders. You're the idiot. You wouldn't tell nobody else the Boss' name and you'll go down as the only one responsible for dealing in drugs, laundering money, dealing in stolen property and murder." Cassidy was almost shouting by this time. He sat smugly looking at Morrison and then gasped horrified when Morrison leaped across the table and wrapped his hands around Cassidy's neck. Small, wiry Morrison attacking tall, thin Cassidy.

Three deputies ran into the room to separate the men and place handcuffs on both of them.

"I was a fool to ever get involved with you," Morrison sputtered. "I suggested the Boss include you as a favor to me because we'd been friends so long. Now we're all in hot water thanks to your loose mouth and stupid, rash actions."

Sharon and Lynn were both shaken by what they had observed. David stood between them with an arm around each one. "Where's Keanu?" he whispered as he looked around to see why the young man had not come to Lynn and Sharon when they gasped.

Belasic rushed out of the room and came back with an angry, red-faced young man. "I found him at the end of the hall asking how to get into that room."

"I was afraid they'd get away," Keanu muttered sullenly.

David looked sternly at him. "You wanted to get your licks in. Sharon and Lynn needed you and you weren't here for them.

"Aw gee," Keanu looked ashamed. "I'm sorry. I'm so mad at those jerks. I've seen their kind all of my life and ---"

"I understand, little brother," Sharon said hugging him even though she was still trembling. "I'm sure there are enough officers around to do their duty without outside help."

"Besides, you made us a promise," Lynn reminded him. "It doesn't matter that you're taller than us, we're older. We're your sisters and you need to start listening to us." She laughed trying to help everyone relax.

Sheriff Howell and Deputy Belasic looked perplexed at each other and then at Keanu.

"Our parents are adopting Keanu and he'll be our little brother," Lynn said bending her head back to look up at him. "Shee-u. I didn't realize how much you'd grown just since you came to live with us."

"Well, David smacked his hands and looked pleased. "It looks as if we have the goods on those questionable friends of yours. Murder, attempted murder, drug dealing, destroying private property, harassment, stalking, and we'll find much more."

"But what's the deal on stolen property that Cassidy mentioned?" Belasic asked.

"I can answer that," David said. "Over a period of several months, we've found stolen cars with evidence that drugs were transported in them. Apparently this ring would steal a car out west, fill it with drugs and drive it across to the east. We couldn't find any prints except the owners, so, we surmised they were wearing gloves and plastic bags on their feet. That way none of their own cars were involved. If they were stopped, they would get out and run and there'd be nothing to identify them."

Sharon gulped and wiped the tears from her eyes before they could run down her cheeks. "Sheriff, Morrison is the shorter man I saw with Jeremy and Cassidy that day in town. Do you think Jeremy was part of their group? Why would he even be friendly with low lives such as that when he had more than the average person?"

"I think I can make an educated guess," Lynn spoke. "Jeremy was spoiled rotten by his mother and was never restricted for anything. He was never at fault for anything that happened. In the military he had to follow rules just like everyone else and had to answer to officers who would not excuse him. He probably got bored and started taking drugs as a defiance. It was exciting and a challenge for him to steal cars and sell drugs. It was his way of thumbing his nose at authority. He was more than likely in deeper than he ever intended to be."

David continued. "The drugs and alcohol caused his mood swings. He must have felt so sick at times and couldn't let on."

Keanu put an arm around Sharon. "We've done all we can do for the time being. Let's go home. I'm sure the sheriff will be in touch as soon as he knows what will be done next."

Sheriff Howell thanked them and told Sharon he was sorry that she had to be exposed to such happenings. David and Keanu hurried Lynn and Sharon out to the car before they might run into the two criminal again. It was a quiet ride home.

David reined in his thoughts. He wanted so badly to pressure Sharon into making a commitment, but he knew the time was not right. She was trying to sort out her past and, what she considered, her considerable mistakes. He struggled to find the words to reassure her that she was being harder on herself than anyone else was.

Keanu had mixed thoughts. He wondered how the students in Zephyrhills High would accept him next week and he fretted that he might miss out on some of the excitement of the arrests, the investigation and the trial.

CHAPTER TWENTY-ONE

Two months passed as the investigation gained momentum. The people at the stable were anxious and felt it was going slowly. David reassured them and reminded them that it was better to be thorough and break up the ring and get all those involved than to hurry and make mistakes. "Do you want to know these people are in prison where they belong, or do you want them out on the street and not know when you're safe? Besides these two are just little frogs in a big pond. We want to find the head honcho and put them out of business." Everyone assured him they would be as patient as possible because they wanted everything cleared up.

Lynn had the end of summer party for the volunteers and put on a show for the parents and friends so the students could demonstrate what they'd learned. Leland was so excited that he almost bounced off his horse when he got to ride alone even at a walk and slow trot over poles. Even though Kara had a backrider, she was able to show exercises she had learned to do on horseback. The spectators were in awe and suitably impressed when "George" showed her riding skills even with one leg and one arm. Awards were presented to every special student.

Following this, the regular students held a jumping presentation and showed what skills they had learned. Each of them received an award.

The volunteers were brought into the ring while Lynn told of their faithful, valuable service. The applause was deafening as the spectators showed their appreciation.

Everyone was then invited to tour the stables and go to the lounge for refreshments. Lynn was happy to answer numerous questions about the program. She even welcomed reporters from various papers who took pictures of the students and told of the riding for the handicapped. All were relieved when nothing was said about Sharon's past.

The volunteers cleaned up and put equipment in proper places in the stable and came to the office. Some of them bid tearful goodbyes because they were off to college and wouldn't be working until next summer. Some promised to visit when they could.

Everyone was tired but happy for the day. Sharon was still staying with Lynn because David felt that it still wasn't safe for her until all of the perpetrators had been apprehended.

Night fell gently on tired but happy people. They were up early the next morning to do the chores and get ready for church. Horses and people rested and enjoyed the day. David had been in Tallahassee all week working with federal officers with more investigation. He had made one quick trip to Texas to pick up some records.

Monday about ten o'clock David drove up, parked and came running in obvious excitement. The stables were closed on Monday. "Where's Sharon? She won't believe this." David said, a little out of breath.

"Sharon's in the office helping Sheilah. What's happened, David?" Lynn asked concerned.

"Everybody. In the office and I'll tell the story to everyone at once." He turned striding quickly to the office. Keanu, Jake and Gordon were right at his heels. Lynn paused to make sure all the horses were in safely and quickly followed them.

"David!" Sharon jumped up and hurried to meet up. Seeing the excitement in his eyes and his grin she blurted, "Has something happened?"

He put an arm around her and turned to see if everyone was present. Lynn rushed in out of breath and full of curiosity. "What's the big news that has to be told to all of us at once?"

"Well, it depends on whether you think it's big news or not," David grinned.

"If you don't hurry and tell us, I'm going to make newsprint out of you," Keanu threatened.

"Okay, okay. Sharon, you'd better sit down."

"Uh oh. Is it bad news?"

"Well, that too depends on how you view it." David was still grinning.

"Are you going to tell us or are we going to have to beat it out of you?" Amelia asked.

"The local police," he began, "the state police and the federal officers have taken turns questioning Morrison and Cassidy separately so they wouldn't know what the other said. Morrison is smarter than Cassidy and soon realized that he was in deep for drug dealing, money laundering, stolen cars, murder, you name it. He had Cassidy kill Millhouse on orders. He finally broke declaring that he would not go down alone. He didn't know the name of the man called Boss, but he had the phone number where he always contacted him here in the state of Florida. He gave the number to us and the federal officers found the number and the person at the other end. You will find it hard to believe who it is." He hesitated with a big grin. "Needless to say, I'm thrilled."

Keanu held his fist under David's chin. "You're pushing my buttons too far." David smiled and pushed Keanu's fist aside, then became solemn.

"Yes, it's mean of me to keep you in suspense. I was astonished when I found out who the leader is and I knew all of you would be, too. Truthfully though, I am elated, I feel vindicated and all the hallelujah words you can think to use."

"Is it someone I know fairly well?" Sharon ask weakly. David nodded.

"It is." He knelt beside Sharon's chair. "Honey, I'm sorry, but it's Larry Dauber."

There was a stunned silence and then a cacophony of astonished voices. Keanu whistled shrilly. "I knew I didn't like or trust that man. I **knew** he was a phony."

Sixteen pairs of eyes fastened on David. He looked at Sharon's white face and wide eyes. "He's being held in Tallahassee. I don't know, at this moment, when any of us can see him, if you want to see him." He turned questioning eyes on Sharon's agonized eyes and wished he could have spared her this news.

"How dumb can one person be? Jeremy **and** Larry. I sure can pick them." Sharon jumped up and stumbled to the stairs. Everyone's heart was hurting for her. David watched sadly as she ran. Keanu started after her but Lynn caught his arm and shook her head.

"I know all of you love her and want to help, but the best thing we can do now is let her have time to digest this and come to grips with her own emotions. She's feeling as if she has made every mistake in the book. I'll go to her in a little while." Lynn then turned to David. "How much will be required of Sharon? She knew nothing of Jeremy's activities and she sure knew nothing about Larry or she would not have had anything to do with him."

David shook his head. "I don't know right now, but I'll find out and spare her all I can. I would advise her to obtain the services of a good attorney just in case she will need representation."

Dad and Uncle Malcolm will want to be with her." Lynn said thoughtfully.

David placed an arm around Lynn. "I know they will, but she should have someone living closer. I was thinking of Martin. In fact, it would be a good idea for you to call him and fill him in as soon as possible. He'll need to do an investigation of his own and set up a plan of action. We know Sharon knew nothing about what was going on, but she was married to Jeremy and she'll be questioned. Thankfully the District Attorney knows both of you and he'll be sympathetic."

Lynn called Martin and told him all that she had heard. She then called Sean and told him of the developments. Sean said he would talk to Malcolm and they would come up as soon as Martin wanted them.

Twenty-five minutes later Martin pulled his car in and came in the office. "I had my secretary cancel appointments for the rest of the day. Lynn, you're the one that called me. Is Sharon willing to talk to me?"

"I don't know, Martin, but I guess she will as soon as she has time to calm down and go through all of this in her own mind."

David warned everyone to continue to keep the information to themselves until the officers were sure they'd gotten the heads of the ring. He told them that others might be implicated and he would share information as he received it.

David looked over the group. "Amelia, Bernie, come here, please. I would appreciate it if you would go to the phones and call the rest of the kids, the volunteers who were here, and ask them to come out this afternoon at six for some special news. Please don't discuss anything over the phones. Maybe by then I'll have more to tell all of you. They deserve to know since they were here and supported Sharon."

With affirmations of loyalty and awareness of responsibility, the group of young people went out to continue the chores and make the calls. Lynn's eyes were misty as she spoke to David. "I am so blessed to have such competent, loving young people willing to care about others such as these have. I'm going up now and talk to Sharon. Martin, I'll call you if she feels she can talk to you". I know you and David have a lot to discuss."

David and Martin had a long discussion and planning strategy. Martin agreed that Sharon needed representation and that her dad and Malcolm would be a valuable resource.

At two Sharon and Lynn were still in the apartment, so, David met with the volunteers and told them about Larry

Dauber. There was a resounding cheer from the group and cries of, "I knew it". They left reluctantly but promised to be on hand if needed for anything. They also agreed to not discuss what they knew with anyone until the investigation was completed.

A somber group finished the afternoon chores. Jake sent all of them home early because the wind had picked up and there was a threat of a storm. "The weather people say that there is a possibility of a tornado in Zephyrhills. Everyone go on home safely. See you tomorrow morning, at least those who will be returning. Thanks everyone."

Sheilah went home early, very sad because she hadn't gotten to say more to Sharon.

"David, Lynn knows I love her and care what happens to her. Please tell her to call me if she needs me before morning."

The four men ate supper in their shared kitchen/dining room. After making a last check on the animals all of them settled for the night. Lynn and Sharon were in bed.

The sky became quite black with a roaring wind and rain hitting like gravels on the windows and building. Trees twisted and groaned. Thunder rolled causing vibration on the ground and lightning kept the area light enough to see where to walk.

At five the next morning the men hurriedly ate breakfast and went down to see about the animals. A couple of trees were uprooted, flowering bushes were flattened but not destroyed, and the driveway was a running creek. The ground was too wet to work outside, therefore, lessons would be in the indoor arena, if anyone showed up.

The few volunteers started straggling in excitedly telling of the damage in down town Zephyrhills. An Italian restaurant lost its roof and six private planes at the airport had been turned upside down and a couple planes had rolled. A local weatherman stated that some had said a tornado had hit Zephyrhills, but in his opinion, it was just a big wind.

"Oh, fry that," Darrell Huff scoffed. "How can a big wind just touch here and there? A wind would have hit in a wide area, not bounced on a roof and then over to the airport.

It was a tornado. They must think we're real dummies."

Darrell was a senior at Zephyrhills High and he and Keanu had become good friends. He was eager to show Keanu over the school buildings and introduce him to his friends.

This morning he had come out to work with Keanu and ride. Because of the bad weather, they had to ride indoors, but the boys didn't mind. Keanu gave Darrell his first jumping lesson. Darrell vowed he would be out to work as often as he could.

About ten thirty Sean and Malcolm pulled in. They had a long discussion with David and made arrangements to meet with Martin. Their hearts ached to see Sharon's red, baggy eyes and pale face. Lynn wasn't much better. Both girls were forcing themselves to move and be sociable.

"It's no surprise that Lynn feels Sharon's pain. They have always been close and fiercely loyal to each other." Sean explained to the group.

Sean and Malcolm had lunch with the girls and then left for a conference with Martin and the D A. They ate together at The Village Inn and then Sean and Malcolm went back to Fort Lauderdale.

That evening some of the volunteers gathered at The Clock to eat together and discuss all that had happened. They were very careful to not be overheard as most of them wanted to testify for Sharon, especially against Larry Dauber.

It was the afternoon of the second day before Sharon came out to the stable and listlessly picked up a brush and started to curry a horse. Lynn felt so proud of her young people exhibiting a lot of maturity and going about their business as usual. Everyone waited for Sharon to initiate a conversation. Sharon answered if it was necessary for someone to speak to her but otherwise was silent. She couldn't look at David, and when he came near her, she'd turn her back. She was so ashamed of her behavior. He wisely left her alone but watched her carefully.

On Thursday night Sheilah stayed to have dinner with Lynn and Sharon. She tried to be lively and entertaining telling of a woman who had visited that day scared to death of the horses. A large pony had walked by her and she had shrieked and jumped aside saying, "But why are they so big?"

Sharon politely looked at her but didn't change expression or say anything. Finally Sheilah got disgusted. "Well, I can see I'm not needed or wanted, so, I'm leaving."

Sharon said, "Hmmm," as Sheilah whirled her wheelchair and headed out.

Lynn raised her voice. "Sharon, snap out of it right this minute. You're not the only person in the world that's ever made a mistake or had a shock or disappointment. This isn't like you. The Sharon I grew up with would be shocked and then get angry and make the best of the situation."

Sharon said nothing just stared morosely into space. Lynn grabbed her shoulders and shook her. "Sharon! It's been five days and everyone is suffering because you won't fight back. You've crawled in a shell and dared anyone to care about you."

"Lynn, what are you babbling about?" Sharon was now paying attention.

"If you'd come out of that poor little me phase and look around you, you'd see what I'm babbling about."

"Lynn, you're too rough on her," Sheilah observed worriedly.

"No, I'm not. Someone had to shake her out of those doldrums. Sure she's had a shock; we all did. That doesn't excuse this behavior of hers."

Sharon stared at Lynn and then burst out bawling and shaking with deep sobs. She drew painful breaths and started again. Sheilah hurriedly wheeled to her and tried to take her in her arms.

"I'm truly sorry," Sharon sobbed. "I was not only in shock, but I've been embarrassed because of the way I treated David. I was the stupid one who called Larry and told on David. I blew his cover and could have gotten him k-k-killed," she sobbed.

"But that didn't happen," Lynn soothed her. David is a strong, emotionally mature man. He was too alert and well trained to allow Larry to get the upper hand."

"You're right," Sharon said firmly. "I'm going to find David and have a talk, if he's still speaking to me." She hurried out of the office and didn't see Lynn and Sheilah grinning at each other and giving a high five.

Larry Dauber had been a detective working in the state attorney's office, therefore, he knew how to argue and how to try to cover his tracks. The evidence was too strong and others had begun to break and confess, including Morrison.

Another month went by before Larry realized that he was in too deep to dig out. He broke one day and shocked everyone by telling who the Big Boss was. A federal officer called David and informed him. David stood so long holding the phone and looking down in the mouth that Jake got worried. "David, boy, what's up? I can tell it's bad news. Would it help to talk about it? Does it have anything to do with Sharon?"

"Lynn and Sharon will find it hard to ever trust anyone again. Why do some of the rotten criminal have to hold respectable, responsible jobs and make a mockery of them?

How can I make the girls understand that only a small percentage is bad? The largest part is trustworthy and worth cultivating as a friend."

Jake didn't know what to say. "Uh oh. I guess that means someone else they know and trusted has been in the slime with the ring."

"Yes. Dr. Zimmerman was arrested today for being accessory to the fact and her only, spoiled rotten son, like Jeremy, is the ring leader. Mitchell Zimmerman, known as Mitch is on the run, but there's an APB out on him. He won't get far."

"The Dr. Zimmerman who inspects therapeutic riding stables?!"

David nodded his head and placed his hands in his back pockets. "I'd better go tell the girls, and how I hate to tell them this on top of the Larry Dauber news."

Sheilah, Sharon and Lynn all looked as if they might faint. Lynn finally mumbled, "Mitch Zimmerman-- and his mother knew. She's part of a group selling drugs and damaging innocent young lives when her job requires her to protect them. Dear God in Heaven, how easily some of those people could have walked in here and killed, or set the place or fire or --"

"And we would never have been on guard or suspected them," Sheilah finished. "Why? Why would Dr. Zimmerman risk getting involved in something that she was supposed to be fighting against?" Lynn agonized.

"Greed. Power. Excitement." David said. "If we knew why, we could stop some of these people before they did so much damage. I was told that she learned her son was involved and, instead of turning him in, she kept quiet."

Mitch Zimmerman was caught in Indiana and brought back to Florida. Sharon testified that she had never met him, but she believed him to be the second tall man that was with Jeremy, Cassidy and Morrison when she saw them on the street.

January through April of the following year, the separate trials seemed to go on forever. Sharon attended as much as she could and still keep up with college classes and helping Lynn. She was back in her own home which she loved. David had convinced her that their future together deserved a fighting chance. She did accept an engagement ring from him after taking him to Fort Lauderdale to have a discussion with her parents and Malcolm.

Thankfully the doctors agreed that Agnes was too sick and dangerous to be out of the hospital for the insane, so, Sharon didn't have her around to worry about.

Lynn received a large jade ring surrounded by diamonds from Martin who was now walking with only one crutch. Sharon's ring was a special order of a heart-shaped diamond with three small diamonds on either side. Plans were being made for late summer weddings. Lynn would have a gold wedding band and Sharon's would have small diamonds across the top.

Mitch, Larry, Morrison and "Duke" all got life in prison with no chance for parole.

Larry insisted on seeing Sharon before he was sent away. She reluctantly agreed to talk to him. He swore that he truly loved her and would never have hurt her or allowed anyone else to do so. He explained that Duke had acted on his own. Sharon reminded him that others could have done the same thing and he was not a protector for her.

Dr. Zimmerman was given forty years which would put her in her nineties when she got out. Of course she might get some years off for good behavior but she could never again work with children or in any program where peoples health and lives were at stake.

The adoption of Keanu went off without a hitch and he graduated as Keanu Rodriguez Donnelly with an A average and awards in baseball and basketball. His plans were to attend the University of Florida in Gainesville to start his studies to be an attorney.

Sharon completed her third year of college with top grades. She and Lynn were disagreeing on weddings. Lynn wanted a double wedding, but Sharon insisted that Lynn deserved to have her own wedding and be the only bride.

David had been offered a job in the state's attorney's off ice and was also getting requests from the DEA to remain with them. Sean and Malcolm had told him they would be delighted to have him join them. Martin had said he could use a partner. David told everyone that he and Sharon would discuss their future and make a decision together in a short while.

CHAPTER TWENTY-TWO

In June David, Keanu and Gabe built a beautiful wooden diamond-shaped arch, twelve feet high and ten feet wide, and painted it white to be placed in the front lawn covered with flowers. Sharon, Sheilah, who was now walking, and some volunteers planted flowers that were the envy of every prospective bride. The front lawn was made into a fairy scene straight out of a romantic movie. Mounds of various colored flowers gave a sweet scent to the air and the topiary shrubs in tubs were a wonderland.

Singers from the Baptist Church were ready to perform and Dennis, although a music director was also an ordained minister, agreed to perform the ceremony. Folding chairs were borrowed from the church which the volunteers covered in white and placed multi-colored roses on the back of each chair. Long tables, covered in white cloths with lace borders, were set up in a corner of the huge lawn. An extension cord was run out from the stable so that a fountain of cold fruit juice could be available at all times.

A three-tiered bride's cake, German chocolate with rich pecan frosting was on a small table at one end. A bride and groom figure was on the cake and candy flowers were all around it. A groom's cake, vanilla with pistachio icing was on another table. Sheilah and Ashley were at a table to greet guests and have them sign the bride's book. Several photographers were mixing in the crowd taking pictures of the decorations and of the people. Two were ready, one with a still camera and one with a camcorder to record the actual wedding.

Everyone was seated and eagerly waiting for the wedding to begin when the youth band played and Dennis rode in on Banjo to take his place under the arch. He was dressed in an old-fashioned suit with a big bow tie. He dismounted and handed the reins to one of the volunteers who had come to be part of the wedding of their much loved Lynn. They had all leaned to love and respect Martin.

Martin, wearing an old fashioned white suit that looked like the middle 1800s, rode in on Fleetwood beside David who was in similar dress of light blue riding Cutter's Gold. The bright red Fleetwood and the gorgeous dark Palomino, Cutter's Gold were an eye-catching pair. Sharon and three college friends of Lynn rode side saddle wearing pastel dresses and wide-brimmed hats. The attendants' dresses were pastel blue, green, lilac and pink. David grinned at Sharon thinking that in her lilac, she was the most beautiful of all. The wedding party remained mounted.

Megan was too proud of her girls to cry and was sitting on the front row feeling so relieved and happy that, at last, life was worth living for them. She said a silent prayer for all of them, especially the bride and groom.

The musicians played the wedding march and everyone stood and turned to look toward the back. Oooos and ahhhs broke out all over the large crowd. Lynn rode side saddle wearing her grandmothers white satin and lace gown with a short veil and an arch of peach roses across her head. The skirt of her gown was so full that it covered the horse's back. Her Palomino horse, Gold Nugget, had a blanket of peach roses across his rump. He tossed his head proudly as if he knew his importance for the day.

When Dennis said, "Who gives this woman?" Malcolm and Sean both answered, "Her mother and we do." They then dismounted and gave the horses to some teens who took them carefully away while Sean and Malcolm sat on either side of Megan It was a beautiful wedding. Lynn and Martin had written their own vows which would be placed in the bride's book.

The sun was out bright, but the big trees gave enough shade, and a slight breeze wafted over the flowers bringing sweet relief and breath-taking odors. Butterflies floated merrily over the flowers and some birds even sang in nearby trees as if they knew they were adding to the festivities.

Jardine was in charge of the volunteers who were taking care of the refreshments. She was nervously moving around hoping that everything would be beautiful for Lynn. The young men volunteers, under Keanu's direction, had served as valets to park cars for people in the adjoining pasture. All of them wore black trousers, white shirts, black ties and black Eisenhower jackets.

The horses were brought back for Sean and Malcolm so that group pictures could be taken. Lynn got her first look at the crowd and gasped when she saw reporters and television cameras at work. *What are they doing at my wedding?* She thought.

As soon as Lynn was able to get away, she and Sharon tapped Sheilah on the shoulder and the three young women went up to the apartment to change clothes. They could hardly dress for hugging each other and exclaiming how well everything went and how beautiful everything was. Gifts were piled on one of the twin beds; some unopened.

"I can never find words to thank you two for all of your help and your support," Lynn wiped her eyes.

"Don't start waterworks," Sheilah ordered. "This is a happy day for many, many reasons. Sharon, I know you thought David as best man was sooo handsome."

"Sure I did, but Martin has won a place in my heart for loving Lynn and being so good to her." She lifted Lynn's left hand to see the gold band now with the jade and diamond ring. "I have a good feeling that this will be for life. I bet it won't be long until we'll be raising some of our own little volunteers around here," she teased.

"Zip your mouth," Lynn grinned. "We both want children in a couple of years. Martin needs to get well established and I just need to get used to being married."

Bird seed was thrown in the air as Lynn and Martin hurried to hug Sean, Megan and Malcolm and all the others. They then ran to get in Martin's decorated car in which their luggage had already been placed. Lynn turned to give yet more instructions to Sharon.

"Go. Go. I know what to do and have plenty of help. Your stable will be well taken care of and all your four-legged babies will be well and happy to see you when you return.

Relax and have fun you two. Take loads of pictures and take good care of each other," Sharon yelled as they pulled out. She turned and walked into David and Keanu standing behind her.

David grinned. "Still want our wedding in July or do you want to elope?"

Keanu yelped. "You'd better not elope. This will be the first time I've gotten to be best man." Laughing, the three went back to the stable to join the family for dinner.

Long tables had been set up in the back room beyond the office. Counting family and volunteers, plus Dennis and Peggy, there were fifty-two people seated for dinner. Ladies from the church had volunteered to help with the dinner for which Sharon was very grateful. They had ham, fried chicken, potato salad, three bean salad, peas, celery sticks with strawberry cream cheese filling, carrot sticks, tomatoes, onion rings, olives, peppers, fresh yeast rolls and a choice of coffee, ice tea, lemonade or water. Pineapple upside down cakes had been baked for this occasion.

Sharon had carefully placed the top layer of the wedding cake, with the bride and groom on it, in a special box to be frozen. Lynn and Martin would decide what they wanted to do with it although most people saved it for their first wedding anniversary.

The next day Sharon, Sheilah, Ashley and Jardine were in the apartment looking at the gifts that had been opened. Sharon and Sheilah were making a list of gifts so that Lynn could write thank you notes when she returned. Amelia ran in.

"Here's the mail. There's several envelopes for Lynn and Martin. I bet there's checks in some of them. Where should I put them?"

"On the bed with the rest of the gifts and envelopes," Sharon told her. "I sure hope they're having a great time and staying well and happy."

Jardine stood up sticking her lower lip out and blowing up to get stray hairs out of her eyes. "Where did they go for a honeymoon? I don't remember anyone saying."

Sheilah and Sharon grinned at each other. Sheilah answered, "They had discussed going to the Canary Islands and Morocco in North Africa, but with all this world turmoil, they decided to see more of our own country. They'll be in Wyoming and North and South Dakota. Since they're driving, they'll take their time and sightsee between there and here."

"That's marvelous," Ashley exclaimed. She squatted back on her heels and shoved trash into a bag. "Where are you going on your honeymoon, Sharon?"

That's a secret, but I will tell you that we'll more than likely do the same and tour our own country. David and I both believe in buying America." She emphasized the last two words, stood and saluted. "Now my wedding is rushing toward me like a run away freight train. If you still intend to help me, let's polish up the plans."

All three young women affirmed that they were ready and willing to help. They looked alarmed at Sharon when she suddenly sat in the floor and looked so dejected.

"What are you thinking, honey?" Sheilah asked gently.

"My wedding to Jeremy. My parents went all out and spent a tremendous amount of money. Loads of people came, brought gifts and were happy for us. Sometimes I get a little afraid to plan another wedding, but David deserves the best. It's his first wedding and I do feel that this one will be for life."

"You bet," Ashley and Sheilah answered together laughing cheerfully.

Four young heads bent over papers with plans written on them and made themselves comfortable on the floor. They lost track of time until Keanu walked in sweaty, tired and smelling of sawdust and fresh air.

"Eeuw," Jardine waved a hand in front of her face. Ashley stood up by him declaring that she thought the smell of fresh cut wood was delightful. "What have you been doing?" Jardine asked.

"Didn't you tell them, Sharon?" She shook her head. "I guess you've had too much on your mind. Before they left, Martin and David discussed plans for a house. David has drawn the blueprints. Lynn chose the pasture where we parked the cars to build them a new house. Martin thought they would start after Sharon and David's wedding, but David wants to surprise them and have it well started when they return. We've put out the stakes for the borders and measured for lumber, which I've been cutting. Several of the boys offered to come back and help. We'll have cement poured for the flooring before the inspectors from the county have checked for plumbing and wiring. Then we can lay the bricks and get it started."

"Wow! Zowie!" Jardine chortled. "What a great surprise that'll be. Sharon, where will you and David live?"

"In my house in town until we decide what job David will accept and where we'll be most of the time. I hope to get a job teaching wherever we live. Too, I have another year of college to finish." The girls jumped around hugging each other and laughed when Keanu ran before anyone could hug him.

Riding lessons, trail rides, cook-outs and daily activities went on as planned. Everyone was pleased with the progress. Three weeks passed and Lynn and Martin returned looking rested, happy and eager to go on with their life. They were astonished that David and the boys had almost finished their house. They were very pleased with what had been done and were eager to finish the house and furnish it. Lynn and the girls planned together for the landscaping.

Keanu had already put up a lovely picket fence across the front, with a swinging gate, and painted it white. A country-style fence of a bar top and bottom between posts with two poles making an X centering was planned for the sides and back.

Only two more weeks until Sharon and David's wedding on July 3rd. There would not be as big a crowd because Sharon didn't want the attention. She had requested no gifts on the invitation that she had sent. However, gifts galore kept coming in with good wishes.

The same white arch was used with multi-colored flowers on it. A low stand was placed in the center for the minister to stand on. Again chairs were borrowed from the church but were not covered. Wide, white satin bows with a flower in the center of each was placed on the side of each chair making the center aisle. A white carpet was rolled out for the center aisle.

Again the long tables held refreshments and the traditional cakes. The bride's cake was four alternating vanilla and chocolate layers with white cream icing and a ring of candy roses around the top layer and at the bottom. A bride and groom were on the top. The groom's cake was butter pecan with butter cream icing.

Martin and three of the male volunteers served as ushers and Keanu was the very proud best man. "You'll be my brother-in-law, so, you might as well get in this shindig from the beginning," David grinned at him.

Again news reporters and TV cameras were present. The editor of the Zephyrhills News hugged Sharon and said, "Just relax and ignore it, honey. You're as much a celebrity around here as they have in Hollywood. Everyone knows your story and is so pleased for you that this is turning out to be a fairy tale ending."

David wore his dress Marine uniform because technically he was still a marine. He had been released on special permission to work with DEA on drug enforcement. He planned to seek an honorable discharge. Much to his embarrassment, he shed tears when Martin told him that he had had David's mother and sisters flown out for the wedding. They came the morning of the late afternoon affair and would be staying with Lynn for two days. Several of his superiors were present.

Keanu looked like a fashion model in his full dress tux of light blue. He made quite an impression with his coal black hair, beautiful dark eyes with long lashes, copper complexion and standing proudly straight and tall. A grin never left his face.

All of the volunteers were invited to participate if they wished. The boys made a line on one side of the aisle in their dress suits and ties. The girls in a gown of their choice made a line across from them. Megan did cry from happiness this time.

A dear, sweet, elderly man Manley Wakefield, from the church, an ordained minister, performed the ceremony. Singers from the church performed and the youth orchestra provided the music.

Two of the young women volunteers met people and kept the Bride's book. This left Sheilah, Ashley and Jardine to serve as bridesmaids. They wore Victorian-styled dresses of lime green, sky blue and pink. George was a hit on her coal-black Hanoverian stallion. Her bright red Spanish-style dress stood out on the black horse. She sat proudly to lead the carriage in.

Two large, pure white Andalusian stallions were brought in special to pull the white carriage that Sharon rode in with Sean and Malcolm. Silver ribbons and flowers decorated the carriage. They dismounted and Sharon stood between the two men. Her ivory satin gown with ivory lace and short veil were complimented with white elbow length satin gloves. She carried a white Bible with two white orchids on it.

Sharon and David, too, had written their own vows. At their request, the congregation sang, "My Lord Is Near Me All The Time". A friend played "Amazing Grace" on the bagpipes.

When Sharon turned her back and threw her bouquet, much to the amusement of the crowd, ninety-nine year old Eliza Younger caught it.

David yelled that he needed help to pull Sharon from Keanu's arms. He hugged her so many times that she began to think she'd never get away.

At the reception, the volunteers and Keanu surprised everyone by performing skits, which they had written, about David and Sharon. The television news reporters got a charge out of this and put it on the late news. Too, pictures of the young volunteers and exclamations of what they were doing, were placed in all the newspapers.

The newlyweds left for a tour of New England and a trip to Niagara Falls. Sharon put her head on David's shoulder and prayed aloud, "Thank you, Heavenly Father, for this wonderful man. I know you put us together. You've given me so many blessings that I can't name them all."

David finished, "And, Lord, we promise to have a Christian home and raise any children that you bless us with in a Christian atmosphere. Guide me in a choice of a job and be with us and all of our family and friends.

EPILOGUE

Months went by with the usual joys and tears. Sharon looked around the room with satisfaction. It was almost frightening, after all they'd been through, how relaxed and at peace everyone was.

She was justifiably proud of the fact that she had completed college and had a Masters in Guidance and Psychology and was now teaching at Zephyrhills High. *I'm happy I turned down the job of Guidance Counselor. I love working with the youth in classrooms.*

Keanu was well into his studies for an attorney with the promise that he could train with Malcolm and his father, Sean. Keanu had developed a keen interest in investigations and, later was going to solve the mystery of the horse rustling in Pasco County.

Lynn, with all the publicity around the two weddings, had become well known and had a much bigger practice run successfully with Sheilah as a partner. Ashley and Jardine were working closely with Lynn hoping to become part of the business when they finished college.

Martin came in one day fairly bursting with news and beaming as a kid does at Christmas. He was so excited that it took several gulping breaths for him to share his news. "Lynn and I have known for several weeks that we're pregnant." he had to pause until the cheers and congratulations were called. "We didn't tell our news because we wanted to wait for a sonogram. Well, we've had one and ---" he hesitated and looked around with a big, silly grin, "it's twin boys!"

Everyone shared the joy with them and the room was filled with laughter and good wishes. When Lynn walked in there were more cheers, whistles and hugs, as well as tears of joy.

Sharon was so pleased for Lynn and Martin. She kept smiling as she kept her news to herself. She didn't want to take the attention away from Lynn. David didn't even know yet that he was going to be a father. She was so thrilled that she could hardly contain her joy. She knew everyone would assume she was so pleased for Lynn, and she was. Their babies would grow up together just as she and Lynn had.

Sean, Megan and Malcolm walked in to join in the joyous news. Lynn had already called them and told them her good news. Sean and Megan were overjoyed at the news. "You didn't think we could stay away when we're expecting our first grandchild," Megan was thrilled.

Malcolm was overjoyed for the happiness of his two precious girls. Agnes would never again be healthy and sane. She would remain in the hospital for the remainder of her life.

The Soaring Eagle was filled with peacefulness, love and joy. Some of the mares had new little foals and all was going so well that Sharon felt there was surely a glitch going to happen.

Lynn had sold two acres to David and he and the young men had built a house for him and Sharon on the property. Sharon was breeding big draft horses with Thoroughbreds to develop some good heavy hunters. Her favorite was a big nineteen hand Shire stallion that was bred with a beautiful Thoroughbred. Both sire and dam had such easy-going temperaments, and were so easy to work with, she was sure she'd have a gorgeous little fellow to raise and train. Her joy was complete.

CPSIA information can be obtained at www.ICGtesting.com
Printed in the USA
LVOW100751310312

275579LV00002B/37/P